MELISSA ALYSE

A Place To Belong

First published by Empty Nesting On Purpose 2025

First edition

ISBN: 979-8-9986787-1-4

This book was professionally typeset on Reedsy.
Find out more at reedsy.com

Dedication

For the sister holding this story in her hands—
I hope you find whispers of hope tucked between the lines,
a spark of joy that makes you smile (maybe even laugh out loud),
and extra grace when you need it most.
You are deeply loved by a God
who is with you every step of the way (Psalm 139: 7–12)
and who made you just as you are, on purpose. (Ephesians 2:10)
I've been praying for you.
Big hugs, sweet friend,
-melissa. ❤
P.S. Let's stay in touch, www.melissaalyse.com/friends

Chapter 1

The black dress fit like it had been waiting for this exact night.

Sammy twisted in front of the mirror, adjusting one curl, then another, trying to ignore the flutter in her chest. The girl in the mirror looked ready. But something in her eyes . . . Was that nerves or doubt?

She had packed most of her dorm room earlier that afternoon. Only one suitcase remained open—just enough space to carry her through the weekend. The rest was already sealed and labeled: *Books*, *Linens*, *Dresser*, *Shoes*. Only the essentials were still out.

Tonight, she didn't need much: the dress, the heels, a little courage, and the plan.

Once upon a time, Sammy Thomas had big, bold plans—travel, teach overseas, maybe even write a book about faith and education. Her journals from high school had been filled with plans, dreams, and bucket lists.

But somewhere along the way, the dreams had gotten smaller. Not in a sad way. Just *simpler*. She considered them "realistic plans," and they looked something like this:

Graduate with honors.

Get married to Richard.

Be a strong, steady, Proverbs 31 wife.

And tonight, if everything went the way she prayed it would, that life—the one she'd carefully reshaped around him—might finally begin.

She stepped over the box marked *Shoes*, reaching into another for her perfume. Her fingers brushed something soft and unexpected. She pulled out a cheap nylon lei, faded and tangled.

A laugh slipped out.

Back-to-School Luau, sophomore year.

She could still see it: lukewarm punch, paper lanterns, the awkward shuffle of feet in a too-bright gym. Amanda had made a beeline for the dance floor. Sammy had hovered near the wall, fingers clenched around that lei, planning her exit.

And then she'd spotted Richard, a quiet guy in her English class the year before. He noticed her and gave a slight nod and two finger wave.

She'd crossed the floor, heart hammering.

"I wish someone would ask me to dance."

"I don't dance," he'd said, flat and sure.

"Well, I wish you would."

He sighed, looking around the room, "Only if you promise never to ask again."

They'd danced. Offbeat. A little awkward. Perfect.

Now, holding the lei, a quiet ache tightened in her chest. That night had felt light. Easy. Somewhere along the way, the ease had disappeared.

She folded the lei gently, set it back in the box, and spritzed her wrists with perfume. Then one last look in the mirror.

"You're ready," she whispered.

In the living room, Amanda sat on the floor between two half-taped boxes, swiping on lip gloss with the reflection from a baking sheet.

When she looked up and saw Sammy, she let out a low whistle. "Okay, wow. You look like a plot twist in a Hallmark movie."

Sammy laughed, nerves softening. "Thanks. I think my hands are permanently clammy."

Amanda stood, brushing off her jeans. "Clammy hands mean something big's about to happen." She motioned toward the couch. "Now sit. Your hair has to be perfect for dinner at The Luxe."

Sammy sat obediently. Amanda twisted and pinned with practiced precision.

"Did Richard give you any kind of hint about what tonight is about?" Amanda asked.

"Just that he wanted to celebrate us," Sammy said with a dreamy gaze. "Where we started, where we are, and where we're going."

Amanda's hands paused for half a second.

"You two are the most spreadsheet-loving couple I know," she said carefully. "I bet he's got a tab somewhere labeled 'After Graduation Steps—Q2 Goals.'"

Sammy giggled. "Plans help us stay focused on what we want."

Amanda pinned the last curl, then stood back, eyes scanning critically, then warmly as she helped Sammy up too. "Well, whatever tonight holds, you look stunning, sweet sister."

"Thank you." Sammy breathed out, smoothing her dress.

Even as she said it, a flicker of something uncertain twisted low in her stomach.

Her phone buzzed.

Richard: *I'm here.*

She looked up. "Gotta go." She wiggled her eyebrows in excitement.

Amanda lifted a brow. "He's not coming to the door?"

Sammy smiled, grabbing her clutch. "You know, he's not the grand gesture type."

Outside, campus buzzed with post-finals energy. Students hauled boxes to waiting cars. Laughter echoed across the lawn. But Sammy's focus narrowed to one thing.

Richard's red BMW, the graduation present his parents had bought him.

It gleamed beneath a streetlamp like a promise. He raised two fingers acknowledging Sammy walking up with a quick wave before finishing the text on his phone.

She opened the door and slid in. The leather seats were cold against her skin.

"Hey," she said nervously.

He looked up as he put his phone away. "Hey. You look nice."

Sammy smoothed her dress, "Thanks."

Tonight was going to be perfect.

She just knew it.

Chapter 2

Soft, ambient light shimmered across crystal and polished silver, catching on the rim of her champagne glass like it had something to say. Velvet curtains dulled the sound of laughter and silverware clinking. The piano in the corner played something slow, unhurried, like the night had nowhere to be.

It was perfect.

She smoothed her dress as the waiter pulled out her chair. Across the table, Richard already looked comfortable. Two champagne flutes waited between them, bubbling quietly.

He lifted his glass. "To three wonderful years. You've made college a lot more fun than I expected."

Sammy raised her glass on reflex, but the words caught somewhere in her chest.

Fun? That's all?

"To us," she said softly, and their glasses clinked.

He sipped, then opened the menu. "My parents are covering tonight. Order whatever you want."

She kept her smile in place. "They're proud of you. You earned that graduation medal."

He shrugged. "Yeah, well, it was all part of the plan."

The plan.

His life was full of those—neatly stacked, forward-moving, uninterrupted.

She tilted her head, trying to find the version of him that used to pull her off campus to get ice cream at midnight. "Do you remember the luau our sophomore year?"

He didn't look up. "What?"

"Our first unofficial date. You wouldn't dance. I made you."

He arched a brow. "You didn't make me."

"Ok, fine. I begged you."

His smirk faded. "Yeah. I remember."

"I found the lei tonight in one of my boxes," she said, her voice quieter now. "It made me think about how easy everything felt back then."

He looked down at the menu again. "That was a long time ago."

Still, she tried. "If you want to break your no-dancing rule tonight, I wouldn't mind."

"You know I don't dance."

And that was that.

Dinner arrived. They barely touched it. Richard checked his watch—twice. Her stomach, once light with nerves, now sank with dread. A different kind of knowing bloomed in her chest the longer this night went on.

And then he looked up.

"Samantha," he said, voice low but steady, "there's something I need to tell you."

She set down her fork. "Okay."

"I got the fellowship in D.C."

Her heart paused.

He cleared his throat. "And honestly, it made me realize some things. Every time I imagined my life there, moving forward, you weren't . . . in it."

She blinked, as if that might make the words make more sense. "What?"

"The nonprofit I mentioned? My dad reached out to a contact. It moved fast."

"You applied?"

"A while ago."

Her eyes narrowed slightly. "And you already accepted?"

He nodded. "Three weeks ago."

Her hands went still.

"I didn't want to distract you during finals," he added. "I wanted to tell you in person."

She stared at him. "So you're moving to D.C. And what—breaking up with me?"

He nodded again. Calm. Certain.

Like he'd done this math already and the result was clean.

"I thought we were planning a life together."

Richard's expression didn't shift. "I've been thinking a lot about the future, Samantha. About what I really want."

She searched his face. "And I'm not part of that?"

He didn't answer. He didn't have to.

Her voice wavered, but she pressed on. "You've known. You've known for weeks and didn't tell me. I turned down a job thinking we'd be here, starting something. I mapped out a future in pencil, waiting for you to draw the lines in ink. And all this time, you were already gone."

He looked away, raised a hand for the check.

She leaned in, voice low. "Richard, can't we at least talk about this?"

He hesitated, just a flicker.

Then: "My parents were right," he said softly. "They always saw things clearly. You and I . . . we were good in college. But that's not the same as being right for the long run."

Her heart sank. "What are you saying?"

He glanced toward the waiter bringing their check, then back at her. "It's time to breakup."

Something in her cracked.

Not from the cruelty—he didn't mean it cruelly. That was the worst part. He meant it like truth. Quiet and logical. A final slide into place.

She sat still, stunned. And then slowly, the memories flooded in.

Shrinking.

Tucking herself neatly into corners at his family gatherings. Crossing her legs just so. Laughing lightly at the right times. Speaking only when spoken to. Making sure her makeup was subtle. Her posture perfect. Her opinions soft-edged.

Not because anyone told her to. Because it was the only way to fit. Because it was the only way to be *acceptable.*

She folded her hands in her lap, hiding the tremble in her fingers.

Her voice, when it came, was thin but sure. “I spent three years trying to make myself small enough to belong in your world.”

Richard looked at her blankly.

“And I thought maybe if I was quiet enough, polished enough, agreeable enough—I’d earn my place in it.” A pause. Her throat tightened. “But I see it now. I was never being chosen. I was just being tolerated.”

He didn’t deny it. And that hurt the most.

The waiter set the check on the table. Richard signed it, unhurried, as if closing a contract.

“I’ll be in the car.” He stood and walked out of the restaurant.

She stayed seated.

People were watching, but she couldn’t move because if she stood, it would be real. And she wasn’t ready to let go.

But Richard already had.

Her hands curled into her dress.

She had lost him.

The future she’d imagined—*the one she’d made room for him in*—was gone.

And for the first time, she had no idea what came next.

Chapter 3

When Sammy stepped inside her apartment and found no lights glowing, no music playing, no laughter echoing off the kitchen tile, she felt a strange sense of comfort. She let the door click softly shut behind her and followed the streetlight streaking through the blinds, weaving between taped-up moving boxes scattered across the floor.

In her bedroom, she shut the door and let the silence wrap around her like a blanket pulled too tight.

And then she broke.

She collapsed onto the bed in one graceless motion and buried her face in the comforter. The sobs rushed in—loud, heavy, unstoppable. Her shoulders shook, fists clutching the covers, her tears soaking everything as if her grief needed somewhere to live.

This wasn't just heartbreak. It was the kind of devastation that rearranged your insides.

She hadn't simply lost Richard. She'd lost a life she thought she was building. A place she thought she held in someone else's story.

And somewhere along the line, she'd let herself believe that being loved meant being smaller.

What's wrong with me? Why wasn't I enough?

The questions circled like hawks, never landing.

Why did I ignore all the signs?

His distracted glances. The gentle but constant corrections. The way he'd smile and change the subject when she got too excited about something he didn't care about.

The memories flickered—his crooked grin, the old inside jokes, the night she first told him she loved him and he said, *"Let's wait for our first kiss until we're married."*

She had thought it was romantic.

Now she wondered if he'd just wanted to keep his distance.

She'd ignored the way he made her feel like an accessory instead of a partner. Like she was something lovely he wore in college, but not something he'd carry into real life.

Her sobs slowed only when her body couldn't hold them anymore. Her throat was raw. Her limbs, aching. She sat up slowly, wiped her eyes with the edge of her comforter, and wandered toward the kitchen.

A hallway mirror caught her as she passed.

She stopped.

The girl staring back looked older. Not wiser. Just . . . worn.

Mascara streaks lined her cheeks. Her curls hung in a tangled mess. But it was her eyes that startled her most.

Empty.

Like she didn't recognize herself without his name attached to hers.

She turned away.

In the kitchen, she filled a glass with water and sank onto the couch. She hadn't even lifted it to her lips when the front door opened.

"Sammy, you have to hear what happened—"

Amanda's voice froze in mid-laughter.

She stepped inside and saw her curled on the couch, glass forgotten in her lap, face blotchy, body limp.

"Oh no." Amanda's tone softened in an instant. "Sammy . . ."

She crossed the room and dropped onto the couch beside her like a sister would. No demand for answers. No rush.

Just presence.

Sammy blinked, her voice cracking. "He broke up with me."

Amanda's brows pulled together. "What?"

Sammy nodded. "Tonight."

Amanda's eyes filled with quiet disbelief. "But you were going to The Luxe.

He made a reservation and everything."

"I think," Sammy whispered, "that was his parting gift."

Amanda was silent for a moment. Then, gently: "What happened?"

Sammy stared at her hands. "He's moving to D.C. Said he talked to his parents and decided I'm not part of the life he wants."

Amanda let out a slow exhale filled with anger and sorrow and restraint all tangled together.

"I thought we were building something real," Sammy said, her voice breaking. "But I guess I was just filling space."

Amanda reached out and took her hand.

Sammy blinked, her eyes filling again. "I thought if I just . . . blended in enough, they'd accept me. Him. His family. All of it." She gave a soft, broken laugh. "Remember that red dress with the flowers? The one I used to wear with confidence?"

Amanda nodded.

"I wore it to his parents' anniversary dinner. His mom looked at me like I'd shown up in a circus costume. After that, I started buying beige. Pale blue. Soft pink. Nothing too loud."

She swallowed. "I stopped wearing hoops. Started wearing pearls. Bit my tongue when I had something to say. And thought I was being too sensitive when jokes stung. I made myself smaller. Gentler. Quieter. And I told myself it was worth it."

Her voice dropped to a whisper. "But I was never being chosen, Amanda. I was being measured. And eventually, I came up short."

Amanda put her arm around her friend and squeezed her shoulder, firm and unflinching. "Love should make you bloom, not vanish."

Sammy leaned into her, eyes wet. "I don't know who I am without him."

Amanda rested her chin lightly on Sammy's head. "Then maybe now is the time to remember. Not because he's gone, but because you're still here."

They sat in silence—the kind that doesn't ask for anything. Amanda rubbed Sammy's arm.

After a while, Amanda spoke, brushing Sammy's hair from her face. "I know this isn't the plan. And I know how you love your plans."

Sammy let out the barest of laughs, tears still clinging to her lashes.

"But maybe this isn't the end," Amanda said. "Maybe this is God's way of clearing the path for what comes next. Something better. Something you don't have to shrink for."

Sammy didn't answer right away. Her head remained on Amanda's shoulder, but something inside her—something small and bruised—stirred.

"What if there's nothing better?" she whispered.

Amanda didn't hesitate. "Remember Jeremiah 29:11? With God, there is always something better." Amanda kissed her forehead and stood. "Love you, Sammy. Always."

Sammy nodded, the lump in her throat too thick for words.

As Amanda disappeared down the hall, the apartment fell quiet again. Outside, dawn began to stretch across the sky, casting soft light through the blinds. Sammy stayed curled in the cushions, her arms wrapped around her middle, holding herself together the best she could.

The ache in her chest hadn't gone.

It still pulsed—deep, steady, and real.

She stared at nothing for a long time, her breath slow and uneven.

Trying to picture life tomorrow.

Next week.

Next year.

She tried to look at the future ahead of her, and it was blank and unfamiliar.

And that absolutely terrified her.

Chapter 4

Gloria Thomas—"Glory" to most, especially her grandkids—woke with a start at five o'clock that morning. The hum of the air conditioner and the faint scent of last night's coffee greeted her as she reached for her well-worn Bible on the nightstand.

A familiar tug in her spirit whispered a call to pray for her granddaughter Sammy.

Glory never ignored that voice. It had guided her through storms and blessings alike.

Opening her Bible to Psalm 91, she bowed her head and prayed softly, "Lord, I trust You with the details, even when I can't see them. Whatever Sammy is facing, give her strength to stand firm. Guide her steps to the coffee shop, and help me be exactly what she needs today—a listening ear, a steady hand, or simply quiet comfort."

By the time Glory finished her prayer, the first rays of morning sunlight crept across the horizon.

She trusted the Lord to guide Sammy's steps, even if she didn't know what the day would bring.

* * *

As Sammy pulled into the coffee shop, she was so grateful for their standing coffee date when Glory came to town. It had been a lifeline, a steady point in her suddenly chaotic world for these past four years of college.

Sammy caught her reflection in the rearview mirror: puffy eyes and a pale complexion. She sighed, brushing a stray curl from her face.

"Yep."

She looked tired, but at least Glory wouldn't care.

Through the window, her grandmother's steady presence felt like a lighthouse in a storm: strong, constant, and impossible to miss.

That was all the courage Sammy needed to step out.

Glory rose from her seat and came to the sidewalk to meet Sammy, pulling her into a warm hug. The faint scent of lavender and coffee from her sweater made Sammy's throat tighten.

"Oh my goodness, sweet Sammy, so proud of you! Happy graduation day!" Glory said warmly. But as she pulled back, her gaze swept over Sammy's tear-streaked cheeks. "Oh goodness, are you okay?" she whispered.

Sammy nodded, her throat too tight for words.

Glory squeezed her hand. "Want to go somewhere else?"

"How about we walk?" Sammy suggested.

Glory nodded. "Let me grab you a coffee, and I'll meet you back out here."

With steaming coffee cups in hand, they strolled down a quiet neighborhood street, the morning light filtering through the trees.

For a while, they walked in silence, the rhythmic crunch of their footsteps grounding Sammy.

She broke the quiet first, her voice tentative. "So, Glory, what's been keeping you busy these days?"

Glory's eyes twinkled. "Well, Nelda and Lora are absolutely cleaning me and Ethel Sue out at bridge, and between you and me, I think they're practicing on the sly." She winked, sniffing a blooming pink rose along the sidewalk. "Oh, and they send their love and congratulations, of course."

Sammy chuckled softly, her first genuine laugh in what felt like days. "That sounds about right. Anything else?"

"Oh, I've been porch gardening," Glory replied.

"Porch gardening?"

"Yes, that's what I call sitting on my swing with sweet tea and marking pages in seed catalogs. It feels very official, even if nothing ever makes it into the ground."

A soft giggle escaping despite herself. "Oh, Glory."

The warmth in Glory's humor began to thaw the edges of her sorrow, melting into something lighter, if only for a moment.

Glory looped her arm through Sammy's, her touch gentle but steady. "Oh, my Sammy, it's so good to hear you laugh. It's been far too long."

Sammy's smile faltered as fresh tears welled. Her throat tightened, and the emotions came rushing back. "Glory, I don't even know where to start."

Glory slowed their pace. "Take your time, sweetheart."

Sammy inhaled shakily. "As of nine o'clock last night, I'm single." She laughed, but it was dry and hollow. "Apparently, Richard decided I'm not marriage material. Three years, Glory. How do you spend that long with someone and only *then* figure that out?"

Glory's heart ached as she listened. "Oh, Sammy."

"I've spent the last three years twisting myself into knots, trying to fit into his world, making his life easier while forgetting my own. And now, it's like none of it even mattered." Her voice cracked. She shook her head, its weight pressing down on her chest.

They walked a little farther in silence. Leaves stirred in the trees above them, sunlight slipping between branches. When Sammy finally spoke again, her voice was quieter.

"What if I spent so long helping him chase his future . . . that I lost mine?" She shook her head. "I wish I would have listened to you when you said you knew Grandpa was the one for you because he always knew when to ask you to dance."

Glory stopped and turned toward her, eyes shining with tenderness. She reached out, resting a hand on Sammy's cheek. "You didn't lose your future, love. It's still waiting."

Sammy looked away, blinking against the tears. "It doesn't feel like anything's waiting."

"I know," Glory said gently. "But that's what grief does. It blinds us to what's next. You're still in the fog, sweetheart. But that doesn't mean the road is gone. It just means you need time to see it."

Sammy was quiet for a moment. Then she whispered, "I feel so empty."

Glory gave a small, knowing look. "Then that is where you begin. Empty is not the end. Empty is room for God to fill." She nodded to herself as she searched the trees in front of her for a thought. Then it came to her. "It reminds me of something I read in Matthew recently," she said. "One of the Beatitudes." She turned toward Sammy trying to find the verse, "It goes something like, 'Blessed are you when you're at the end of your rope. Because that's where God meets you. With less of you, there's more of him.'"

Sammy looked at her, eyes still puffy with tears, a trace of confused amusement behind them. "What Bible are you reading?"

Glory tilted her head, eyes twinkling. "The Message version. Nelda's got us 'expanding our horizons' with all these modern translations lately."

As they passed a vine-covered fence, Glory leaned in and sniffed a cluster of hanging wisteria, her expression soft and thoughtful. "Good things take time to grow. God isn't finished with you yet, sweet Sammy," she added, wrapping her arm around her.

They continued walking, the silence between them now more comforting than heavy.

They turned the corner back to where they started, and Glory gave her arm a gentle squeeze. "One step at a time, sweetheart," she said. "Maybe it doesn't feel like much, but that's how every journey begins."

Sammy pulled her into a hug. "I love you, Glory."

"I love you too, my sweet Sammy," Glory said, smoothing a curl from her granddaughter's cheek. "I'll see you at graduation."

Sammy watched her walk away, the scent of lavender lingering like a promise in the morning air.

The ache hadn't vanished.

But something else had taken root. Something small, quiet and unshakable. She was certain she would not shrink herself to belong again.

Chapter 5

As the graduates waited for the ceremony to begin, Sammy took a deep breath and scanned the crowd. When her family spotted her, they started waving and beaming proudly, as if she'd won a Nobel Peace Prize instead of a private school teaching degree. The sight made her chest tighten with gratitude as she waved back.

First in line of chairs were Jonathon, Katie, and Jeremy, ages seven, nine, and ten, who were sitting nice and straight.

Next came her mom and dad, with her mother holding the newest addition, little Lucy, now almost one and absolutely adorable.

Then there was little Carol, six, who kept switching from her chair to her dad's lap and back to the chair again.

Then Glory, and finally, there was Chris, twenty-one, sitting tall at the end of the row.

Sammy's let out a breath. *I'm so glad he could make it.*

Sammy had been about to start middle school when her parents announced they were having more kids. As the babies came, priorities shifted, and Chris and Sammy often found themselves filling the gaps. Without realizing it, they became a team, taking turns with diaper duty and feedings like pros when Mom and Dad had dates or church commitments.

Once, when Sammy was about fifteen and babysitting felt endless, Chris snuck into her room, balancing a bowl of popcorn and a borrowed DVD. "Siblings' Movie Night," he declared, his grin infectious. They'd giggled at the cheesy dialogue, popcorn spilling between them, and laughed until their sides hurt. For a moment, the chaos felt far away, their bond unshakable.

She thought of those late nights spent rocking babies to sleep while Chris reheated leftover mac and cheese for dinner. It wasn't just the sleepless nights or endless chores; it was the quiet realization that no one had time to ask how she was doing or what she wanted. In the whirlwind, Sammy learned to make plans and find order when everything else felt overwhelming.

She blinked, pulling herself back to the present.

They hadn't always been able to support her in the ways she sometimes needed financially or even emotionally, but they had tried. And they were here today.

And that was what mattered.

"Greetings, graduating class! What a ride, right?" The valedictorian's voice rang through the speakers, met with scattered cheers and whoops from the crowd. "This is an amazing time to be heading into the 'real world,' as my mom calls it. Like somehow, until now, we've been living in a 'fake world'?"

He raised an eyebrow, waiting for the laughter. A ripple of chuckles moved through the graduates.

"But she makes a good point," he continued. "Until now, shelter, clothing, food, education were just there. Provided for us. And I never really had to think about my purpose because it was handed to me: get good grades, go to college, find a job."

He paused, drawing a deep breath, his voice rising with conviction. "As we've heard Dean Sanders say again and again over the years at college, our purpose is clear—to love God and love His people. That has never changed. But today, we take it one step further.

"It's time to leave behind the fairy-tale world, the one where most of our decisions have been made for us, and step boldly into the calling He has for each of us."

Cheers erupted around Sammy, but she sat frozen, her heart pounding.

Ha! But what if I don't know my calling? she thought. *And what if every plan I had for my future was ripped out of my hands at 9:00 p.m. last night?*

As if hearing her thoughts, the speaker continued, "And if you're not sure what your calling is yet, take heart. This is the perfect time to figure it out. Seek Him, search your heart, and don't be afraid to start small. Clarity will come as you move forward, one step at a time. But never wonder. Just like Jeremiah 29:11 reminds us, God has great plans for us."

He went on to quote authors and encourage involvement in the community and local government, but Sammy found herself repeating the words: *"Figure it out, one step at a time."*

And then, she wished she could raise her hand and ask, *"But where do you start when you don't even know where you're going?"*

The speaker's voice rang out with conviction, drawing Sammy back to the present.

"And class, until we meet again, don't give up! Press hard on the race marked out for you, fixing your eyes on Jesus, the author and perfecter of our faith. Now go and make your mark on this world for Him!"

He paused, took his hat off, and said, "Here's to the real world!" And with that, his and the other graduating hats went flying.

As the crowd dispersed, Amanda found Sammy.

"Sammy! We did it!" Amanda squealed, throwing her arms around her in a tight hug before pulling back to snap a selfie.

Sammy forced a smile for the camera, but Amanda didn't miss the flicker of something in her eyes.

She studied her best friend for a moment before lowering her phone. "Okay, spill."

Sammy blinked. "What?"

Amanda crossed her arms. "That look. The one that says you're thinking so hard you might actually combust. I thought tonight was supposed to be a celebration."

Sammy laughed softly, but it didn't quite reach her eyes. "Yeah, it is. I just thought I'd have more figured out by now."

Amanda's playful smirk faded. "You're not supposed to have everything figured out. That's the whole point of this next season, Sammy. You get to explore. Try new things. Make mistakes. You don't have to have the perfect plan."

Sammy swallowed. "I've always had a plan."

Amanda softened, squeezing her hand. "I know. And I get it. But maybe, just maybe, God's about to show you a better one."

The words settled between them, weighty and unshakable.

Amanda exhaled, shaking off the heaviness. "Look, I'll check in on you from Michigan, but you better promise me you'll keep me updated on all the amazing things you're about to do."

Sammy hesitated, then nodded. "I promise."

Amanda grinned. "Good. Because best friends don't ghost each other, even across state lines."

Sammy let out a genuine laugh this time. "Never."

And just like that, Amanda was off, disappearing into the sea of graduates and their families.

Sammy took a deep breath, squared her shoulders, and turned toward her family, pasting on her best "happy to see you" face.

"Sammmmmmmy!" The excited squeal came from a tiny redheaded blur racing toward her. Sammy scooped little Carol up in her arms, grinning.

"Well, hello there, sweet pea! How are you?"

"Oh, I'm good. I don't have to sit still anymore." Carol grabbed Sammy's cheeks with dramatic flair. "I really thought I was going to die if I had to sit still another second!"

Sammy laughed. "Well, darling, then I am also glad your sitting time is up. I would hate for you to die over such a thing!"

She took off her cap and placed it on Carol's head before setting her back down.

Carol gasped in delight, then immediately ran off to show the other siblings her new treasure.

Sammy watched with quiet joy as her little brothers and sisters ooh-ed and ahh-ed over the magical cap their oldest sister had just worn on stage.

Oh, how cute are they? she thought, wishing she could freeze this moment forever. They were all growing up so fast.

"Samantha!"

Her mom appeared, taking her hands and squeezing them tightly. "We are all so incredibly proud of you! A degree in teaching and nothing but *everything* ahead of you!"

Right, Sammy thought. Her doubts flared like warning lights, but she shoved them aside. "Oh, thanks, Mama," she said, hugging her.

Her dad stepped up next, pulling her into a big, warm papa-bear hug. "We know you are going to go far, kiddo!"

Chris, her oldest brother, slung an arm around her shoulders and gently steered her away from the crowd.

"So," he said, keeping his voice low. "We thought we'd take you out to dinner to celebrate and, you know, really get the scoop on where you're heading next." Then, glancing back to ensure they were out of earshot, he added, "I got your text. I'm sorry about Richard."

His voice was low, sincere. "He's a putz, Sammy—plain and simple. You deserve someone who sees how incredible you are, not someone who takes you for granted." Chris squeezed her. "And you? You're going to do amazing things, with or without him. Don't ever doubt that."

As they walked back to the group, Glory linked arms with Sammy.

"I've got Sammy!" Glory announced, patting her arm. "We'll meet y'all at the restaurant."

Sammy watched as her family piled into their van, a flicker of peace settling over her.

She had no debt.

$8,000 in savings.

And a supportive family by her side.

She still didn't know what came next, and the uncertainty gnawed at her like an ache she couldn't shake.

But as she glanced back at her classmates one last time, the day's chaos fading into the distance, she whispered, "Okay, Lord. I don't have any plans this time. Please, just show me the next step."

Chapter 6

On the ride to the restaurant, Sammy stared out the window, her mind racing. She kept rehearsing how to tell her family.

Hey, Mom and Dad, I have no clue what I'm doing. Can I move in and babysit to pay rent while I figure out my life in our small town?

But no matter how she framed it, each attempt sounded worse than the last. The knot of dread in her chest only tightened.

Glory's voice cut through her spiraling thoughts. "I've been thinking about our talk this morning," she said, her hands steady on the wheel. She glanced at Sammy, her tone calm but purposeful. "And I'd like for you to consider a proposition."

Sammy froze. "Proposition?" She eyed her grandmother warily. "Glory, what are you talking about?"

Glory took a measured breath, as if gathering her words. "At last week's bridge game, it came up that while our church wants to host a food pantry to help the community, we can't actually have one until someone steps up to spearhead the project."

Sammy blinked, unsure where this was going. "That's really neat that your church is so outreach-focused."

"Well, we want to be that focused," Glory admitted. "But right now, we're just a church with nice thoughts about reaching others. Without someone to take the lead, it's all just talk." She pulled into the Italian restaurant's parking lot, parked the car, and turned to face Sammy with hopeful eyes. "Here's my proposal: think of it as a respite while you figure out your next move." She let the words settle before adding, "This afternoon, I called

Pastor Mark and shared the idea with him, and he said to ask you."

Sammy's eyebrows shot up. "Me?"

Glory's tone grew more animated. "There's such a need in our community. We are the second fastest-growing city in Texas—the Hill Country is booming! But more and more, we're seeing families who can't make ends meet and kids going to bed hungry. It breaks my heart." She hesitated momentarily, then continued, "After our walk this morning, while I was praying, the food pantry and our conversation came to mind, and, well, I think you'd be perfect for this."

Sammy blinked, her stomach fluttering. "Perfect for . . . ?"

"The part-time, temporary position of food pantry coordinator," Glory clarified. "It'll take some time to really establish the pantry—maybe six months to a year. It needs someone who can dedicate twenty to thirty hours a week. We'd take care of your room and board and give you one hundred dollars weekly too."

Sammy stared at her, stunned.

A food pantry? How would I even start? I've never led something like this. What if I fail?

The doubts came rushing in, twisting her stomach into knots.

But alongside the hesitation, something else stirred—an almost imperceptible spark. *Maybe this is what I need.* A chance to prove to herself that she could handle something bigger.

Glory leaned forward, her hands warm as they enclosed Sammy's. "You've always had things planned out, Sammy, but sometimes life calls us to step into the unknown. I think you're ready for this."

Sammy swallowed hard. Was she?

Glory sat up straighter, her tone turning playful. "So, with all that said, would you like the six-to-twelve-month, part-time, temporary job as food pantry coordinator for Grace Chapel?"

Sammy's head spun. She hadn't seen this coming. Every instinct told her to stall. She needed time to think, map out a plan, and see a year or more into the future.

But this?

There wouldn't be time to analyze, to weigh every possibility. She would have to jump—or miss out.

And then, for the first time in a long time, a different thought whispered: *Why not?*

Sammy took a deep breath. Then, before she could second-guess herself, she met Glory's gaze and nodded. "Yes," she said, softly at first, as if speaking to more than just her grandmother. "Ok."

The confidence in her voice surprised even her. But as the words settled in her chest, they felt right.

Glory's face lit up, pride shining in her eyes. "That's my girl," she said, gently squeezing Sammy's hands. "You've got this."

After making the decision, they got out of the car and joined the family at the restaurant's door.

The warm, garlicky scent of breadsticks filled the air as they walked inside, and there was a hum of conversation and clinking glasses all around.

She sat between Carol and Chris at the circular table, surrounded by the comforting buzz of family.

Karen, Sammy's mom, broke through the chatter. "Oh, sweetie," she said, her voice a mix of concern and love. "We heard about Richard. I don't know what happened, but I want you to know you're always welcome to come home." She gave an empathetic look. "You can stay in the girls' room as long as you need. And I'm sure the daycare down the road would happily hire you until you get back on your feet. We just want you to know you have a place no matter what."

Sammy's stomach tightened.

She could already picture it. The floral bedspread, the closet packed with princess dresses, and the faint scent of candy and Barbies strewn across the floor. That cozy world was safe—but stepping back into it would mean becoming a smaller version of herself.

And that wasn't her plan.

Not anymore.

Sammy straightened, forcing herself to speak. "I do appreciate the offer, Mom, but actually—" She cleared her throat, feeling the weight of everyone's attention shift to her.

A week ago, her future had been mapped out. A perfect plan. A safe plan.

Now she was saying yes to something she never even imagined.

But it didn't feel wrong.

She met Glory's gaze, steady and reassuring, then squared her shoulders. "I have an announcement," Sammy said, the words catching slightly.

The table quieted.

All eyes turned toward her.

She swallowed hard. "Glory's church in Willow Creek is looking for a part-time, temporary food pantry coordinator." She breathed, adding, "And I've agreed to take the position."

Her mom blinked. "So, you'll be volunteering at Glory's church?"

Sammy's stomach clenched. *Is that how they see it?*

Before she could answer, Glory spoke smoothly, her voice kind but firm. "It's actually a paid position, and one that our church desperately needs right now. Sammy's exactly the person to get this off the ground."

Chris leaned back in his chair, a proud grin spreading across his face. "Wow. So, you're heading to Glory's town to start a food pantry? That's incredible, Sammy. I knew you'd do something amazing. It's just who you are."

Sammy's chest warmed at his words. "It feels like the right thing," she admitted. "I love tackling projects, and this one has a real purpose."

Her mom hesitated. "Do you really think you're ready for something this big on your own?"

Sammy took a deep breath, steadying herself. "I know it's sudden, and I'm sure I'll have much to learn," she said. "But it's time. And I'm ready."

She glanced at Glory, then at Chris. Their encouraging faces gave her the confidence to add, "Oh, and bonus?" Sammy added with a sparkle in her eye. "I get to live with Glory too."

Carol's eyes lit up. "I want to live with Glory too!"

Laughter rippled around the table, breaking the tension like sunlight through storm clouds. Sammy glanced at Glory, who gave her an encouraging smile. Nodding back, she turned to catch Chris's eye, his grin as proud as ever.

Toward the end of the meal, her dad raised his glass of tea, his eyes warm with pride. "Here's to Sammy, our firstborn and very own world-changer. I always knew you'd do big things, kiddo."

* * *

That night, after loading her boxes into Glory's car, Sammy lay awake in the stillness of her hotel room.

She stared at the ceiling, replaying the day in her mind, each moment feeling like a step forward. Deliberate. Uncertain. Leading toward something she couldn't quite name.

It was nothing like she had imagined just a week ago. But maybe that wasn't a bad thing.

With each passing hour, the breakup felt less like a loss and more like a release. Her carefully laid-out plans had crumbled. Yet she wasn't as devastated as she thought she'd be.

But she needed a new plan.

She reached for the journal her mother had given her as a graduation gift and flipped to the first page. Clicking her pen open, she hesitated just for a moment before pressing the tip to the paper and jotting down her top-of-mind goals, while her thoughts chimed in with their opinions.

> **NEW PLAN**
>
> **1 - Get a job.**
>
> *Done. That feels good.*
>
> **2 - Set up a real plan for the food pantry.**
>
> *Where do I even start? I should probably look at what other churches are doing and make a list of resources.*
>
> **3 - Meet people.**
>
> *Surely the town has grown a little since I was last there. But are there actually people my age?*
>
> **4 - Read more about calling.**

Where can I find something on this? A Bible app? A devotional? Maybe I should just spend more time in the Word?

5 - Make Glory's house feel like home.

6 - Give myself grace.

Funny how that's the hardest one.

With a quiet sigh, she closed the journal and tossed it—and her tumbling thoughts—onto her open luggage.

It wasn't much, but it was a start.

Chapter 7

"Only one more hour," Glory said, sipping her coffee and tapping the steering wheel in rhythm with the praise song playing softly on the radio.

"You sure you don't want me to drive? This has been a long road trip," Sammy offered, watching her grandmother with concern.

"You took the first half, and now it's my turn." Glory winked, her eyes bright with determination.

"All right," Sammy said, leaning back in her seat. The music flowed around her, and memories of Willow Creek returned, quiet and vivid, like pages turning in an old photo album.

She thought of summer afternoons spent visiting Glory and Grandpa. There was always a walk to Wilson Pharmacy—the place she had called the bubblegum shop as a child—for a piece of gum. She could almost hear the crunch of gravel under her sneakers and feel the sun warming her face as she and Chris kicked a rock down the road, laughing while the grown-ups chatted on the porch.

Her favorite memory rose to the surface. One Fourth of July, she and her cousins walked to the pharmacy by themselves for the first time. They had bought their favorite sodas, proud of their independence. On the way back, Chris cracked a joke that was so funny that she laughed mid-sip, and soda came out of her nose. They laughed the entire way home.

She loved that memory, but her thoughts were interrupted by a sprawling construction site on the side of the highway.

"Whoa, Glory." Sammy reached for the volume dial, turning the music down. She leaned forward, eyes widening. "What is that?"

Glory chuckled and glanced over. "That, sweet Sammy, is what progress looks like."

"Progress?" Sammy frowned as she stared at the cranes and bulldozers.

"New apartments. We're up to twelve thousand people now. Town ran out of room, so they're building on the edge," Glory said, easing off the highway and turning toward town. "Nelda could tell you more. She's been on the zoning committee for years."

"Wow," Sammy said, still watching the construction fade behind them. "I remember when the population sign said three thousand."

"That was more than a decade ago. Time moves faster than we think."

Sammy fell quiet. Familiar roads passed outside the window, but they didn't feel familiar anymore. Had it really been that long? She used to know this place like the back of her hand—holidays at Glory's house, walks to the bubblegum shop, quiet afternoons on the porch. Then, one year, the visits had just stopped.

"Why did we stop coming here for the holidays?" The question escaped before she could pull it back.

Glory gave her a gentle look. "When your parents started having more kids, your father and I talked. It was the year after your grandpa passed. He said, 'Mom, we love you, but the holidays already feel different with Dad gone. And with all the little ones, traveling is getting hard. Would it be all right if we hosted from now on? You'll always have a room, and we'd love for you to stay as long as you want.'"

Sammy let the words settle. For so long, she had assumed the visits stopped because something had gone wrong. That no one had cared to keep the tradition, but it hadn't been a falling out. It had just been life. Messy. Complicated. Human.

The ache in her chest eased, replaced by something quieter. Maybe it wasn't about what they had lost but what could still be rebuilt.

Glory slowed at a red light. "You'll notice a lot of changes on Main Street. That's where everything started to shift." She pointed towards a billboard for Main Street. "Do you remember Luke Foster? He owned the Foster Ranch."

Sammy thought for a moment. "A little. I remember the name."

"He was one of the kindest men you'd ever meet. Loved this town like it was family. Turns out he'd been quietly saving for years. When he passed, we found out he had left the entire amount in a trust for Willow Creek—with one request." The light turned green. Glory flicked on her signal and turned onto Main Street. "He wanted Main Street to be a place people would remember."

Sammy's breath caught as they drove forward.

The old, faded storefronts were gone. In their place were cheerful awnings and freshly painted buildings. String lights stretched across the street. Flower beds burst with color along the sidewalks. People moved easily between shops, talking and laughing. It was still Willow Creek, but it sparkled.

Her eyes landed on a storefront with a soft blue-and-cream-striped awning. The words were painted on the window in delicate, looping script: *Coffee With Your Cream Café. Pouring coffee, kindness, and second chances daily.*

Sammy leaned toward the glass. Inside, a pastry case gleamed beneath warm lighting, with golden croissants and cinnamon rolls stacked in inviting rows. A chalkboard sign outside the door caught her eye: *Today's Special: Cinnamon Swirl Latte and a Little Extra Grace.*

"Oh, Glory, there's a coffee shop now?" she asked, twisting in her seat.

"Yes, ma'am. And you'll love the owner, Lisa Bennett."

Sammy laughed. "I need to go. I can already picture myself there one morning this week."

Just as the café faded from view, another storefront caught her eye. She gasped. "Is that a bookstore?"

Glory nodded. "Oak and Ink. You'll love that place too. They do story nights and book clubs and even have a reading nook in the back."

Sammy's heart gave a hopeful flutter. "Between the coffee shop and the bookstore, I think I've found my two new favorite places."

Sunlight spilled on the sidewalks, casting gold across the windows and pavement. For the first time, she saw Willow Creek not just as a memory but as a place full of possibility.

They turned onto Glory's road, and a warm familiarity settled over her like an old quilt. The trees lining the narrow street looked taller, the sky somehow wider. Even the crooked, hand-painted mailbox felt like a friend waving her home.

When they pulled into the gravel driveway, Sammy took a slow breath.

Glory's home looked just as she remembered. Maybe sweeter. As if it had been waiting for her to come back. The porch wrapped around the house in a welcoming embrace. Lace curtains fluttered in the windows. A rocking chair creaked in the breeze.

She stepped out of the car slowly, the scent of honeysuckle surrounding her. As she climbed the steps, a quiet wave of nerves rose inside her.

This wasn't just a visit. This was a beginning.

Inside, the house smelled faintly of lemon polish and cinnamon. The Glory blend, Sammy always called it. The hallway walls still held faded photos, a cross-stitch that read *Love grows best in houses just like this,* and the old runner rug that always bunched up under fast footsteps.

Upstairs, her room had been cleared out and made new again. A soft quilt in calming blue tones covered the bed. A small vase of daffodils and irises sat on the dresser. The light through the window felt gentle.

On the nightstand rested a folded note.

You are not behind. You're just on a different road. Welcome home, sweetheart.

Sammy blinked quickly, a lump rising in her throat. She set her bag quietly by the door and sat on the edge of the bed, fingertips brushing the careful stitches of the quilt.

She didn't feel steady. She didn't feel strong.

But she felt held.

Later, downstairs, the scent of rosemary and garlic greeted her as she stepped into the kitchen.

"This all came together while I was away?" she asked, easing onto a stool.

Glory nodded from the stove. "My bridge club ladies helped. Nosy. Sneaky. Fantastic with throw pillows." They chuckled, and Glory poured more tea and glanced over with a gentle expression. "Settling in upstairs?"

"All unpacked," Sammy said, setting her fork down. "Thank you for everything. For letting me figure this out here."

Glory's eyes softened. "This is your home too. Stay as long as you need."

"Thanks," Sammy whispered, stifling a yawn.

Glory laughed. "It's been a long weekend. Before you turn in, can you meet with Pastor Mark and the board at ten in the morning? They want to get everyone on the same page about the food pantry."

"That sounds perfect," Sammy said, rising from the table. Fatigue pressed in on her limbs. She moved on autopilot.

Sammy tossed her plate in the trash without thinking.

Glory's soft laugh filled the room.

Sammy froze. "Oh no."

"Tired much?" Glory teased.

"Just a little," she said, retrieving her plate with a sheepish grin. She rinsed it properly and loaded it into the dishwasher. "That's my cue to call it a night."

"You've earned it. Sleep well."

Back upstairs, Sammy caught her reflection in the mirror. Shadows circled her eyes. A few strands had escaped her ponytail.

"One step at a time," she whispered.

She opened her journal and wrote a simple list:

> **Morning Routine**
>
> 1 Morning jog.
>
> *That one might hurt, but maybe it will help clear my head.*
>
> 2 Coffee and quiet time.
>
> *Absolutely necessary.*
>
> 3 Get to work.
>
> *Do I have an office? A schedule? Am I just figuring it out day by day?*

She studied it for a moment then sighed and closed the journal, placing it on the nightstand. Her body ached, but her spirit felt steadier.

Tomorrow was the first meeting. Her stomach fluttered. What if she wasn't what they were hoping for?

Still, she believed she could do this.

Slow. Steady. One step at a time.

She climbed into bed, pulled the quilt around her shoulders, and turned out the light.

Tomorrow, she would take the first step.

Chapter 8

The next morning, Sammy woke to her alarm and pulled on her running clothes before her brain had time to protest. Earbuds in, sneakers in hand, she tiptoed through the house, trying not to wake Glory.

"Good morning," Glory greeted from the kitchen, her voice bright and cheerful.

Sammy paused, startled to find her grandmother already up and sipping on coffee. "Good morning!" she said, tying her sneakers tighter.

"Have fun jogging. Coffee will be ready when you get back." Glory replied, smiling warmly.

"Will do," Sammy said, kissing Glory's cheek quickly and heading out the door.

The crisp morning air stung her cheeks, carrying the faint scent of honeysuckle on the breeze. As Sammy jogged past quiet houses, she smiled at a neighbor feeding chickens. This was exactly how she'd pictured life in Willow Creek.

Her legs ached when she reached Glory's walkway again, but her spirits felt lighter. Slowing, she spotted Glory on the porch swing, with her coffee and Bible. Sammy snuck past, offering a nod before slipping inside.

Inside, she poured herself a cup of coffee, went upstairs, and grabbed her journal from her nightstand. She took a deep breath and sat on her bed, feeling beat but accomplished.

She flipped to a fresh page, wrote the date, and gave a quick update:

> First jog today. I did it. Still no closer to figuring out my purpose, but at least I checked one thing off my morning routine plan.
>
> First meeting with the food pantry board this morning. Pretty sure I have no idea what I'm getting myself into. Why did I say yes to this again??
>
> Well, it's time to get ready. Hoping to start reading my Bible more—maybe even find a reading plan about figuring out my calling. Note to self: add that to the list.

God, I'm not sure what I'm doing here, but help me take it one step at a time.

She closed the journal and set it aside, stretching her legs before pushing herself up from the bed. The day was just beginning, and there was plenty ahead.

She grabbed her go-to outfit: jeans, sneakers, and a simple top. It was casual but put together, and it would do for a first meeting, hopefully.

Catching her reflection in the mirror, she noticed the tension in her shoulders. Sammy took a slow breath, held it, and then let it out, willing her body to ease.

"You've got this," she said aloud, hoping the words would root themselves somewhere deeper than her throat.

"Maybe if I keep saying it, I'll actually believe it." She said under her breath on the way downstairs.

* * *

As Glory pulled into the freshly paved parking lot of Grace Chapel, a wave of nostalgia and curiosity swept over Sammy. The church's brick facade and tall white steeple remained unchanged, evoking memories of childhood Christmas Eve services. Yet the addition of a few extra buildings and the upgraded parking lot hinted at a church that had subtly evolved over the years.

The meeting room was simple but inviting. Mismatched chairs circled a large, well-worn table. A bulletin board near the door overflowed with colorful flyers for Bible study groups, 4-H events, and community potlucks. Sammy's gaze paused on a framed photo of a younger Pastor Mark shaking hands with a man Glory had mentioned earlier, Luke Foster.

Pastor Mark greeted them warmly, enveloping Glory in a hug before turning to Sammy. "You must be Samantha. We're so glad you're here," he said, his voice rich with warmth.

Before Sammy could respond, Lora breezed in, balancing a tray of cookies that filled the air with a buttery sweetness. "Hope you're ready for these!" she declared, setting the tray down with a flourish, Ethel Sue behind her.

Pastor Mark chuckled. "Careful, Lora's cookies are addictive. One bite and store-bought will never cut it again."

"He's not wrong," Nelda said, reaching for her second. "If blue ribbons were handed out for baking, Lora would need a trophy case."

Sammy recognized Lora, Nelda, and Ethel Sue as her grandmother's bridge group friends. Over the years, she'd met them through Glory, their laughter and spirited conversations always filling Glory's kitchen like sunshine. The familiarity eased her nerves as she reached for a cookie, letting herself settle into the room's cheerful energy.

The door opened, and a young woman about Sammy's age stepped inside. Every movement, every detail of her presence felt deliberate, as if she had spent years perfecting the art of effortless grace.

Her loose brown curls framed her face with almost deliberate precision, and her immaculately pressed blouse—tucked neatly into freshly starched, perfectly fitting jeans—made Sammy suddenly self-conscious of her outfit.

The woman's gaze swept the room, her features were polished to perfection. But when her eyes landed on Sammy, they lingered just a fraction too long—long enough to make Sammy glance down at her own simple outfit. Then, as if catching herself, her expression softened into something almost pleasant.

"Welcome," she said smoothly. "Love your casual style. So . . . effortless."

Sammy opened her mouth to say thanks, but instead, as she wasn't sure it was a compliment, she nodded.

Then, just as quickly, she turned to Pastor Mark, her expression shifting—light, easy, as if she'd simply been scanning the room all along.

"Michelle! So glad you could make it," Pastor Mark greeted her.

Michelle strode forward, extending a graceful arm for a side hug. "Of course, Pastor. Always happy to be here," she said smoothly. Her voice carried the easy confidence of someone who never questioned whether she belonged.

Sammy's stomach tightened. Maybe this wasn't such a good idea after all. She shifted slightly, the weight of uncertainty pressing down, but a familiar voice pulled her back before she could dwell on it.

"Sammy, there you are!" Nelda appeared beside her, the warmth in her expression cutting through the tension like a welcomed breeze. She gave Sammy's arm a gentle squeeze, grounding her in the easy familiarity of an old friend.

"So, how are you finding Willow Creek?"

Sammy exhaled, grateful for the distraction. "It's just as charming as I remembered. In fact, on my jog this morning, I waved to a neighbor feeding chickens in their side yard."

"Oh, that's Mrs. Harper," Nelda said, a flicker of amused recognition lighting her eyes. "She's a sweetheart, but her rooster, Biscuit? That's another story. He's made the most wanted list in town for the chaos he's caused."

Sammy frowned, half laughing. "A rooster? What could he possibly have done?"

Ethel Sue leaned in, her voice dropping to a conspiratorial whisper. "Let's just say the mailman still refuses to deliver to Mrs. Harper's front door."

Lora nodded sagely. "And don't forget the mayor. Biscuit the Third sent him running straight up the steps of City Hall."

Sammy's jaw dropped. "What? He chased the mayor?"

"Not just chased," Ethel Sue corrected, raising an eyebrow. "He cornered him at the top!"

"Oh, it was a full-blown standoff," Lora added. "The mayor barely made it inside. Biscuit was right on his heels."

"And the best part?" Ethel Sue said, her eyes twinkling with laughter. "Once the doors shut, Biscuit just stood there. Watching. Waiting. Like he knew this wasn't over."

The group erupted into laughter, their chuckles bouncing off the walls, lingering like the warmth of a shared memory. Sammy wiped a tear from the corner of her eye, shaking her head at the absurdity of a town terrorized by a rooster.

Pastor Mark cleared his throat as the laughter faded, his voice rising above the cheerful buzz. "Alright, everyone, let's go ahead and find our seats."

The lighthearted energy lingered, but the group began to settle, shifting their focus as the meeting prepared to begin.

Once everyone had settled, Pastor Mark opened with a prayer, thanking God for guidance and the opportunity to serve their community. Sammy clasped her hands in her lap, soothed by the familiar rhythm of church life.

"Everyone, I'd like to introduce y'all to Samantha Thomas, our new food pantry intern," Pastor Mark said, motioning toward her. "Samantha, would you tell us a little about yourself?"

Sammy nodded, smiling. "Sure." She cleared her throat and hesitated. *What do I even say? Hi, I'm Sammy, and my whole life plan just blew up. I have no clue what I want to be when I grow up.* She quickly decided against that route.

"Hey, everyone." She lifted a hand in a casual wave. "My name is Samantha, but everyone calls me Sammy."

"Noted," Pastor Mark said, jotting something on his yellow pad.

"I grew up in a family of nine in Rogers, Arkansas."

Eyebrows raised around the table, and Michelle spoke first. "Nine?"

Sammy grinned. "Yep. We were a family of four for about eight years, and then the Lord called my parents to have more. I'm the oldest, so I've had plenty of practice with organizing chaos." She paused, her tone softening. "I always thought I'd be a teacher, so I went to college and got my degree in education. I just graduated last weekend."

A chorus of congratulations rose from the room.

"I thought I had plans lined up after graduation," Sammy continued, "but they fell through. So, I'm here now and excited to help get this pantry up and running. I love a good project."

The group responded with smiles and encouraging nods. Sammy sat down, feeling a little steadier.

Pastor Mark passed the meeting agenda around the table. "Sammy, we're so grateful you're here. No one in Willow Creek has done this before, but I have a buddy up in Denton who started a pantry, and he said setting a soft launch six months out gave them a good target."

As Pastor Mark praised Sammy's role in the food pantry, Michelle's fingers drummed lightly on the edge of her planner. The movement was small but steady, tapping a quiet, measured rhythm. Sammy caught it—the only tell in Michelle's otherwise perfect composure.

Michelle's expression faltered for a fraction of a second as she noticed her tapping, her lips pressing just a little too tightly together. Frustration? Annoyance? Sammy wasn't sure. But just as quickly, Michelle exhaled, stilled her fingers, and flipped a page in her planner, as if nothing had happened.

She found the date she was looking for, her tone smooth but pointed. "A soft launch is a smart idea." She said starring the date, "Gives you some breathing room in case things get overwhelming."

Sammy's grip tightened around her pen, her fingers pressing into the smooth barrel. The word hung in the air—sharp, uninvited. *Overwhelming.* She swallowed hard, her pulse quickening. Was that how they saw her? Like a stopgap, not a real solution?

She nodded, a pleasant mask in place, as if the comment hadn't landed. *It's fine. It doesn't matter what Michelle thinks.* But a quiet voice in her mind whispered, *What if she's right? What if you can't do this on your own?*

Before she could dwell on it any further, Pastor Mark spoke up, his voice warm. "Sammy, any progress you make toward this goal is a win."

She inhaled slowly, willing her shoulders to ease. Maybe she wasn't as confident as Michelle, but she'd committed to this. And that had to count for something.

Clearing his throat, Pastor Mark looked around the table. "This meeting is for you all to get to know Sammy and share your heart and ideas with her," he said. "After that, we'd love your support and prayers as she steps into this role and follows where the Lord leads."

Sammy picked up her pen and circled the launch date. *It's just for now. Just until I figure out what's next.* But even as she thought it, something in her chest tightened. She shook it off. This was just another task, another thing to manage, not a permanent stop. She could organize a pantry. She could coordinate volunteers. But that didn't mean she was staying.

As suggestions began bouncing around the table, Sammy leaned in, her pen poised. She could do this. A plan always made things feel more manageable.

"We should add hygiene products," Lora suggested. "Toothpaste, soap, even diapers. Those are just as important as food."

Nelda leaned forward, her voice firm. "She's right. I know a family who had to choose between buying groceries and diapers last month. This pantry isn't just about food; it's about dignity."

Sammy nodded, scribbling notes as the group's passion lifted her spirits.

"You know," Michelle began. "Summers in Willow Creek can be dull for kids. What if we organized a summer camp? Sports, crafts, Bible lessons. It would be such a gift to the community."

Pastor Mark nodded thoughtfully as others chimed in approvingly. "That's an ambitious idea, Michelle. What do you think, Sammy?"

Sammy hesitated, feeling the weight of the room's gaze.

"That's a great idea," Sammy said, lighting her tone. "Would you be open to helping me with logistics?"

Michelle lit up, amusement threading her voice. "Oh, I'd love to see it happen! But between my role as Sterling Ridge Ranch ambassador and everything I juggle at the ranch, I barely have time to breathe."

She exhaled dramatically, then softened her tone, offering a polite, almost pitying expression. "But I can definitely offer suggestions. If you need guidance, of course."

Sammy forced a grin. *If* she needed guidance. The way Michelle said it made it sound like she already did.

The room responded with polite chuckles, the kind that filled silences more than expressed amusement. Sammy, however, caught the artful dodge beneath Michelle's polished response. She wasn't refusing outright, but her words had neatly sidestepped any real commitment. It was a graceful deflection, dressed in charm, and Sammy couldn't help but wonder if anyone else noticed.

As the meeting wound down, Pastor Mark outlined the next steps. "Glory, would you help Sammy familiarize herself with the church this week?"

Glory nodded. "Of course."

Pastor Mark's gaze softened as he looked around the table. "This is a big task, but with God's guidance and everyone's effort, I believe we can make a real impact. Let's close in prayer."

The group bowed their heads, the room falling into a calm stillness as Pastor Mark prayed for guidance and unity in their work.

As everyone started to get up, Michelle's phone buzzed. She glanced at the screen and sighed before answering.

"Hi, Mom. Yes, I'm still here." A pause. "Yes, of course, I'll be at the fundraiser early. Yes, the dress is steamed. No, I haven't forgotten about the guest list—"

Her voice lowered slightly, and Sammy barely caught the next words. "I know, I will."

As she hung up, she put her phone in her purse and Sammy noticed her eyes seemed distant now—tired, tight around the edges.

"Well, I have a full schedule today. See y'all next time," Michelle said lightly, waving as she breezed out the door.

As others began to disperse, Glory's friends lingered behind. Nelda leaned toward her, a knowing glint in her eyes. "Michelle's sweet, but bless her heart, she's all ribbons and parades. She doesn't always see the work behind the sparkle."

Lora chuckled, nodding in agreement. "Her heart's in the right place, but she's never had to roll up her sleeves. Just remember, you've got a whole team of people who are ready to get their hands dirty."

Sammy's eyes sparkled with amusement. "So, take her ideas with a grain of salt?"

"Honey, take 'em with the whole saltshaker." Nelda winked.

The group burst into laughter, the sound warm and unpretentious, settling Sammy's nerves.

As the laughter faded, some of the tension in Sammy's chest slipped away. She hadn't expected it, but Glory's bridge friends—Lora, Nelda, and Ethel Sue—already felt like her kind of people. Women who didn't need to impress anyone, who believed in showing up, rolling up their sleeves, and doing the work. No wonder they were Glory's closest friends.

Glory looped her arm through Sammy's and led her deeper into the church.

"Come on, sweet girl," she said, her tone warm and steady. "Let's go look around."

Chapter 9

The building was older, and its age was evident in the details. The 1960s wallpaper, yellowed with time, seemed to beg for mercy, and the carpet looked like it might've been installed not long after. Still, the church had a charm about it, a sense of history and resilience that spoke of faith, community, and steadfast perseverance.

As they descended the creaky basement stairs, Sammy noticed a series of Sunday school classrooms. Each bore signs of years of faithful use: bulletin boards filled with faded construction paper crafts, shelves crammed with well-loved Bibles, and tattered hymnals. She could almost hear the echoes of children's laughter and the warm hum of devotion woven into these walls.

Glory stopped at the last room, the only one that stood empty. The fluorescent light flickered as Glory nudged the door open, casting uneven shadows across the room.

"And this, my dear sweet Sammy," Glory said, her voice filled with pride and excitement, "is where the food pantry will be."

Sammy stepped inside, her eyes drawn to the burnt-orange carpet. The room was plain: bare walls in a faded blue color, a faint scent of dust, and a single window high on the wall, letting in just enough sunlight to cast golden streaks across the space. It was quiet, unassuming, and brimming with potential.

But Sammy couldn't ignore the tightening in her chest. It wasn't just the room that felt empty; so did she. She always had a clear vision, a checklist, and a next step. But this? This was uncharted territory. There was no syllabus, no study guide, and no guarantee of success. What if she let everyone down?

What if she let God down?

Glory turned to Sammy, her gaze steady and kind. Taking Sammy's hands in her own, she bowed her head and began to pray, her voice soft but unwavering. "Lord, we are so excited to see what You will do with this room, with the food pantry, and with Sammy while she's here. Lord, we place it all in Your hands and thank You for the blessings You've already set in motion. In Jesus' name, amen."

As Glory prayed, Sammy's throat tightened, her emotions swirling in a mix of doubt and longing. But something about the steady cadence of Glory's words and their quiet confidence began to shift something inside her.

When Glory said, "Amen," Sammy whispered it back, her voice carrying a quiet reverence. As Glory prayed, Sammy's chest tightened, but not with fear this time. It was something softer, a nudge, or a whisper in her heart that encouraged her that just taking life one step at a time was okay.

* * *

After wrapping up at the church, Sammy borrowed Glory's car to run errands. She hoped keeping busy might keep the doubts at bay.

Tightening her grip on the list, she stepped into the local grocery store. The cool air and comforting aroma of freshly baked bread welcomed her.

"New town, new start," she muttered under her breath.

But as she maneuvered her wobbly cart down the produce aisle, it became clear that a "new start" might not include mastering the art of grocery shopping.

"Bananas, milk, eggs . . . something green," Sammy murmured, scanning the shelves. She reached for a perfectly crisp green apple just as her cart veered sharply to the left, as though it had a mind of its own. She tugged it back, but the front wheel stuck, sending the cart forward with an alarming thunk.

Her eyes widened as a towering stack of oranges teetered, then cascaded to the floor, the fruit scattering like bowling pins. Sammy froze, horror mixing with disbelief as shoppers dodged the rogue citrus.

"Oh no," she whispered, crouching to gather the escapees.

She managed to catch one only for another to roll directly into her path. She stumbled back, her hand gripping the cart for balance.

"Great. I'm being attacked by citrus," she muttered, wondering if this was how she'd make her mark on Willow Creek, as the girl who declared war on the produce aisle.

A low chuckle broke the tension behind her.

"Need a hand?"

Sammy whipped around to see a tall, broad-shouldered man with warm brown eyes and an easy grin leaning casually on his cart. He looked as though he was trying very hard not to laugh outright.

"I've got it, thanks," she said, aiming for confidence as she clutched an armful of fruit.

There was a strange, unexpected familiarity about him. Not like she knew him, but like she was supposed to. The thought was ridiculous, but it unsettled her just enough to make her fumble the orange in her grasp. It slipped free, bouncing cheerfully across the floor.

The man raised an eyebrow, his eyes dancing with amusement.

"You sure about that?" he asked, bending down to grab the runaway orange.

Sammy reached for another piece of fruit, her mind scrambling to find a witty comeback, but all she managed was a breathy "Thanks." Her cheeks warmed as if her brain had forgotten how basic human interaction worked.

She sighed, unable to suppress a small laugh. "Okay, fine. Maybe I could use some help."

Together—with two employees joining in—they managed to corral the rogue citrus, a few still rolling lazily under the shelves.

"I've gotta say," he said, handing her the last orange, "this might be the best grocery store entertainment I've seen in a while."

Sammy turned red but couldn't help smiling. "Glad I could liven up your shopping trip."

He tilted his head toward her cart, which now wobbled precariously again. "That thing looks like it's about to give up on life. Want me to grab you a new one?"

Sammy hesitated, glancing at the offending cart. "Honestly? That's probably the best idea I've heard all day."

He disappeared for a moment and returned with a fresh cart. "Here you go. Guaranteed to behave—well, mostly."

Sammy accepted it with a light nod, amusement flickering in her eyes. "Thanks. I owe you one."

"Don't worry about it," he said, a teasing glint in his gaze. "Just promise you won't launch another fruit assault anytime soon."

Her laugh was light, genuine, and a little self-deprecating. "I'll do my best."

As he walked away, Sammy caught herself still watching. She blinked, forcing her gaze to her cart instead. But the warmth of his grin lingered, the way some people just leave a trace of laughter in the air after they're gone.

Just as she reached for her shopping list, a flicker of movement caught her eye. She glanced up just in time to see him cast a quick look over his shoulder, his gaze finding hers for the briefest moment before he turned the corner.

Her breath hitched, her fingers tightening around the cart's handle.

When she glanced at the curved produce mirror, her reflection met her gaze, her smile brighter than it had been in weeks.

Maybe this next chapter wouldn't be so bad after all.

* * *

Back at Glory's house, Sammy spread the meeting materials across the dining table, her notes organized in neat stacks. But a dozen questions hummed in her thoughts beneath the Sharpie-inked words and neatly typed agendas. *What if no one showed up to volunteer? What if the community doesn't support it? What if I failed before I even began?*

"This is big," she whispered, tapping her pen against the table.

She spent the afternoon going through the packet again and then Googled food pantries to get a clue about what they might look like. By evening, she was ready to call it a night.

Glory appeared with an extra cup. "Sweet tea, my dear? I usually end my days on the porch swing and watch the sunset. Would you like to join me?"

"I would love that." Sammy sighed as she got up and stretched.

As they got settled, Glory asked, "So, what did you think of your first day here?"

Sammy leaned back in the swing, letting the cool evening air brush against her face. She sipped the sweet tea, savoring its familiar comfort before answering. "It's been good. A little overwhelming, but good. I knocked over an entire stack of oranges at the grocery store, so, you know, just making sure everyone knows the new girl's here."

Glory chuckled, her eyes sparkling in the golden light of the setting sun. "Well, if you wanted to make an impression, you've succeeded."

"Mission accomplished," Sammy said in mock celebration. "But honestly, it's been nice to stay busy. The meeting this morning was helpful, and diving into all those notes this afternoon gave me a little more confidence about what I'm supposed to do here. I think."

She hesitated, her fingers tracing the rim of her glass. "I'm still not sure I'm the right person for this."

Glory leaned forward, her voice gentle but firm. "Sweetheart, we never feel ready for what God calls us to do. Nothing would ever get done if we waited until we were certain."

"But what if I mess it up? What if the pantry never gets off the ground, and I let everyone down?" Sammy glanced at her grandmother, her doubts reflected in her eyes.

Glory reached over, placing a warm hand over Sammy's. "Then you learn from it, and you try again. This isn't about perfection, Sammy, it's about obedience and faith. God doesn't call the equipped; He equips the called."

Sammy let the words settle over her, their weight both comforting and challenging. She nodded slowly. They sat in companionable silence for a while, the swing creaking gently as they rocked, the sky painted in streaks of orange.

Sammy went inside, and before exhaustion could set in, she made a quick journal entry.

God doesn't call the equipped; He equips the called.

Here's hoping I am called to this, she thought as she closed her journal, exhaled slowly, and let the day go.

* * *

Across town, the same sunset stretched over Martinez Ranch, its golden hues settling over miles of open land. Jake finished his last chore of the day, wiping his brow with the back of his hand. He would never call ranch life easy, but he would always call it good.

Leading Zeke up the worn path to the ridge, he felt the day's weight begin to ease. This was his favorite time, the world softening around the edges, the sky painted in shades of pink and gold, and the quiet hum of crickets rising with the evening breeze.

Most evenings, he'd take a moment here, letting the quiet of the land settle his mind. He'd pray, listen, breathe. But tonight, his thoughts kept wandering back to her.

The woman with the green eyes and the laugh that seemed to lift the weight of the world, if only for a moment.

He chuckled, the sound low and warm in the cool evening air. Who would've thought a simple trip to the grocery store would leave him thinking about a girl juggling oranges like she was in some kind of slapstick routine? Yet, here he was.

Sure, the oranges were comedy gold. But it was how she carried it—light and a little self-conscious, like someone who knew how to laugh at life.

At the crest of the hill, Jake swung down from the saddle. Zeke wandered off to graze, and Jake sat on the old fallen tree he'd come to think of as his spot. He pulled off his hat, let the breeze cool his skin, and looked out over the fields stretching far and wide.

He'd been coming to this ridge since he was a kid, back when his *abuelo* would take him on horseback rides, pointing out the land that had been in their family for generations. His grandfather owned the ranch, rose with the sun, and worked until the light faded. Jake had moved in full-time after college, helping with the heavy lifting and keeping an eye on John, who lived in the dry cabin behind the main house.

John had become part of their little family, working odd jobs around the ranch and sharing quiet meals at the big kitchen table. There was something sacred about the life they'd built, a rhythm of hard work, good food, and stories shared over cups of Abuelo's strong coffee.

Jake had prayed many times on this hill, his words drifting into the wide Texas sky. It was here, on a clear summer night, that he'd first asked God to guide his steps.

"I'm ready, Lord. I'd like someone to share this life with. Someone to love."

God's answer had always been the same: "Trust Me."

And Jake had tried. He'd held on to that promise through countless weddings of friends, well-meaning setups from folks at church, and quiet dinners at his kitchen table with Abuelo and John. He'd trusted, even when the waiting was hard.

But tonight, sitting under the streaks of twilight, he felt something shift.

"What is it about her, Lord?" His voice was soft, barely more than a whisper. "It was just a moment, but it felt like more."

The question lingered, carried by the breeze, woven into the songs of crickets and the gentle rustling of leaves.

Jake sighed, his heart aching with the familiar mix of hope and doubt. Was he just being foolish? Was he reading too much into a chance encounter in the produce aisle?

He let the thought go, lifting his worries to God. The answer came as it always did—gentle, steady, and true. "Trust Me."

A soft smile tugged at his lips. Jake didn't need all the answers. He didn't need to know why today felt different. He only needed to take the next step, whatever that looked like.

He stood, brushing the dirt from his jeans, and whistled for Zeke. The horse's ears perked up, and he trotted over, ready to head home.

As they started back down the hill, Jake kept the pace slow, savoring the quiet. The rhythm of Zeke's hooves against the earth felt like a heartbeat, steady and sure.

"Lord, I trust You."

He didn't know if he'd see her again. He didn't even know her name. But if God was in this, if today had been a nudge in a new direction, Jake was willing to follow.

As he neared the barn, he spotted the warm glow from the main house. The soft hum of John sitting on the porch, his old guitar in hand, picking out a tune as the crickets joined in. And he was sure Abuelo would be out there too, whittling on his latest creations.

He took a deep breath, letting the comfort of home settle over him.

And maybe, just maybe, he'd see those green eyes again.

Chapter 10

Sammy arrived at the church just after 9:00 a.m. and headed straight for the pantry room. The quiet air greeted her as she stepped inside, the faint scent of old wood and paper lingering in the space.

She set her things down and eased onto the floor, letting the stillness wash over her. But the quiet didn't erase the doubt pressing at the edges of her thoughts.

What if I can't do this? What if I mess it up?

What if they realize I was never the right person for this in the first place?

She swallowed hard, her fingers curling around the fabric of her jeans. The weight of it all, this project, this town, this unexpected new path, felt impossibly heavy.

She closed her eyes. *I trust You, Lord.* The words felt more like a question than a declaration. But still, she whispered them into the stillness. "Guide my steps."

The hum of the air-conditioning filled her ears as she waited for clarity. For something, *anything*, to tell her she wasn't about to fail at this. But after a moment, her thoughts drifted not to her growing to-do list, but to the guy from the grocery store.

Warm brown eyes. An easy grin. That dimple when he smiled.

Why am I thinking about him? She shook her head with a self-deprecating laugh. *Focus, Sammy. You've got bigger things to figure out.*

With a deep breath, she pulled out her new food pantry notebook and tapped her pen against the blank page of the spiral.

"Alright," she murmured. "Let's figure this out."

She began jotting down everything that came to mind.

FOOD PANTRY—IMMEDIATE NEEDS

Food—nonperishables, fresh produce if possible

Shelving—sturdy enough to hold bulk donations

Permits & Inspections—do we need government approval?

Partnerships—local food banks, grocery stores, suppliers

Sponsors—businesses willing to support or donate regularly

She glanced around the room, chewing the end of her pen.

"This is just the beginning," she said to herself.

Sammy loved a good list. She always saw checklists as roadmaps to success. If she could just figure out every step, then maybe she wouldn't fail. Maybe then, she'd prove she could do this.

She made a few more notes, closed her notebook, and stretched, rolling the stiffness from her shoulders. The list was a start, but the real work was ahead of her. She needed a moment to breathe, to think, maybe even to feel excited about the possibilities. And if anything could help with that, it was coffee.

The café wasn't far, just a nice mile-long walk from the church. She grabbed her things, hopped up, and embraced the walk as a chance to clear her head.

As she reached the café, the chalkboard sign had a new special: *Today's Special: Peppermint Latte with a side of Kindness.*

Sammy exhaled as she reached for the door, she already liked this place.

The bell above the door chimed as she stepped inside Coffee with Your Cream Café. The rich and inviting scent of fresh espresso and cinnamon curled through the air.

Sunlight streamed through the tall windows, spilling golden rays across rustic wooden tables, where mason jars of local honey sat in neat rows. The place had a heartbeat—soft chatter, the occasional scrape of a chair, the low hum of a vintage radio playing an old tune in the background. It was not loud, not overwhelming, just warm, just right.

Her gaze flickered to the counter, where a curvy woman in her late forties with short brown hair streaked with soft blond highlights was wiping her hands on a checkered dish towel. She had the kind of presence that filled a room without trying—steady, welcoming, like she'd seen a thousand stories unfold over cups of coffee. When her eyes landed on Sammy, her expression lit with a kind of warm mischief—like she'd already decided she liked her.

Lisa leaned casually against the counter as Sammy approached. "Well, well. Glory's granddaughter finally made her way in."

Sammy blinked, then let out a soft laugh. "Word travels fast."

Lisa grinned. "Oh, honey, I run a coffee shop. That means I know everything." She winked. "Before it even happens."

Sammy shook her head, smiling as she scanned the menu. She should probably stick with something simple like she always did.

But instead, she found herself blurting out, "I'll take the Cinnamon Swirl Latte."

Lisa's grin widened. "Good choice. That one's like a hug in a cup." She turned to start making the drink, her movements fluid, and practiced. Then, glancing over her shoulder, she asked, "You settling in alright?"

Sammy let out a small breath, considering the question. "Let's just say my boxes are unpacked, but I'm still working on the rest."

Because settling in wasn't just about where things went; it was about where she fit. And she hadn't quite figured that out yet.

Lisa gave a knowing hum as she dusted cinnamon over the foam and slid the cup across the counter. "Well, take your time. Willow Creek has a way of showing people exactly what they need, whether they're looking for it or not."

Sammy nodded politely, but the words stuck with her longer than she expected. She wasn't looking for anything more than a fresh start. Right?

Lisa rested her elbows on the counter. "Heard you're working on the food pantry over at the church."

Sammy raised a brow. Small towns really didn't waste time, did they?

She wrapped her hands around the warm cup and nodded. "Yeah. Still in the early stages, but I'm hoping to get things up and running soon."

Lisa's expression softened, and there was something like approval in her eyes. "That's good work, honey. And trust me, folks around here will be glad for it. Let me know if you need anything: coffee, volunteers, a little extra grace." She winked. "We're all in this together."

Sammy nodded, warmth spreading through her chest. "I really appreciate that." She hesitated, then added, "I'm actually about to brainstorm some ideas and dreams for the next year, and I'll definitely keep you in mind."

Lisa's eyes lit with enthusiasm. "Please do."

Sammy took her drink to a cozy corner table by the window, the cup's warmth seeping into her fingers. She exhaled slowly, letting the moment settle.

What do I want this pantry to look like a year from now?

She opened her food pantry notebook and began writing:

> **FOOD PANTRY—1 YEAR FROM NOW**
>
> Fully stocked shelves—no empty spaces.
>
> A walk-in fridge for fresh produce, milk, and eggs.
>
> A network of regular donors—businesses, farms, and local families.
>
> A system in place for emergencies—families in crisis never leave empty-handed.
>
> A volunteer team that runs like a well-oiled machine.
>
> Community involvement—maybe even an annual fundraiser to keep it sustainable.

Her gaze drifted to the café counter, where Lisa chatted easily with a customer. Then she continued, her pen gliding across the page as more ideas surfaced.

> **Beyond Food—What Else Can We Offer?**
>
> Hygiene products: diapers, toothpaste, soap, deodorant.

School supplies for kids in need.

A resource board for job listings, housing assistance, and crisis hotlines.

A prayer box so people leave with more than just groceries.

She paused and circled "prayer box". A small thing, but maybe the most important one on this list. This wasn't just about meeting physical needs but also about caring for hearts and offering hope too. And if there was one thing she knew about this town, it was that the prayer warriors would be all over it, covering every request with faith and love every week.

Sammy sat back, staring at the list. It was ambitious, but she *wanted* it to be.

She took a sip of her latte, the cinnamon warmth curling through her chest as the town of Willow Creek bustled outside the window—shopkeepers chatting, neighbors laughing, kids skipping along the sidewalk.

Maybe Lisa was right.

Maybe this town wasn't just a stop along the way. Maybe it had something to show her. Something she hadn't even realized she was looking for.

But for now, she had a plan. And for now, that was enough.

Chapter 11

As Sammy worked through her plans, word spread fast in Willow Creek, and by the time Glory sat down for her regular bridge game two weeks later, Sammy's efforts had become the latest hot topic.

"Your Sammy is such a worker bee!" Ethel Sue declared at the bridge table one afternoon. "She's only been here a few weeks, and already that old Sunday School room is spotless!"

"And did you see her painting?" Lora chimed in. "She said the color's called Alpine White, and I'll tell you, that burnt-orange carpet never looked so good!"

The ladies burst into laughter, the kind that only longtime friends could share.

"I really appreciate your kind words," Glory said, shuffling the deck. "I think Sammy's the most surprised at how much she's enjoying this—and how well she's doing."

Always the practical, Nelda set down her cards and tilted her head thoughtfully. "Ladies, I've got an idea. That utility closet across from the pantry room—do we even use it? What if Sammy turned it into an office? A fresh coat of Alpine White, a desk, maybe some shelves. Even after she moves on—though heaven knows we hope she doesn't—it could still be the food pantry's office."

The others nodded in agreement, their enthusiasm bubbling over.

"Nelda, that's brilliant!" Lora exclaimed. "But instead of having Sammy do it, let's surprise her!"

"I love surprises," Ethel Sue said, her voice rising excitedly. "I just saw the cutest idea for a desk on Pinterest. It's a dining table repurposed as a desk. What do y'all think? Want to go garage sale shopping this weekend?"

By the time they finished their card game, permission had been granted, plans were in motion, and a Pinterest board was taking shape. Glory smiled as she listened to her friends buzz with excitement. She couldn't wait to see Sammy's face when they revealed the surprise.

* * *

Sammy and Pastor Mark were in their weekly morning meeting to discuss the pantry project. As he scanned her updated to-do list, his eyes widened.

"Wow," he said. "Hard to believe you've only been here three weeks, and already this mountain is starting to move!"

Sammy nodded, her voice easy. "I just asked the Lord to guide my path, and He's kept things rolling."

"So, what's next for the room?" he asked.

"I've cleaned it out and painted the walls. Now I need to install shelves on the north and west walls, two feet apart," she said, flipping to her sketch.

Pastor Mark's face lit up. "You may not know this, but your church family loves a good workday. Could you use some help assembling those shelves?"

"Oh, Pastor Mark, do you know how to make shelves?" Sammy asked, her voice hopeful. "I was just going to buy a kit and figure it out, but if you're offering . . ."

"Am I ever!" he said with a grin. "I'm heading into the city later today. If you give me the measurements, I can pick up supplies."

"That would be amazing!" Sammy said, relief washing over her. "Just let me know if there's anything I can grab. I'm at Walmart often these days," she admitted sheepishly.

"I'll let you know," he said, jotting down notes. "But let's get this on the calendar. How about a workday next Sunday? We'll do a potluck—your grandmother's bridge ladies are just the team to organize it—and then spend the afternoon working on the shelves and any other repairs around the church."

"Wait, the whole church?" Sammy hesitated, chewing her lip. "I don't want to take up everyone's Sunday afternoon."

"Sammy, none of us can do everything alone," Pastor Mark said kindly. "This church wants to help, and this is their chance. So, are we good?"

Sammy hesitated, then exhaled deeply. "I'd definitely move faster with help . . . deal."

"Deal," Pastor Mark said, practically beaming. "Just wait—half the congregation will be lining up with drills and donut boxes."

* * *

As the church workday approached, Sammy again found herself at Walmart, scanning the aisles for the last potluck supplies.

"Hey, you're Sammy Thomas, right?"

Sammy looked up, startled but smiling. "That's me! And you are?"

"I'm Sarah Shoreman." The woman tucked a strand of blond hair behind her ear, a friendly glow in her expression making her seem instantly approachable. "We haven't officially met, but we go to the same church, and I just wanted to say hi."

"Well, hello!" Sammy said warmly. "It's so nice to meet you, Sarah."

Sarah's eyes flicked to Sammy's cart, taking in the piles of paper plates, napkins, and serving trays. "Looks like you're getting ready for the workday."

"Yep. Pastor Mark's idea to turn the church workday into a potluck-slash-shelving party was brilliant," Sammy said with a laugh. "He's gathering all the work supplies and put me in charge of paper goods." She leaned in slightly, lowering her voice with a conspiratorial grin. "I think I got the easy part of the list."

Sarah's eyes sparkled with enthusiasm. "Maybe for a shopping list, but my friend on the food pantry board says you've blown the timetable out of the water! Way to go, Sammy!" She held up her fist for a bump.

Sammy chuckled as she tapped her fist against Sarah's, only to be met with giggles from the cart beside them.

"Oh, and these two," she said, gesturing to her kids, "are Michael and Adeline."

Sammy crouched down to the little boy's level. Michael had shaggy red hair, bright blue eyes, and freckles that seemed to multiply as he blushed.

"How old are you, Michael?"

"I'm six!" he said proudly, then added quickly, "And a half."

"Well, six and a half is a very important age," Sammy said, holding her hand for a high-five. Michael grinned and gave her a quick slap.

"And this little cutie?" Sammy asked, nodding toward the blond toddler sitting in the cart's seat.

"This is Adeline," Sarah said. "She just turned three."

Adeline, with a loose ponytail and sunglasses perched on her head like a movie star, held up three fingers triumphantly.

"Hi, Adeline!" Sammy said, shaking the toddler's tiny hand. "I'm Sammy. It's great to meet you!"

Adeline giggled, then stuffed her sunglasses back on her face.

"We're just grabbing a few things before heading to the pool," Sarah explained. "But I had to say hi when I saw you. I've been meaning to introduce myself."

"Well, I'm so glad you did," Sammy said, genuinely touched by Sarah's friendliness.

"Willow Creek really is a wonderful town," Sarah said, lowering her voice. "But even though it's growing, it can feel small sometimes. If you ever need someone to talk to or just a friend to grab coffee with, I'm here."

Sammy blinked at the kind offer, and Sarah pulled a card out of her purse. "That means so much, thank you," Sammy said as she took the card.

Sarah nodded, her tone warm as Adeline fidgeted beside her. "It was so great meeting you, Sammy. And seriously, let's get together sometime for coffee," she added, steering her cart forward with a friendly wave.

"I'd love that," Sammy called after her, watching as Sarah and her kids made their way to the checkout.

As Sammy loaded the last box of napkins into her cart, she glanced down at Sarah's card. Realtor was printed in bold beneath her name. But it wasn't the profession that stood out—it was the kindness. In just a few moments, Sarah had offered her time, encouragement, and even a glimpse of the support Sammy had been longing for.

Sammy slipped the card into her wallet, an unexpected wave of gratitude washing over her. "Lord, I think I just made my first friend in town."

As Sammy drove home, Sarah's words echoed in her mind. *"If you ever need a friend . . ."* It was a simple offer, yet it felt like a lifeline.

When Sammy arrived home, she found Glory on the front porch swing with two glasses of sweet tea on the side table.

She joined her, sinking into the familiar comfort of the swing, and marveled at the streaks of gold and crimson stretching across the sky. The warm evening breeze stirred her hair as she exhaled, letting the stillness settle over her.

Pulling out her phone, she glanced at the verse she had read earlier:

"For we are God's handiwork, created in Christ Jesus to do good works, which God prepared in advance for us to do." —Ephesians 2:10 NIV

She *wanted* to believe that. That she was created for something meaningful. That God had prepared something for her. But how did she *know* what it was? And what if she missed it?

Sammy hesitated, then glanced at Glory. "I've been working through a devotion called Still Becoming to help me figure out what I'm called to do, and today, I was looking at Ephesians 2:10." She traced the rim of her cup, the words sitting heavy on her heart. "I guess what I'm really wondering is, How do you *know* what you're called to do, Glory?"

Glory chuckled softly, setting her tea down. "Hmmm, let me see if I can do it justice." She folded her hands in her lap, her gaze thoughtful. "I've learned that when it comes to knowing what the Lord is calling you to do, it isn't always a straight line."

She paused as if looking back on a life full of twists and turns. "I love how your dean at college reminded you all that our purpose as Christians is to love God and love people. It is so true. But discovering the specific work He had for me to do, my calling? That took focus and changed over time."

"Really? How?" Sammy asked, leaning in.

"I had to pay attention. I had to look for the doors God was opening and be brave enough to walk through them. Sometimes, I was thrilled, like when I married your grandpa. Other times, I was nervous, like when I served as mayor pro tem for that year." She chuckled quietly at the memory, then looked Sammy in the eye. "But I've found that when I focus on walking through the doors God opens, it gets a little easier to stay in step with Him."

She reached for her tea, taking a slow sip before continuing. "And these days? I think supporting you is part of my calling."

Sammy blinked, caught off guard. "What do you mean?"

Glory's gaze softened. "Our bond isn't accidental. God brought you here, to this house and town, for a reason. And, Sammy, His timing is impeccable."

Sammy let the words settle, their weight both comforting and daunting. "It feels like I'm just fumbling in the dark."

Glory leaned forward, her voice steady with a wisdom Sammy could only hope to have one day. "That's where the Lord's mystery shines brightest. Our callings aren't always revealed in grand gestures. Sometimes, it's in the small steps, the trust to keep moving forward, the faith to listen for His voice, even when you don't have all the answers."

Sammy stared into the horizon, her fingers tracing the rim of her cup. "It's hard to believe that stumbles could be part of God's plan," she said softly. "But I guess when I look back, every step, no matter how messy, has led me here."

Glory reached over, resting a hand gently on Sammy's arm, her eyes shining. "Exactly. Trust the process, Sammy. The Lord is shaping you, even now."

As Sammy reflected on her day and the conversation with Glory, one thought settled in her heart—something she didn't want to forget.

She picked up her pen and wrote in her journal:

> Maybe my calling, the work God has for me to do, isn't something I have to figure out all at once. Maybe it's just about walking through the doors He opens, one step at a time.

Chapter 12

Everyone wore their work clothes to church that Sunday, the cheerful hum of fellowship buzzing through the sanctuary. Sammy couldn't help but wish the whole world responded with such joy when asked to lend a hand.

After the service, Sarah's son, Michael, bounded over, his red hair bobbing as he announced, "I'll save you a seat, Sammy, since you're new!"

She laughed and ruffled his hair. "Thanks, buddy. I appreciate that."

He grinned before racing back to his mom, and Sammy followed the crowd into the fellowship hall, where the delicious aroma of a potluck lunch greeted her.

Pastor Mark stepped to the front, his deep voice carrying easily over the room. "Well, everyone, we're so glad you're here! The ladies have prepared a wonderful meal, and the shelving materials are all set up in the food pantry room. Let's say grace and get this day started."

He paused, scanning the crowd. Then, with a warm smile, he gestured toward Sammy. "And a special thanks to Miss Sammy Thomas, who's been taking charge of the food pantry project. She's been working hard to prepare everything, and we're grateful to have her here."

She waved and nodded while the families gave her a quick applause, which she was pretty sure Sarah had started.

Jake's gaze followed Pastor Mark's gesture, and then he saw her. He did a double take, catching those bright green eyes, and just like that, his hope turned into reality.

And she has a name, Sammy.

His breath caught, recognition flickering like a spark. *Lord, You've got to be kidding. She's here. Right here.*

For a split second, he hesitated. Was this a sign or just a coincidence? But the words came quickly. *Trust Me.*

That was all the push he needed.

The room quieted as hands joined in a circle. Pastor Mark continued, "Lord, thank You for the food we're about to enjoy. Bless the hands that prepared it, and protect those that will build Your shelves today. In Jesus' name, amen."

The fellowship hall erupted into motion as if *amen* meant *ready, set, go* to the entire congregation. Conversations picked up, chairs scraped back as some saved seats, and a quick but polite rush formed toward the food tables.

Well—everyone *except* Jake.

He quickened, then slowed his pace, weaving through the crowd just enough to land exactly where he wanted to be.

Right behind her.

Sammy turned as a soft throat-clearing behind her caught her attention.

She froze. It was him—the guy from the grocery store debacle. Only now, there were no runaway oranges, no wobbly cart—just a confident, easy grin and brown eyes that made her pulse jump. She had wondered if she'd ever see him again. She just hadn't expected it to be here.

"Hi, I'm Jacob," he said, his voice steady and warm, breaking the silence.

"Jacob," she repeated, her cheeks flushing at the memory. "It's nice to meet you."

His smile widened, and with a slight shake of his head, he added, "You can call me Jake."

Sammy grinned, recovering some of her composure. "I'm Samantha. But you can call me Sammy," she said, her tone lighter as she extended her hand.

Jake took it, his grip warm and firm. "Well, Sammy, truth be told, I half expected you to give me an orange instead of a handshake."

Sammy groaned, shaking her head with a laugh. "You're never going to let me live that down, are you?"

He shrugged. "Not unless you prove you can walk past the oranges without causing another fruit stampede."

She laughed, the tension between them easing. "So, you go to church here?"

"Been here a while," Jake said with an easy smile. "Sometimes it is hard to get away from the ranch for church, but I wasn't going to miss helping with the food pantry project." He slipped his hands into his pockets. "I know we're all excited for it to get up and running. I hear it's really coming together."

"It really is," she said, suddenly self-conscious. "It's been a lot of work, but I've loved working on this project. And bonus, I get to hang out with my grandma too."

Jake raised an eyebrow, amused. "'Bonus,' huh? Who's your grandma?"

"Glory," Sammy said, a glint of pride in her eyes.

"Glory's granddaughter?" Jake's brows lifted. "I should've known—you've got her fire." He shook his head, chuckling. "Well, now I really have to be on my best behavior. She's been looking out for me since I was a kid." He shook his head with a grin. "Again, so good to meet you, Sammy."

Now, it was Sammy's turn to be amused. "You too, Jake." She crossed her arms, tilting her head slightly. "So, tell me a bit about you. What do you do?"

"I work on a ranch outside of town," Jake replied.

"So, you don't usually spend your days shopping for produce at the grocery store?" she teased, feeling herself relax.

"Not most days, but I will forever be glad I was that day. Sammy, that moment was just so fun!" he continued, "But my favorite part of the day usually involves bringing the cows in at sunset. No traffic, no noise—just me, the sky, and the Lord. It's something else."

"Wow," Sammy said softly. "That sounds amazing."

A voice—smooth, practiced—cut through the conversation. "Oh, Sammy, you don't mind if I steal Jake for a second, do you?"

Sammy turned, startled. Michelle had appeared beside them.

Jake blinked, stepping back just half an inch, but Michelle had already shifted the conversation toward him.

Sammy hesitated. "Uh, sure, go ahead."

"Thanks!" Michelle slipped between them, her smile fixed firmly on Jake. Sammy saw her arm brush his as she leaned in, her voice dropping into an almost sing-song tone.

Jake offered a polite nod, but discomfort flickered across his face even with his best attempt to hide it. Sammy hesitated, something unsettled stirring in her chest. It wasn't her business, but still . . . She took a step back, deciding it was time to move along.

After picking out a meal that would rival any Thanksgiving table, Sammy carefully balanced her plate as she weaved through the crowded tables toward Michael. The hum of conversation and the clinking of silverware filled the room, the warmth of community settling over her like a well-worn quilt.

Sarah introduced her to her husband, Phillip, and a few others at the table before excusing them to grab dessert.

As soon as they were out of earshot, Sarah looped her arm through Sammy's and leaned in with a knowing smile. "You look a little flushed. Wouldn't have anything to do with a certain Mr. Jacob Martinez, would it?"

Sammy felt her face warm as she shook her head. "It was just a nice conversation," she said, reaching for the lemonade pitcher and pouring a little too fast, nearly spilling over the rim of her cup.

Sarah raised an eyebrow, unconvinced. "Mmm-hmm. Sure looked like a *real* nice one." She wiggled her brows, her teasing light but pointed.

Sammy shook her head, fighting a smile. "You're worse than my college roommate, Amanda."

Sarah gasped dramatically. "I *aspire* to be worse than Amanda."

They laughed but the moment replayed in Sammy's mind as they returned to the table. The way Jake had looked at her. Easy and open, like she was someone worth noticing.

And then, just as quickly, Michelle's hand on his arm flickered into her thoughts.

Her smile faltered for half a second. *Is she always that . . . assertive?* Probably. And honestly, why did it even matter? Sammy barely knew Jake. She had no right to feel—

She sipped her lemonade, shaking off the thought before it could take root.

As she picked at the last bites of her meal, a feeling stirred at the back of her mind, an unmistakable sense of being watched. She glanced up, her gaze drifting across the room until it landed on Jake.

He was sitting at a table across from hers, mid-conversation, but his eyes were on *her.*

For a brief second, neither of them looked away.

Then, with a small, knowing smile, Jake tipped his head before returning to the discussion at his table.

Across the room, plates clinked as people finished their meals, the low hum of conversation giving way to a familiar buzz of anticipation. Pastor Mark's booming voice rang out as Sammy set her glass down, commanding the room's attention. "All right, everyone! Time to break into our groups. The team helping with the food pantry, Sammy has a plan and we're going to follow it."

Movement spread through the crowd as chairs scraped and people stood. Sammy stepped forward, grabbing her clipboard from Pastor Mark. All eyes turned to her, but instead of nerves, she felt a steady surge of determination.

"Thank you all for being here," Sammy began, her voice steady. "Here's how we'll tackle this:

"Team 1 will measure and cut boards outside, then lacquer them and set them out to dry."

A group of volunteers nodded enthusiastically, reaching for measuring tapes and saws.

"Team 2," Sammy continued, holding up a bag of hardware. "You'll install anchors in the walls. If you're good with levels and hammers, this is your job."

Jake stepped forward, a smile playing on his lips. "I'll take Team 2," he said.

Sammy handed him the bag, their fingers brushing briefly. "Thanks, Jake," she said, her cheeks warming.

The room sprang into action. The sharp snap of a measuring tape snapped through the air as one of the volunteers stretched it across the wall. Outside, the rhythmic thud of hammers and the occasional scrape of a saw echoed through the open door. The scent of freshly cut wood drifted in, mixing with the warm breeze.

Jake led the anchor team, his easy confidence contagious as they worked together to secure the foundation for the shelves. A few feet away, Pastor Mark adjusted a level against the wall, nodding in approval before driving a screw into place.

As the day progressed, Sammy moved from team to team, stepping over scattered toolboxes and stacks of wood, fielding questions, and ensuring everyone had what they needed.

When she passed by Team 2, she noticed Jake frowning at an anchor that wouldn't stay in place. His fingers pressed against the metal, his jaw tightening as he tested the hold.

"We're going to need something stronger here," he muttered, frustration flickering across his face.

Sammy stepped in, clipboard in hand. "Try these; they're rated for heavier loads," she said, handing him a bag of anchors.

Jake looked up, impressed. "Thanks, boss."

By 4:30, the transformation was almost complete. The once-empty walls now stood lined with sturdy shelves, their fresh wood gleaming under the overhead lights. Volunteers wiped the sweat from their brows as they packed away tools, the air buzzing with satisfied chatter and the occasional clatter of a hammer being put back in its place.

Sammy took a deep breath, letting the moment settle in. The room, once dusty and forgotten, now felt like something real. Something built with purpose.

Pastor Mark clapped Sammy on the shoulder. "You did a great job leading this, Sammy. And look—your vision is coming to life."

Sammy smiled, her tired muscles easing as pride swelled in her chest. She scanned the room, taking in the laughter and shared sense of accomplishment. For weeks, she had doubted herself—unsure if she could pull this off. But now, surrounded by people who had trusted her vision and worked alongside her, she realized her hard work had mattered.

A sudden commotion erupted near the doorway. A group of volunteers who had been enjoying the fresh air outside came barreling into the room, wide-eyed and breathless.

"*Run!*" one of them gasped. "*Biscuit's loose again!*"

Someone yelped. A chair toppled. And somewhere outside, the unmistakable *flap-flap-flap* of furious wings cut through the shouts, followed by an outraged, rapid-fire "buk-BUK-buk-BUK!" that could only mean one thing.

Biscuit was on the warpath.

"Oh, for heaven's sake," Pastor Mark muttered.

Jake, tools still in hand, tilted his head, amusement sparking in his eyes. "You ever wrangled a rogue rooster before?"

Sammy exhaled a laugh, already bracing herself. "No, but I have a feeling I'm about to."

Jake glanced toward the utility closet, then back at the open door. With a casual roll of his shoulders, he strode across the room, yanked open the closet, and pulled out a length of rope.

Sammy's eyebrows shot up. "You *do not* think—"

But Jake was already heading for the door, twirling the rope into a practiced loop.

"I'll be back," he said, flashing her a confident grin.

She followed him outside, stopping just short of the porch steps. And there, in all his feathery fury, was Biscuit.

The notorious rooster stood in the middle of the yard, chest puffed, tail feathers ruffled, his sharp eyes scanning for his next victim. A group of volunteers had scrambled onto the picnic tables for safety. In contrast, others hovered near the entrance, torn between fear and morbid fascination.

Biscuit let out another sharp, ear-piercing crow, flapped his wings violently, and locked eyes with Jake.

It was a *true* Western standoff.

Jake gave his rope a slow swing. "All right, Biscuit," he murmured. "Let's see what you got."

The rooster's beady eyes narrowed.

Then he charged.

A collective gasp rippled through the crowd. Sammy's breath hitched. But just as the rooster lunged, Jake flicked his wrist, the rope sailing clean through the air. And in one fluid motion, he *lassoed* that ornery bird.

A chorus of cheers and laughter erupted as Jake tugged the rope just enough to stop Biscuit in his tracks. The rooster flapped wildly, letting out an outraged, high-pitched screech that sounded downright offended.

Sammy clapped a hand over her mouth, torn between shock and uncontrollable laughter. "I *cannot* believe that worked."

Jake approached, grinning as he carefully loosened the rope to scoop Biscuit up under one arm. The rooster squawked in protest, still grumbling a string of angry "buk-buk-buks," but Jake didn't seem fazed.

He turned back to Sammy. "Guess you can cross 'rooster wrangling' off your bucket list."

Sammy shook her head, laughing. "That was *insane*."

"You mean *impressive*," he corrected, adjusting his grip on the still-flailing Biscuit.

"Yeah, yeah." She waved a hand, still grinning. "Let's just get him back to Mrs. Harper before he adds another name to his hit list."

As they walked back inside—Jake with a *very* disgruntled Biscuit in his arms—Sammy caught his eye again. This time, she didn't look away so quickly.

She hugged her clipboard to her chest, laughter still bubbling just beneath the surface. The day had gone off the rails, but somehow it had never felt more right.

Chapter 13

Sammy wiped her hands on her jeans, watching as laughter floated up from the far corner and someone mimed Biscuit's dramatic escape. The tension in her shoulders loosened, finally.

Across the room, Jake was handing Biscuit—still squawking indignantly—back to Mrs. Harper, who cradled the rooster like he was the crown jewel of the barnyard.

"Now, Biscuit," she scolded lightly, adjusting his feathers, "we've talked about chasing people."

Biscuit let out a final, defiant "buk-BUK," fluffing his feathers like he had no regrets whatsoever. Then, slowly, he turned his head and fixed Jake with an unblinking, beady-eyed stare.

Jake huffed a laugh. "You planning your revenge already?"

Biscuit narrowed his gaze.

The room erupted in laughter again, and Sammy shook her head, grinning as the last of her tension melted away.

From the corner, she spotted Glory standing nearby, arms crossed in that way that meant she'd been waiting for just the right moment. Her grandmother's eyes sparkled, filled with a knowing mischief.

"Well," Glory said, amusement threading through her voice, "now that rooster catching is officially checked off the to-do list, I've got a little surprise for you." She took Sammy's hand and led her down the hall. "You've got quite the knack for seeing the big picture," Glory said. "Maybe you can tell me if anything's missing."

She opened the door to what used to be a dusty old storage closet.

Sammy stepped inside—and froze.

A warm lamp glowed softly on a desk. Clean, labeled file folders lined a shelf. A small collection of supplies had been arranged with care. It wasn't extravagant. But it was intentional.

And it was for her.

A lump rose in her throat.

She had spent so much of her life trying to prove she belonged—meeting expectations, being useful, and fitting into a role that made sense. But this? This wasn't something she had to earn.

It was simply given.

Her hands trembled slightly as she touched the edge of the desk, and she was so grateful for their kindness, love, and acceptance.

Glory broke the silence. "Oh wait—I know what's missing. *You!*" she giggled as Nelda and Lora popped around the corner.

"Glory, you did it!" Nelda beamed. "You kept the secret!"

Lora slipped an arm around Sammy's waist. "We all decided you needed a proper office. A place to keep things organized. And"—she winked—"a spot where you can actually leave work at work."

"Yes," Ethel Sue chimed in, taking Sammy's hands. "We hope you see this as a thank-you. You've done so much already, and we're ahead of schedule."

Sammy swallowed hard, pressing a hand to her chest. It was a small room—a desk, a chair, a lamp. But somehow, it felt like a promise.

A promise that she mattered. That she was seen. That she belonged.

She turned to the women, her voice trembling. "I feel like I've been searching for a place like this my whole life."

Ethel Sue squeezed her hand. "That's because this is where you were meant to be, sweetheart."

Sammy nodded, her throat tight. "Thank you," she whispered. "Y'all are angels." Regaining her composure, she looked around again, joy bubbling up. "I can't wait to start working here tomorrow."

The women laughed, wrapping her in a group hug.

Later, as Sammy stepped outside to help cleanup, the sunlight warmed her face. She exhaled deeply, letting the moment settle.

She'd walked into this job thinking she needed to prove herself. Now, she saw—she'd already been invited to the table.

* * *

Jake wiped the sweat from his brow as the evening air cooled. The day at the church had been satisfying, but nothing felt more natural than being back on the ranch.

From the barn door, John's voice rang out. "So . . . orange girl's got a name now, huh?"

Jake smirked. "Yep."

John crossed his arms, a smug smile starting to show. "She seemed real nice at the workday. What's the story?"

"No story," Jake said as he checked Zeke's feet.

John chuckled low. "Uh-huh. No story yet. But you were grinning like a fool all afternoon."

Jake kept his head down, tightening Zeke's saddle. The quiet rhythm of the ranch filled the space between them. Then, more to the horse than to John, he muttered, "It just feels . . . different."

John finished tossing hay, still grinning as he shook his head. "Yeah," he said casually. "I figured."

Zeke snorted as Jake swung into the saddle. He adjusted his hat and gave a short nod. "Later."

John lifted two fingers in a lazy wave, knowing smirk still in place. "Good luck out there, cowboy."

Abuelo waited by the fence line, astride Rico. He gave a slight nod, and the two rode off together toward the western pasture, the sun dipping into gold behind them.

The sun dropped low over the western pasture, painting the hills in soft golds and pinks. The breeze whispered through the tall grass, brushing past Jake like a benediction. He and Abuelo rode side by side, their horses falling into an easy rhythm, hooves a steady percussion against the earth.

They didn't speak at first. They didn't need to.

But after a while, Abuelo tugged at the brim of his weathered hat and said, "It's funny how the heart works, isn't it?"

Jake lifted a brow. "How do you mean?"

Abuelo shot him a sidelong look, a glint of humor flickering in his dark eyes. "Not every man ropes a rooster in front of a crowd. And it's certainly not every man who does it with that look in his eye."

Jake huffed a short laugh and looked away. "You noticed?"

"Of course I noticed," Abuelo said, his grin deepening. "*Mijo*, you can keep your hands busy all you want. But your eyes? They give you away every time."

Jake didn't argue. He bent slightly over the saddle horn, brushing a hand along Zeke's neck like the gelding could offer a buffer from this conversation.

"You remember what you told me back when you and Michelle decided to be friends?" Abuelo's voice had gentled, more reflective now. "We were checking fences. You couldn't have been more than seventeen."

Jake nodded faintly. "I said I'd trust God to show me who He'd picked for me when the time was right."

"And I told you," Abuelo added, "God's in the business of true love. And when you meet her, you'll know."

Silence stretched between them; it was not heavy, just waiting.

Jake took a breath, eyes on the horizon. "Today felt like . . . something."

Abuelo didn't push. He waited.

Jake's voice dropped. "It didn't start today, though."

He told him about the grocery store. The oranges. The look in her eyes when she laughed. The way something about her had caught his attention and wouldn't let go.

"And now?" Abuelo asked.

Jake's grip tightened slightly on the reins. "Now that I've seen her again, I want more time with her. It's like something picked up right where it left off—even if it never really started." He hesitated, then added, "But Michelle's still in town. Still single. And she literally cut between us while we were talking today. The town? They've practically been planning our wedding since we were kids."

Abuelo's face didn't shift, but his tone grew firmer. "Let me tell you something, Mijo. Other people's expectations don't carry the weight of God's will. If He's leading you toward Sammy, He'll make a way. Michelle's presence, the town's opinions—they don't have the final word."

Jake exhaled. Slowly. Deeply. "You think I'm just imagining all this?" he asked. "Reading into something that isn't there?"

"No," Abuelo said easily. "I think God's been preparing you for this all along. And maybe preparing her too."

They rode in thoughtful silence until Abuelo's voice rose again, softer this time. "Sammy reminds me of someone."

Jake glanced over, curious.

"She reminds me of Gloria," Abuelo said. "Same spark. Same compassion. Same stubborn streak hidden behind a kind smile." He sighed watching the sky. "Gloria and I, we had our season. We were real close friends. But the timing . . . it wasn't ours."

Jake's eyebrows lifted slightly.

"I've never regretted the life I built," Abuelo said, "but I've always respected Gloria. Admired her heart. And now, watching you with Sammy? It feels like God's letting that story continue in a new chapter."

Jake felt something settle inside him—like a piece clicking into place.

"You ever think about reconnecting with her?" he asked quietly.

Abuelo chuckled, then sighed, the sound warm and nostalgic. "I've thought about it. Maybe I've just been waiting for a nudge."

Jake offered a grin. "Guess we both have."

"That's the thing about God's timing," Abuelo said, voice low and full of something unshakable. "It's never rushed. But it's never late, either." A hawk drifted overhead, silent and sure, as if nodding in agreement.

The horses carried them through the tall grass, the fading light gilding everything it touched. And at that moment, Jake didn't need every answer. He just needed this; God's nudge, a steadying word from the man who'd taught him what love looked like, and the slow, growing certainty that maybe this was the beginning of something real.

* * *

The sun was dipping low at Glory's, casting the porch in golden light. Sammy carried two glasses of tea outside and passed Glory a cup as she joined her on the swing.

Glory settled beside her, taking a sip of tea. "So, where's your heart tonight?"

Sammy exhaled. "Today was a lot. A good lot. But still—big."

Glory nodded. "Good days do that. They fill you up and empty you out all at once." She tilted her head. "What was your favorite part?"

Sammy twirled her glass. "The surprise. That office . . . I was so surprised." She shook her head in disbelief, "How did I get so lucky?"

"You didn't get lucky," Glory said gently. "God knew exactly where you needed to be."

Sammy nodded, her voice quiet as she said, "Amen."

Glory eyes twinkling. "Now, I have to say, *my* favorite part was watching you and Jake today."

Sammy covered her face, blushing.

Glory chuckled. "How often do you find a guy who'll lead a team and wrestle a rooster all in the same day?"

Sammy nearly choked on her tea. "Well, there's something else. Jake—he's the guy from the grocery store."

Glory blinked, her glass paused halfway to her lips. "Oh, wow. God wasn't subtle with y'all's introduction, was He?"

"Nope." Sammy smiled. "But at least now, we know each other's names."

Glory's tone softened. "Jake's a good man. And his grandfather Edmund . . . he and I go way back."

Sammy's brows lifted. "You two were close?"

Glory smiled, her voice full of memory. "Very. We were inseparable, the best of friends. I think part of me wondered if there might be more. But then I met Robert."

Sammy leaned in. "And you just knew?"

"I did." She smiled. "And the rest was thirty-eight beautiful years."

Later that night, Sammy curled up with her journal.

> Lord, I didn't expect any of this.
>
> But maybe that's the beauty of it—how You plant us in places we never saw coming, in moments we never planned, and somehow they become exactly what we needed. Today, I stood in a room built by hands willing to help, laughed with people who barely knew me but already believed in me, and felt a sense of belonging I wasn't even searching for.
>
> And Jake . . . I don't know what this is yet. But I know sometimes the best things start with a simple hello, a shared laugh—or, in my case, a rolling cascade of oranges.

She smiled as she closed the journal.

Some things are worth taking one step at a time.

Chapter 14

Willow Creek buzzed with excitement as the Fourth of July celebration drew near. From the coffee shop on Main Street to the Sunday school classrooms in every church, anticipation filled the air. Families huddled over sketches of their parade floats, neighbors swapped secret-ingredient tips for the bake sale, and children counted down the days until they could light their sparklers.

For Sammy, this year felt different. She wasn't just a visitor watching from the sidelines, she was part of it.

On Monday, when she arrived at the office, she found a surprise taped to her new office door. It was a vibrant poster from Miss Ethel Sue's Sunday school class, the words *"We are the hands and feet of Jesus"* painted in bold, cheerful colors. Tiny handprints surrounded the message, each a splash of brightness, with doodles and a few charmingly wobbly stick figures filling in the gaps. Sammy traced one of the little handprints with her finger, a smile tugging at her lips. It was more than just a sweet gift, it was a reminder. She wasn't alone here. She belonged.

Each day brought steady progress. The pantry was moving from idea to reality. Supply orders were finalized, flyers printed, and by midweek, families across town knew about the upcoming food drive.

Thursday, she'd promised herself a day off. But in Willow Creek, a "day off" could mean just about anything. Today, it meant baking. With the Fourth of July festival tomorrow, it was time to get serious about brownies.

When Sammy stepped into Glory's kitchen, she had to pause, taking it all in. Rows of softened butter, neat containers of pre-measured ingredients, and pans covered every inch of counter space. The air was thick with the sweet, comforting scents of cocoa and vanilla.

"Glory, you're a brownie-making machine," Sammy said, laughing as she shook her head.

Glory tied her apron strings tighter, a mischievous grin spreading across her face. "Brownies wait for no one, my dear. We have an assembly line to run!"

They fell into an easy rhythm. Sammy stirred the glossy batter while Glory prepped the pans. The kitchen filled with the sounds of mixing and laughter, especially when Sammy's one-handed egg crack turned into a slimy disaster, or when a puff of cocoa powder left Glory dusted from head to toe.

By the time the last batch was in the oven, Sammy leaned against the counter, brushing a stray hair from her face only to smudge flour across her cheek. Glory chuckled, drying her hands on a towel before reaching out to wipe it away.

"Want to go on the front porch and catch the sunset, my Sammy?" she asked, her voice warm and soft.

Sammy's tiredness melted away at the suggestion. The kitchen still smelled like warm brownies, but the thought of sinking into a rocking chair, watching the sky melt into soft oranges and pinks, sounded like heaven.

"I'd love that," she said, pulling off her apron and following Glory outside.

They settled into their chairs, the porch creaking softly beneath them. The sky melted into pinks and purples, the clouds brushed with silver like a painter's final touch.

They didn't need words. Just quiet, and the beauty of the moment.

When the kitchen timer went off, Sammy started to get up, but Glory stopped her. "Oh, you stay here. Enjoy this sweet moment with the Lord. I'll take care of the brownies."

"Thanks, Glory." Sammy let out an astonished breath. "Lord, that was by far one of the most beautiful sunsets I have ever seen." She looked toward the horizon, then added, "Thank You for sharing it with me tonight."

Sammy had recently found a devotion on discovering your calling, and she had been working through the daily readings and thoughts. Each day felt like another piece of the puzzle clicking into place.

Just yesterday, the devotional had asked: What are the gifts God has given you to serve others? Sammy had written: *Organizing, creating, helping people see what's possible.*

The words had stayed with her, resonating deeply. But they also stirred up questions.

Was the food pantry where she was meant to stay long-term? Or was it just one step on the path God was leading her down?

Not knowing the plan—it was starting to wear her down.

The thought spun in her mind, equal parts exciting and exhausting.

Her thoughts drifted to Sarah. From the moment they'd met, Sarah had already been such a sweet lifeline. Sammy smiled, reaching for her phone.

"Hey Sarah, could I take you up on that cup of coffee and a friend to chat with?" She asked when her new friend answered.

"Yes ma'am!" Sarah said without hesitation. "We just finished dinner. Want to come over now?"

"I would love that!" Sammy said, hanging up. She grabbed her journal and purse, gave Glory a quick kiss on the cheek, and headed out the door.

* * *

"Sammy!" Sarah greeted her with a warm hug, Sammy returned the hug, smiling wide. It felt so good to have a friend in town. "Phillip said he'd hold down the fort tonight, so, sweet sister, the back porch is all ours," Sarah continued her voice light and welcoming as she led Sammy through her charming home.

Sammy couldn't help but admire how every room felt like a warm embrace—soft colors, thoughtful details, and that quiet hum of peace only a well-loved home could carry.

But when they stepped onto the back porch, her breath caught. It was nothing short of a backyard paradise.

The smooth stone patio, curved like a gentle half-moon, flowed seamlessly into a sparkling pool on one side and an inviting outdoor fireplace on the other. A long dining table with sturdy wooden benches sat cozily in one corner, while a matching stone bar with sleek stainless-steel accents stood nearby, four stools lined up neatly beneath it.

Sarah smiled, her eyes twinkling with joy as she pushed a tray towards Sammy. "I brought the Keurig out here so we could make our coffee on the spot. Pick your flavor!"

Sammy couldn't help but grin. "This is amazing." She chose a vanilla hazelnut blend and grabbed a cup, already feeling a bit spoiled by the thoughtful setup.

As the coffee brewed, Sarah pulled her own cup closer. "Alright, sweet Sammy. I'm so glad you called me. What's on your heart?" Her voice held that gentle blend of curiosity and love that made opening up feel safe.

Sammy nodded, pulling her journal from her purse. The pages were filled with scribbles, Scripture, and little prayers. She found her spot and took a breath. "I've been working on figuring out what I've been called to do. Recently, I started a devotion called Still Becoming, and it's been quite eye opening as I have wrestled through the questions and Scriptures.

Sarah's expression softened, a knowing look in her eyes. She passed Sammy her coffee as it finished. "Absolutely. There's something so powerful about reflection. When we let the Holy Spirit bring things to the surface, that's where the breakthroughs happen. What's been standing out to you?"

"Well, first, I realized I've never really given much thought to my calling. Honestly, if the valedictorian speech at graduation hadn't been about that topic, I'm not sure it would even be on my radar." Sammy's voice held a mix of vulnerability and surprise. "Growing up as the oldest of seven, I lived in a bit of chaos, and having a plan was how I kept my sanity. So, I made one—college, a degree, a future in teaching. And somewhere along the way, I convinced myself that was my calling." She hesitated, frustration flickering in her tone. "But looking back, I spent too much time trying to make sure my life fit into a plan. Especially when it came to Richard."

Sarah's eyebrows lifted slightly. "Richard?"

Sammy let out a small, self-deprecating laugh. "Yeah. We 'dated' for three years. But honestly? We were more like friends who occasionally held hands and went out to dinner. It wasn't the kind of love you dream about." She sighed. "But it fit my plan. Until it didn't."

Sarah leaned in, listening.

"The day before graduation, he broke up with me." Sammy exhaled. "At first, it felt like the ground had been pulled out from under me. Like I couldn't breathe."

"Oh, honey . . ." Sarah reached over, resting a comforting hand on Sammy's arm.

Sammy steadied herself, her voice quieter but filled with more certainty. "But losing him forced me to realize something. I'm not here to make anyone else happy. I'm here to follow God's call for my life. I have work to do—like Ephesians 2:10 says." She turned her journal, showing Sarah the verse scrawled in her careful handwriting.

For we are God's handiwork, created in Christ Jesus to do good works, which God prepared in advance for us to do.

Sarah nodded, her expression warm with admiration. "That's beautiful, Sammy."

Sammy took a breath, gathering her thoughts. "And then Glory and the church offered me this internship. I'll forever be grateful. It gave me space to begin this journey of discovering what God's really called me to do." She glanced up at the night sky, the stars twinkling like tiny beacons of hope. "Being here in Willow Creek, living with Glory, working at the food pantry . . . it's like God's been peeling back layers and showing me what He's been preparing me for all along.

"It's been . . ." She paused, searching for the right words, then smiled softly. "It's been like finally stretching after being curled up too long. Uncomfortable at first, but so, so needed."

Sarah's smile widened. "I love that. And how does it make you feel?"

Sammy's lips curved into a soft, genuine smile. "Free."

Sarah's eyes twinkled. "Wow, Sammy. I feel like I'm watching a butterfly emerge from a cocoon. It's incredible to see how God's been shaping you."

Sammy chuckled, brushing a stray strand of hair behind her ear. "Well, I definitely felt like that gooey mess inside the cocoon not too long ago."

Sarah laughed, nudging Sammy's arm. "Well, for what it's worth, I think you're past the mush stage—and totally into the breaking-out-of-the-cocoon phase."

Sammy sighed playfully. "Any tips as I break out? Or is this the part where I just flail around and hope for the best?"

Sarah smirked, tilting her head. "From what I hear, the struggle is part of the process. Makes your wings stronger."

Sammy raised a brow. "So . . . no shortcuts?"

"Afraid not." Sarah grinned. "But hey, you've got people cheering you on. And coffee. Both are essential."

Sammy chuckled, lifting her mug in a mock toast. "To not crashing into porch lights on my first flight."

They clinked their cups together, the moment light and easy—just what Sammy needed.

As the laughter faded, Sammy hesitated, chewing her lip. "I do have a question if we have a little more time." Her voice was a bit more tentative, Sarah's nod reassuring her. "Have you gone through this journey of finding your calling?"

Sarah nodded, setting her cup down. "Actually, yeah. Phillip and I read a book on purpose once, and it really stuck with us. We realized our purpose never changes—it's to love God and love people. But our calling? That shifts as we grow."

"Tell me more," Sammy encouraged, sipping her coffee.

Sarah's expression turned thoughtful. "We're called to be loving spouses and amazing parents first, showing our kids God's love and helping them get to know Him. Beyond that, we try to follow our hearts and the gentle leading—I call them nudges—of the Holy Spirit, just like it says in Ephesians 3:20."

"What does a 'nudge' feel like?" Sammy asked, giving an amused look but pen ready over her journal.

Sarah's smile was gentle. "Usually, it's a thought or idea that crosses our minds out of nowhere and connects with our heart's desires, maybe even a wish we didn't know we had." She paused, thinking. "That's why we chose real estate. It gives us freedom, provides for our family, and lets us be present for our kids."

Sammy jotted down, *Eph. 3:20 . . . nudges . . . a thought that connects with my heart's desires.* She put her pen down, a soft sigh escaping.

Sarah hesitated before continuing. "As Christians, we all long to live the calling God has for us, but that doesn't mean we're all meant to work or volunteer every free hour at the church." She giggled. "I mean, if we all did that, how would we shine in our community?"

Sammy tilted her head thoughtfully. "So, maybe the real question for me right now is, Am I called to work at the church long-term, or is this just a season of preparation for what's next?"

Sarah reached over, squeezing Sammy's hand. "Exactly! And He may be prepping you for a calling in the church. But sometimes, we think we've arrived at the final destination, only to realize it was just a stepping stone. God doesn't always hand us the whole map. He reveals the path one step at a time."

Sammy let out a slow breath, running her fingers over the words she had just written. The weight of her thoughts settled peacefully in her heart

Then, as if sensing the moment needed a shift, Sarah rested her chin on her hand, eyes twinkling with mischief. "Okay, before you go, can we talk about you and Jake at the church workday? Because, girl, y'all were adorable."

Sammy's cheeks flushed as she laughed. "Oh no, but yes, please!"

Sarah leaned in, her eyes alight with mischief. "The way he lit up when you turned around? Total Hallmark moment."

Sammy laughed, a little brighter now. "Actually, the potluck was round two. I finally got his name this time!"

"What? Tell. Me. Everything!" Sarah exclaimed, grabbing her cup with both hands in excitement.

* * *

As Sammy turned in for the night, she grabbed her journal to share her thoughts of the day as had become habit lately.

> I used to think finding my calling meant having a five-year plan and knowing exactly where I was headed. But maybe it's not about knowing—it's about listening.
>
> About paying attention to the little nudges, the open doors, and the unexpected moments that stir something in my heart.
>
> Tonight, over coffee and laughter with Sarah, I realized something: I don't have to figure it all out today. God isn't asking for my perfectly laid-out roadmap. He's just asking me to trust Him with the next step.
>
> She let out a soft breath, and continued writing.
>
> What a curious place to be—not to need to know everything coming up and still feel peace about it. Maybe this is what it feels like when the cocoon starts to crack open, when the wings are almost ready, even if they're not fully stretched yet.

She closed her journal, turned off the lamp, and lay back against her pillow. As her eyes fluttered shut, a quiet peace settled over her. She didn't have all the answers.

And for the first time, she was okay with that.

Chapter 15

"Good morning, sunshine! It's 9:00 a.m., and I come bearing coffee and a reminder that the city parade starts in thirty minutes." Glory's voice rang through the doorway as she held up a steaming mug, a sly grin on her face.

Sammy shot up from her bed, her hair a wild mess. "Oh, Glory, thank you! I'll be ready in just a minute."

She grabbed the outfit she had laid out the night before, dabbed on sunscreen, swiped on mascara and lip gloss, and hurried to the kitchen. Lately, she'd been moving more than she ever had in college, and she was loving how her jeans fit looser as she ran downstairs.

"Wish I could get ready as quickly as you," Glory teased, sipping her coffee.

"Years of practice," Sammy quipped, grabbing the folding chairs as they headed out the door.

Main Street was already buzzing with activity. Sammy followed behind Glory, weaving through the growing crowd as Glory waved, hugged, and greeted nearly everyone they passed.

"Well, so glad you two could join us, ladies!"

Nelda sat with Lora and Ethel Sue under the shade of their usual oak tree, two open spaces waiting beside them.

Glory beamed. Sammy blushed.

"Sorry, ladies, I'm the one running late today," Sammy said as she unfolded the chairs. "Thankfully, Glory made some strong coffee this morning, so I'm ready for the day!"

Laughter rippled through the group as Sammy hugged each of them. She had quickly become an honorary granddaughter, and their warmth made her feel even more at home.

"So, Sammy," Lora asked, adjusting her floppy sun hat, "how's the new office treating you? Was Frank able to fix that vent?"

"He was, and it's much cooler now. Thank you for asking," Sammy replied. "And I think Glory is glad to have her kitchen table back too."

Glory swatted Sammy's arm playfully. "Your mess—whether it's paper, emotions, or dirty laundry—is always welcome at my house."

Sammy laughed, her heart swelling with gratitude. Glory's unwavering support had been her anchor through everything.

Sirens filled the air as the parade began.

The town's police cars and fire trucks led the way, lights flashing and horns blaring. Next came the Girl Scouts, their float covered in glittery signs reading *Never Give Up!* and *Leave a Little Sparkle Wherever You Go!*

Then came the tractors—local grandpas driving their grandkids, all grinning and waving proudly.

Sammy cheered when she spotted Sarah's family. Their float was a full beach scene, complete with inflatable palm trees and The Beach Boys blaring from the speakers.

Phillip tossed foam footballs into the crowd while Michael and Adeline sat in a kiddie pool full of candy, gleefully throwing it to spectators.

"Go, Shoreman family!" Sammy yelled, clapping.

Michael and Adeline paused mid-throw, spotting her. They waved excitedly, then resumed pelting candy into the cheering crowd.

The parade continued with a bike crew of neighborhood kids pedaling decorated bikes, followed by local floats celebrating everything from the library to the high school marching band.

Finally, Sammy's favorite part of the parade approached: the cowboys.

Her pulse quickened as the horses trotted into view. She knew Jake would be riding today, and she couldn't stop herself from scanning the group for him.

And there he was.

Jake sat tall on his horse, wearing crisp jeans, a pearl-button blue shirt, and a well-worn cowboy hat. His confidence radiated as he expertly guided his horse forward with the kind of steady assurance that only came from years in the saddle.

Then, as they drew closer, his gaze found hers.

And held it.

A slow tip of his hat.

A hint of a smile, just for her.

Before she could stop herself, the words slipped out. "Oh my."

Her hand flew to her heart, warmth flooding her chest before she even realized what she had done.

Then—a chorus of giggles erupted around her.

Oh no.

Her eyes widened in horror. She had totally said that out loud.

Glory, Nelda, Lora, and Ethel Sue were all grinning like schoolgirls, their eyes twinkling with delight.

Ethel Sue leaned in, her voice dripping with mischief. "Honey, if that cowboy smiled at me like that, I'd be saying 'Oh my' too . . . and probably a whole lot more."

The laughter exploded, a ripple of pure amusement and teasing affection.

Sammy groaned, covering her face with her hands, but the giggle that escaped betrayed her.

She couldn't even pretend to be embarrassed.

Because, well . . . they weren't wrong.

After the parade, the crowd spilled into the community park for barbecue and festivities. A small carnival occupied the parking lot, with colorful booths selling everything from handmade trinkets to homemade baked goods.

As Sammy entered the park, she passed a long tent with bold signs reading *FREE WATER*. Inside, tables lined the tent, each representing a different church in town. Volunteers handed out cold water bottles, their tables brimming with displays of mission trips, Vacation Bible School flyers, and cheerful decorations.

At the Grace Chapel table, a bake sale was in full swing, with stacks of brownies and cookies disappearing fast. Volunteers also handed out the bright purple flyers Sammy had designed for the food pantry.

The pantry committee had gathered just last Sunday after installing the new shelves to pray over the flyers, asking the Lord to place them in the hands of those who needed them most. As Sammy noticed families holding the flyers, she silently prayed for each one.

Next, Sammy wandered down the handmade market, a path lined with talented artisans and their unique creations. She stopped in her tracks at a booth filled with intricately carved wood pieces.

Front and center stood a magnificent four-foot-tall bear. Its polished surface gleamed in the sunlight, and the detailed features—its expressive eyes, textured fur, and powerful stance—made it seem almost alive.

Sammy ran her fingers over the bear, captivated. "This is absolutely beautiful," she marveled.

"His name is Miguel," a quiet voice said from the back of the booth.

Startled, Sammy turned to see an elderly man seated in a folding chair, a small whittling knife in his hand, his movements calm and practiced.

"Oh! I didn't see you there," Sammy said, blushing slightly. "Did you make this? It's incredible."

"I did," the man replied, setting down his carving. "Takes a while to bring out the life in the wood, but it's worth every moment."

Sammy tilted her head as recognition sparked. "Wait, I've seen work like this before! Glory—my grandmother—has a few of your pieces. A horse, an ornament, and a welcome sign on her porch. She's a big fan."

The man's face lit up with a warm smile. "Ah, Glory, yes. She's been a dear friend for many years." He rose slowly, dusting off his hands before extending one to Sammy. "And you must be Sammy. I'm Edmund."

Sammy shook his hand, smiling warmly. "It's so nice to meet you, Edmund. Your work is amazing."

Before Edmund could answer, the sound of crunching gravel under boots made them both turn.

Jake approached, two cold water bottles in hand. The late-afternoon sun cast a glow along the brim of his cowboy hat, and when he caught sight of Sammy, something flickered in his eyes—recognition, amusement, maybe something else.

"Grandpa, I brought you some water," he said, his voice carrying that same easy warmth as his smile.

Then, shifting his gaze to Sammy, he held out the second bottle. "And I thought I'd better bring an extra, just in case."

Sammy reached for it, her fingers brushing against his as she took it. A simple touch, but enough to make her pulse stutter.

"Thank you," she said, her voice coming out a bit more breathless than she intended. She twisted off the cap and took a sip, welcoming the cool relief. "You must be melting in that cowboy hat."

Jake chuckled, tipping it back just a bit. "It's part of the uniform. Can't disappoint the kids looking for real cowboys in the parade."

Edmund cleared his throat, his weathered hands resuming their gentle whittling. "Sammy was just admiring Miguel."

Jake's eyes flicked to the carved bear, then back to her. "He's a beauty, isn't he? Grandpa's got a real gift."

Sammy ran a hand lightly over the smooth, polished wood, tracing the lines of the bear's face. "He really does. And I hear craftsmanship runs in the family."

Jake's brow lifted. "Oh?"

Sammy's lips curved. "Word around town is you're the man to call when a girl needs shelves hung."

Jake chuckled, shaking his head. "Well, if you ever need more shelves—or if Biscuit decides she wants a second home—you know where to find me."

Their easy banter hung between them, and for a moment, the bustling fair faded into the background. The scent of kettle corn and barbecue lingered in the air, the sound of distant laughter mixing with the occasional clang of the carnival games.

Edmund set down his carving knife, a knowing glint in his eyes. "You two should take a stroll, get out of this heat for a bit."

Sammy hesitated, glancing between them. "I'd love to, but I need to get back to the bake sale soon."

"I could walk you over," Jake offered, his tone casual but his expression hopeful.

"I'd like that," Sammy said, tucking the water bottle into her tote bag.

As they moved through the crowd, Jake kept a relaxed pace, making room for her beside him. "You looked like you were having a good time at the parade."

"I was." Sammy glanced up at him, eyes twinkling. "Your wave was very . . . cowboy-like."

He laughed, the sound warm and easy. "I was going for a mix of John Wayne and slightly less awkward."

"Well, mission accomplished."

They reached the bake sale booth, where the sweet aroma of chocolate and vanilla filled the air. Without a word, Jake grabbed a fresh tray of brownies and helped Sammy set them out.

Their hands brushed once, then twice, each small touch sending a little thrill through her.

Finally, as the rush of customers slowed, Jake stepped back. "I'd better get back to Grandpa before he gives Miguel away."

Sammy wiped brownie crumbs from her hands and glanced up at him. "Thank you for walking me over."

"Anytime." He hesitated for a second, then added, "And I hope we run into each other again tonight at the fireworks."

Sammy's heart fluttered. "Me too."

With one last smile, Jake tipped his hat and disappeared into the crowd, leaving Sammy with an inexplicable warmth that had nothing to do with the summer heat.

When lunchtime rolled around, the mouthwatering scent of barbecue filled the air. Sammy was scanning the seating area when Sarah waved her over.

"Sammy, come join us!"

As she sat down, Michael grinned up at her. "Did you see our float? It was awesome, right?"

"Awesome doesn't even begin to cover it," Sammy said. "You deserve a high-five."

Michael slapped her palm—barbecue sauce and all.

Sammy stared at her hand in mock horror, then burst out laughing. "Well,

I was about to get messy anyway."

Sarah chuckled, shaking her head. "I'll get you a napkin before you start finger-painting."

As the afternoon dragged on, the July heat pressed down.

"Whew, it's getting hot," Sammy said, helping Glory pack up the Grace Chapel table.

Glory wiped her forehead with a napkin. "Tell me about it. Good thing we've got a break until dinner."

Sammy crumpled the paper tablecloth into a ball. "Perfect. A cool shower and a nap are calling my name."

Glory chuckled. "I second that."

As they walked to the car, Sammy took in the sights around her—smiling families, lingering laughter, the last traces of the parade's joy.

This little town, with its quirky traditions and messy, wonderful moments, was no longer just a stop.

It was starting to feel like home.

Chapter 16

Around 5:00 pm, the town started to come alive again. As Glory and Sammy sat on the front porch sipping on some sweet tea, they could hear the band setting up at the park. It was an unspoken tradition that once you heard the band start to practice, you grabbed your picnic dinner and slowly made your way back to the park to enjoy the food you brought on quilts that you shared with your friends.

Glory and Sammy could walk there, but with the picnic basket and quilt and Texas-hot summer heat, they decided to drive and park up close.

They set the quilt up under a tree and got there a little early so the ladies wouldn't have to wait on them this time.

Sammy looked up as the rustling of grass and cheerful voices drew her attention. Nelda, Ethel Sue, and Lora were making their way over, dishes in hand and smiles on their faces.

The ladies had brought a feast fit for queens. Glory's fried chicken and Sammy's sweet tea paired perfectly with Nelda's red potato salad, Ethel Sue's broccoli salad, and Lora's strawberry cream pie. Sammy couldn't help but marvel at the spread as they settled onto the quilt.

As everyone got their plates of dinner and got settled, Nelda said, "So, I saw you in line in the potluck last Sunday." Nelda raised her eyebrows, hinting. "And it looked like you might have met Mr. Jacob Martinez." She smiled, and the other gals oohed.

Sammy blushed immediately. Leave it to her adopted grandmas to embarrass her. "Yes." Sammy found a smile. "I, um, we met in line." She paused. "Why does everyone call him 'Mr. Jacob Martinez'?" she asked as she took a sip of tea.

Ethel Sue answered, "Because he has been Willow Creeks's most eligible bachelor for probably five years now!" The ladies all giggled as Sammy choked on her tea.

Sammy breathed in, feeling her face warm. "Well okay, then." She smiled, shook her head, and went back to eating.

After dinner, the conversation naturally turned nostalgic as the ladies exchanged stories from the past. Sammy noticed Glory growing quiet, her gaze distant.

The fire chief's voice broke through the hum of conversation.

"Y'all having a good time?" he called out with a grin as the crowd erupted in cheers. "Well, good! Ready to see how Sheriff Rosco saves the day this year?"

The crowd roared with excitement, and the fire chief chuckled. "See y'all in five minutes!"

Sammy perked up. "Oh, wow! They still do the old sheriff showdown skit?"

Lora nodded, smiling proudly. "They sure do. It's different every year, but it's always a hoot."

Sammy settled back onto the quilt, already grinning. She'd heard about the annual skit from Glory—how the sheriff, the bandit, and half the town joined in like kids playing make-believe in a backyard. What she hadn't expected was for the bandit to burst onto the stage in a puff of flour-smoke, brandishing a banana like it was a six-shooter.

And she *definitely* hadn't expected the bandit to be Michelle.

Dressed in a too-big cowboy hat, a fake mustache drooping over her lips, and a red bandana knotted around her neck, Michelle looked more like a child playing dress-up than a fearsome outlaw.

"Well, well!" she hollered, her voice an exaggerated growl. "Sheriff Rosco, you best hand over the loot, or I'll peel you like a tater!"

The crowd erupted into laughter as the sheriff—an older gentleman with a potbelly and a badge that looked suspiciously like it had come from the dollar store—stomped forward. "Not on my watch, you no-good scoundrel!"

Michelle twirled the banana, her mustache slipping slightly. "You'll never catch me!" she declared, spinning on her heel and immediately tripping over her own boots.

Sammy couldn't help but laugh, the silliness of it all washing away any lingering nerves. It was impossible not to join in with the crowd's good-natured giggles, especially when Michelle tried to lasso the sheriff with a piece of string that barely reached her own feet.

Her gaze drifted to the edge of the stage, where a few volunteers stood, ready to jump in for the next bit. That's when she spotted him.

Jake stood with his arms crossed over his chest, a broad smile softening his features. His laugh was easy, his shoulders relaxed, and there was a warmth to him that made Sammy's own smile widen.

He didn't look distracted or caught up in Michelle's performance. He looked like he was simply enjoying the show along with everyone else. Whatever history they might share, it didn't seem to hold much weight in this moment.

The sheriff finally "shot" Michelle with a spray of silly string, and she fell to the ground in a slow-motion, exaggerated collapse. The crowd cheered as the sheriff helped her up, and Michelle ripped off her mustache with a flourish, bowing dramatically.

"She's got good comedic timing," Glory said, nudging Sammy gently.

"She really does." Sammy found herself smiling, a genuine warmth settling over her. *Maybe I was overthinking things.*

As the sheriff skit ended and the cast left to cheers and whistles, a group of musicians emerged, getting set up and tuning their instruments. Kids darted to grab water while parents corralled little ones toward the quilts.

Sammy turned to Lora, curiosity dancing in her wide eyes. "Now what's happening?" she asked, glancing toward the stage as the band prepared.

Chapter 17

Ethel Sue leaned past Lora with a knowing grin. "This is the best part, honey. A local band always plays, and we turn this whole park into one big dance floor. We dance 'til the fireworks light up the sky."

Lora nodded eagerly, her smile encouraging. "You'll love it, Sammy. There's nothing quite like a Willow Creek Fourth of July dance."

Before Sammy could respond, the unmistakable fiddle of "Cotton-Eyed Joe" broke through the air, and the crowd erupted with laughter and cheers. Families grabbed hands, couples moved toward the open space near the stage, and a wave of infectious joy swept over the park.

"Come on, Sammy!" Lora called, grabbing her hand.

Sammy hesitated at first, but the lively rhythm and laughter all around were irresistible. She found herself swept up in the energy, stomping, clapping, and twirling along with the crowd. Laughter bubbled out of her, spilling over as she spun and stumbled through the steps. It was exhilarating.

As Lora moved them through the crowd, familiar faces popped up around her. Lisa, the coffee shop owner, spun by with her husband, her braid swinging and a joyful grin lighting up her face. She waved at Sammy mid-turn, nearly tripping over her own feet as she laughed.

"Having fun yet?" Lisa called over the music.

"The best!" Sammy shouted back, her own smile widening.

A few steps away, Jake and John were in the middle of one of the lines, their boots kicking up dust as they moved in sync with their group. Jake's laughter rang out, unguarded and genuine, as John attempted a fancy spin and nearly toppled into the person next to him.

It was one thing to see Jake at church or in passing, but here—surrounded by friends, his face alight with joy—he seemed even more . . . real.

She laughed, but before she could dwell, Glory slipped an arm through hers, and Lora hooked on to her other side.

"Come on, girl!" Lora laughed, her eyes sparkling. "We're not done yet!"

The three of them sashayed forward with the crowd, their steps loose and carefree as they moved to the beat. Sammy let herself be pulled along, giggling as they swayed and twirled together, their quilt forgotten as they became part of the swirling sea of dancers.

By the time the song ended, Sammy was breathless, her cheeks flushed with excitement. She glanced around, soaking in the scene—the crowd clapping, the band's enthusiasm, and the sheer joy on everyone's faces.

As she pulled back from the crowd a bit, her gaze shifted, and then she saw him. Jake stood just a few feet away, his smile soft and steady as he met her eyes.

Sammy's smile deepened despite the sudden warmth rising in her cheeks. She lifted a quick wave, and Jake's expression softened into a crooked smile, his own wave a bit sheepish. Then, with an easy stride, he closed the distance between them.

"So," Jake said, his voice casual but his expression earnest, "are you having a good time?"

Sammy tucked her hands into her pockets, still smiling. "I really am. Growing up, we always seemed to 'miss' the dance." she said, using air quotes. "But now? I don't think I'll ever miss it again."

Jake chuckled, his shoulders relaxing. "Glad to hear it."

The opening notes of "Boot Scootin' Boogie" filled the air, and people hurried to form lines for the next dance. Sammy raised an eyebrow, teasing. "Do you dance?"

Jake's grin widened. "Actually, I do." He pointed toward a group of seniors, where Glory waved enthusiastically. "See the group your grandma's leading?"

Sammy laughed, waving back. "Yes, I see them."

"Well," Jake said, crossing his arms, "I taught them that line dance."

Sammy stared at him, her laughter bubbling up. "You're kidding! How did that happen?"

"Your grandma can be pretty persuasive," Jake admitted. "She knew I took dance lessons back in the day for prom, and she thought the seniors could use some motivation to join the Fourth of July festivities. One thing led to another, and now we meet once a month for lessons."

Ethel Sue caught Jake's eye mid-step, throwing him an exaggerated thumbs-up. Jake grinned and returned the gesture.

As the song ended, the music shifted to a slower ballad. Jake turned back to Sammy, his expression sincere. "Well, Sammy . . . could I have this dance?"

Sammy's breath caught, but she smiled, slipping her hand into his. "I'd love to."

As Jake led her to the dance floor, Sammy felt her heart skip—not from nerves, but from something deeper. His hand was warm in hers, his touch steady and reassuring.

She focused on his quiet confidence, letting him guide her steps. *You're Willow Creek's most eligible bachelor. What on earth are you doing asking me to dance?* Her thoughts spun, a mix of wonder and disbelief.

The soft strains of the ballad wrapped around them, the melody easing the edges of her uncertainty. For a moment, the world seemed to fall away. It was just the two of them, moving in time with the music. This felt different, and that scared her a little.

Am I reading too much into this? she wondered. *Is this just a dance, or could it be that, for the first time in a long while, someone truly sees me?*

As the song drew to a close, Jake spun her gently, his hand never losing its sure grip. Then he bowed with a playful grin. "Thanks, Sammy."

Her cheeks flushed as she smiled back. "Thank you."

"Would you be up for another dance later?"

Sammy nodded, her heart fluttering. "I'd like that."

Jake's grin widened. "Great. I promised Ethel Sue and a few other seniors a dance, but I'll find you later."

As he disappeared into the crowd, Sammy stood for a moment, her feet still planted on the edge of the dance floor, as if the world needed a second to catch up with her heart. She blinked, a soft laugh escaping as she pressed her fingers to her lips. *Did that really just happen?*

She spun around, spotting Sarah just stepping off the dance floor, her cheeks flushed and her hair a little wild from dancing. Sammy threaded through the crowd, reaching for her friend's arm. "Sarah!"

Sarah turned, and before Sammy could say a word, her eyes went wide, her smile blooming.

"Did that just happen?" Sammy asked, breathless.

"Oh, you and Willow Creek's most eligible bachelor dancing the first slow song?" Sarah's voice rose with delight. "Oh, it happened. And, girl, the way he looked at you?" She nudged Sammy's arm, her grin widening. "Mmm, if only Phillip still looked at me like that!"

Sammy let out a soft laugh, the kind that escaped before she could catch it. "It wasn't . . . I mean, it was just a dance." She bit her lip, but the smile wouldn't quite disappear. "But then he asked if I'd save him another dance later."

Sarah nudged her again, practically bouncing on her toes. "Well, I'd start practicing your dance moves, then. You've got another turn around the floor coming up."

Sammy's cheeks warmed, and a shy smile tugged at her lips. "I guess I do."

The band shifted into a lively tune, and the dance floor filled up again. Sammy and Sarah drifted back to their quilt, sharing a slice of Lora's strawberry cream pie and soaking in the music. Every so often, Sammy's gaze wandered toward the dance floor, catching glimpses of Jake as he twirled Ethel Sue or lined danced with a group.

Sarah leaned over, nudging Sammy gently. "He hasn't forgotten you."

Sammy bit her lip, a mix of nerves and excitement bubbling up inside her. "I know. I'm just trying not to think about it too much."

"Good luck with that," Sarah said with a knowing smile.

Song after song played, the evening settling into that sweet spot where time seemed to stretch, every note and laugh lingering in the warm summer air.

Finally, as the band wrapped up a cheerful two-step, the lead singer stepped up to the microphone, his voice easy and warm. "Alright, folks, this is the last song of the night. Find someone special and hold 'em close."

Sammy's breath caught. She got up and walked back to the dance floor, tucking a loose strand of hair behind her ear as her gaze darted through the crowd.

And then she saw him. Jake stood near the edge of the dance floor, his expression open, his eyes searching—until they landed on her.

Her heart skipped. She thought she saw a quiet exhale, a softness that smoothed the edges of his expression as he began walking toward her. His movements were unhurried, his eyes never leaving hers.

Sammy drew in a deep breath, her feet taking a tentative step forward. It felt like the entire evening had been leading to this moment, a gentle pull drawing them together through the sway of lantern light and the hum of the music.

But then she froze.

"Jakey!" Michelle slipped into his path, her voice curling with feigned sweetness. "You wouldn't forget our last dance, would you?"

A muscle in Jake's jaw tightened. "Michelle, I was—"

"It's tradition!" Michelle's laugh was bright, cutting through his words. Her fingers wrapped around his arm, a grip too tight to be casual. "You wouldn't want to break tradition, right?"

Jake's gaze darted to Sammy, a flash of apology in his eyes. His lips parted, a breath away from saying no, but then he straightened. "After you."

Michelle beamed, her hold on him possessive as she led him onto the dance floor.

Sammy's world tilted, the vibrant colors of the night dulling at the edges. *Did I misread everything? Was I foolish to think this night could be something more?*

Her lips curved into a soft, resigned smile, a mask to cover the quiet unraveling beneath. She managed a small nod. *It's okay. Go.*

She took a step back, her mind buzzing with a mix of hurt and determination. *He doesn't owe me anything.*

Sammy exhaled, her prayer a whisper in the quiet space between the notes. *Lord, if this is meant to be, I don't need to chase it—or him. Help me hold this moment with open hands.*

As she turned to leave, her gaze landed on Glory and Edmund Martinez. They swayed together, their steps easy, as if they'd been sharing this dance for decades.

The sight grounded her. Love—real love—was patient. It didn't push its way forward or cling too tight.

Sammy made her way back to their quilt. The fireworks would start soon, and even if the night hadn't ended with a fairy-tale dance, she wouldn't let the spark fade.

Chapter 18

No sooner had she settled than she realized—her new water bottle, the one she'd bought just hours earlier, was still by the stage. She stood up, letting everyone know where she was going.

Ethel Sue replied, "If you can't find us, just meet Glory at the car. It can get crazy once the fireworks start."

Sammy found her bottle and turned around to head back to her seat, thinking Ethel Sue was so right. She walked along the edge of quilts, occasionally stopping to search for her grandmother in the sea of people, but to no avail.

BOOM, crackle, crackle.

As the first fireworks bloomed against the night sky, Sammy found refuge under a sturdy pine tree. It stood a little off to the side, offering a pocket of quiet away from the crowd.

With the warm pine scent wafting through the breeze and crickets chirping in the background, she leaned her head back against the tree and thought, *Life is so good,* as she watched the Roman Candles light up the sky.

A soft crunch of grass, the brush of a branch—then his voice, warm and familiar. "Is this tree taken?"

"The more the merrier," she said and scooted over.

"Hey, thanks," Jake replied quickly, sitting down and bumping his shoulder to hers.

"Anytime," she replied, returning the bump.

After about twenty minutes, the show was almost over and it was time for Sammy's favorite part, the finale. As the sky erupted with bursts of red, white, and blue, Sammy felt a quiet awe settle over her. A month ago, she'd been so unsure of herself, lost in a world that didn't feel like hers. But now, she was building something—relationships, a purpose, and maybe even a future that felt like home.

When it was over, Jake got up and offered his hand to help Sammy up.

"Thanks," Sammy said, taking it and hopping to her feet.

"My pleasure." He scratched the back of his neck, uncertainty flickering across his face, but there was still an openness in his expression—something easy and earnest. "So, I was wondering . . . would you like to go horseback riding with me tomorrow morning?"

His words landed with a spark, and Sammy felt her heart do a little flip. *Horseback riding?* She'd only been a handful of times, and the last experience included a stubborn pony named Daisy who preferred snacking on grass to following the trail. Still, the thought of spending time with Jake, doing something he clearly loved, was enough to push aside any hesitation.

"Really? I would absolutely love that!"

Jake's expression lit up, his shoulders easing as if he'd been holding his breath. Sammy's pulse quickened at the realization that maybe he'd been just as nervous as she was. *He wants this too.*

"Great! Is six too early?"

Sammy nearly laughed. Six was early, but there was no chance she'd let that stop her. "No way! Let's do it." She bit her lip, trying to contain the excitement that threatened to take over her face. "It sounds perfect."

Perfect. The word settled into the space between them, soft and full of promise. Sure, the idea of riding a thousand-pound animal made her palms a little sweaty, but if Jake believed she could do it, then maybe she could. Besides, the chance to watch the sunrise on horseback—something she'd only seen in movies—felt like the kind of adventure she'd been craving.

"Perfect." He grinned. "Want me to pick you up, or would you rather meet me there?"

"If you're up for it, pick me up. I'm still learning the roads outside of town, but I'll be ready at 5:30, on the dot."

"Deal."

As they stood there, Sammy felt a swell of emotions—excitement, a flicker of nerves, but mostly gratitude. For the invitation, for the possibility of a new experience, and for the way Jake's eyes held hers just a beat longer than necessary.

Tomorrow morning. Her mind raced ahead, alternating between images of sun-drenched trails and the not-so-glamorous possibility of needing help just getting in the saddle. Still, she couldn't wait.

"Well, we've reached my truck, but do you see yours?" Jake asked.

"Yep, I am just one more row up."

"Oh, I see it. Let me walk you," he said, easily falling into step beside her.

They continued walking together toward Glory's car, weaving through families gathering up blankets and sleepy kids. The cool night air was a gentle contrast to the heat of the fireworks, and Sammy felt the evening settling around them, soft and unhurried.

After a moment, Jake cleared his throat, his voice a little lower than usual. "Hey, Sammy, about earlier."

She glanced up at him, surprised by the sudden seriousness in his tone. "Earlier?"

He scratched the back of his neck, his go-to move when he wasn't quite sure how to say something. "With Michelle. The last dance."

"Oh." Sammy's gaze dropped to the sidewalk, her sandals scuffing against the pavement. She hadn't wanted to think too much about it—how it had felt to stand by, unsure, while Michelle slid in so easily. "You don't have to explain. It's—"

"I do, though." Jake stopped walking, and Sammy did too, right under the soft glow of a streetlamp. His expression was steady, his brown eyes warm but earnest. "I didn't mean to let her cut in like that. She's just . . . well, she's persistent. And over the years, it's sort of become this habit. One I probably should've stopped a long time ago."

Sammy blinked, processing his words. "A habit?"

Jake let out a quiet chuckle, though his shoulders tensed. "Yeah. Michelle and I have known each other forever. She likes tradition, and the last dance kind of became her thing. I guess I went along with it because it was easier than saying no."

He took a breath, the soft night air swirling around them. "But earlier when she asked, I realized I didn't want to."

Sammy's chest tightened—not with doubt, but with relief. "You didn't?"

"No." His voice softened, and his smile turned a little rueful. He stepped closer, his hand brushing hers for just a moment. "I wanted to dance with you, Sammy."

A soft breeze stirred the summer air, carrying the distant echoes of laughter and the soft hum of crickets. Sammy's heart fluttered, a delicate, hopeful ache. "Oh." The word slipped out, barely more than a whisper.

Her cheeks warmed, and she ducked her head, tucking a loose strand of hair behind her ear. She hadn't meant to sound so unsteady, but something in Jake's gaze unraveled her composure.

"I wasn't sure," she managed, her voice a little stronger. "I thought maybe . . ." She let the sentence trail off, not wanting to put her insecurities into words.

Jake's knuckles grazed over the back of her hand, his touch light but sure. "I know. I should've said something sooner." His voice held a quiet earnestness, the kind that slipped past her defenses.

Sammy drew in a breath, tasting the sweet tang of honeysuckle on the breeze. "I'm glad you did."

For a moment, they stood in the soft glow of the streetlamp, the world beyond them fading to a gentle blur. There was nothing flashy or grand about this moment—no sweeping declarations or dramatic gestures. Just the truth, spoken softly between them.

Jake's lips curved into a smile that made her feel seen, really seen. "Tomorrow, then? Horseback riding at sunrise?"

Her smile blossomed, the nerves settling into something calmer, steadier. "Absolutely."

"Good." His fingers lingered against hers before he pulled away, his warmth still imprinted on her skin. "I'll see you at 5:30."

"I'll be ready."

As he stepped back, the spell between them gently loosened but didn't break. Sammy stayed where she was, watching until Jake disappeared into the flow of people, his easy stride carrying him back into the hum of Willow Creek's summer night.

Her fingers tightened around the strap of her bag, the realization blooming slowly. This wasn't just a sweet exchange under the stars. It was the start of something. Something real.

She breathed in, letting the cool air fill her lungs, and allowed herself the quiet joy of anticipation. Not just for tomorrow's ride, but for everything that might come after.

She slipped into the passenger seat, and as Glory started the car, Sammy buckled her seatbelt, her mind still replaying the evening's moments. The drive home was only a few blocks, just enough time for the memory of Jake's warm smile and the promise of tomorrow to settle into her heart.

Glory shot Sammy a sideways glance as they turned onto their quiet street, the houses dark and peaceful. "Horseback riding tomorrow, huh? Sounds like fun."

Sammy's cheeks warmed, and she couldn't hold back her smile. "I sure hope so."

Glory pulled into the driveway and turned off the engine, her eyes twinkling. "Wishing you a great time, sweetheart."

They climbed out of the car, and Sammy followed Glory up the porch steps with their picnic basket, a buzz of energy humming through her at the thought of seeing Jake again so soon. As she reached for the door, she couldn't help but glance back down the street, as if she might catch another glimpse of Jake's truck under the glow of a streetlamp.

Once inside, Sammy set the basket down and made her way up to her room, the quiet of the house wrapping around her like a well-worn quilt. The evening played back in her mind—the fireworks, Jake's soft, honest words, the way his hand had lingered against hers as they confirmed plans for tomorrow.

He didn't want to dance with Michelle. He wanted to dance with me.

The thought settled in, warm and steady, and Sammy felt a mix of relief and anticipation bloom in her chest. She didn't need to overthink it, didn't need to analyze every word or look. For once, she let herself simply feel the joy of it.

She let out a breath, curling under her quilt. Tomorrow couldn't come fast enough.

Sammy whispered a quiet prayer as she set her alarm and slipped under the covers. "Thank You, Lord, for today. For fireworks, for good friends, and for whatever tomorrow may bring."

With a contented sigh, she closed her eyes, the memory of Jake's voice and the promise in his eyes lingering like the soft glow of the fireworks still echoing in the night sky. Riding a horse might be a bit out of her comfort zone, but if this new chapter had taught her anything, it was that sometimes the best things started with a little bit of brave. And tomorrow felt like the perfect place to start.

Chapter 19

5:30 a.m. came early, but Sammy didn't mind. Not only was she getting to go for a morning horseback ride, but she was spending time with Jake. She slipped out of the house quietly, not wanting to wake Glory, and perched on the front porch steps as the first hints of dawn touched the horizon.

A rumble broke the stillness of the morning, and Sammy looked up to see an old truck rolling up the driveway. It was faded blue with a few dents here and there, but it suited Jake perfectly—steady, reliable, and full of character. As he stopped the truck, she caught a glimpse of his relaxed expression through the windshield. He looked just as happy about this outing as she felt.

Jake hopped out and jogged around to her side, opening the door like a proper gentleman. "Good morning," he said, his voice easy, warm as the rising sun.

"Morning," Sammy replied, unable to stop the lift of her lips. A handsome guy, good manners, and a good dancer? She could hardly believe it.

As they turned off the main road onto an unpaved path, the world seemed to transform around them. The flat, open land gave way to rolling hills dotted with patches of trees. A barbed-wire fence lined the road, and beyond it, cows grazed contentedly, scattered across the field like slow-moving shadows.

Sammy stared in quiet wonder. "How many cows do you think are out here?"

Jake laughed. "Oh, probably a hundred or so. Don't worry, they don't bite."

Sammy chuckled, shaking her head. Finally, they came to a long driveway with a wooden sign that read, *Martinez Family Ranch*.

"Here we are," Jake said as he turned in. "I know it feels far out here, but I promise we're still in Willow Creek." He glanced her way with a reassuring smile. "Up on the right is where we keep the horses. I figured I'd introduce you to my best friend first, and then we'll head out for the tour."

Sammy raised an eyebrow, teasing. "Best friend?"

"You'll see," Jake said with a grin, pulling up to the barn.

When he slid open the heavy barn doors, Sammy's jaw dropped. The space was spotless—dusty in places, sure, but clearly cared for. Ten stalls lined the barn, five on each side, and most of them held horses, their heads poking out curiously.

The first horse, a stunning tan gelding with a blond mane gave an excited whinny and shook his head.

"Hey, Zeke," Jake said, walking over and rubbing the horse's neck affectionately. "Ready to meet her?" Zeke shook his mane again, and Jake turned toward Sammy, his expression bright. "Sammy, meet Zeke. Zeke, this is Sammy."

Sammy stepped forward tentatively. "Can I pet him?" she asked, biting her lip.

"Of course," Jake said, his voice softening. Sammy didn't realize it, but as she approached Zeke, Jake's shoulders visibly relaxed.

The moment Sammy's hand touched Zeke's warm, muscular neck, the horse let out a low whinny and nudged her gently, as if asking for more. Sammy giggled, running her hand along his coat. "You're such a strong boy," she whispered, awed by his beauty.

Jake beamed. "He comes from Kentucky Derby winners, believe it or not. No racing for him, though—at least not officially."

Sammy looked up, amused. "'Not officially'? What does that mean?"

Jake scratched the back of his neck, grinning sheepishly. "Well . . . Zeke and I like to race the wind. I don't know that we've ever won, but we try."

Sammy laughed, shaking her head. "I'll need to see that someday."

"Deal," Jake said, a flicker of hope in his eyes.

He walked across the aisle to another stall. "And this," he said, "is the girl you'll be riding today—Ellie."

Sammy reached out her hand, and Ellie, a sleek bay mare, stepped closer, leaning her head against the gate. "Hello, Ellie," Sammy said softly. The horse snorted gently, scooting even closer, and Jake chuckled.

"She likes you already," he said, his voice carrying something unspoken.

For the next half hour, Sammy followed Jake's lead as they prepped and saddled the horses. By the time Ellie was ready, Sammy's nerves had settled—until she realized it was time to get on.

"Jake," she admitted, holding Ellie's bridle, "full disclosure: It's been ten years since I've been on a horse."

Jake smiled reassuringly. "Full disclosure: That's no big deal. Ellie's got you. Want help getting on?"

"No, let me try," Sammy said, her determination kicking in.

With a deep breath and a small prayer, Sammy managed to swing herself into the saddle. She couldn't believe it. She was on, and she didn't fall off!

"Nice job," Jake said, mounting Zeke effortlessly. "Let's take it slow at first and see how you feel."

Sammy nodded, gripping the reins as Ellie started with a gentle walk. Soon, they were on a wide dirt path, and Sammy felt herself relax into the rhythm of the ride.

"Ready to pick it up a notch?" Jake called.

Sammy grinned. "Let's do it."

As Ellie trotted and then cantered, Sammy felt her nerves melt away. The wind tugged at her ponytail, the horizon opened before them, and wildflowers stretched across the field like a sea of color. It was freedom, pure and simple.

When they reached the hilltop, Sammy gasped at the sight of the old oak tree, its broken branches softened by ivy and time

"Come on down," Jake said, hopping off Zeke and offering Sammy a hand. "This is the place."

Sammy knew her middle name wasn't Grace, and this moment was proof of why. Getting off Ellie felt more daunting than getting on. The ride had been a breeze, almost like no time had passed since her last time in the saddle. But now, all eyes were on her. Well, one pair of brown eyes, at least.

"I've got this," she whispered to herself, though her nerves begged to differ.

"Take your time," Jake said from nearby, his voice low and easy, the kind of voice that made you believe everything would work out fine.

Determined not to make a fool of herself, Sammy stood in the stirrups, ready to swing her right leg over the saddle, just like Jake had done. She lifted her leg with what she hoped was the elegance of a seasoned rider, but it seemed her enthusiasm had other plans.

WHACK.

Her boot connected with something solid, and behind her, Jake let out a startled grunt.

Sammy turned just in time to see Jake stagger back a step, one hand bracing Zeke's saddle while his other rubbed his cheek. His head was tilted slightly, and his mouth was caught somewhere between a wince and a grin.

"Oh no! Jake!" Sammy cried, hopping to the ground in what felt like slow motion. She barely remembered to steady Ellie's reins before rushing toward him. "Are you okay?"

Jake glanced at her, a sheepish smile creeping across his face despite the swelling already blooming on his cheek. "Well, you don't hold back, do you?"

Sammy gasped, her hands flying to her mouth. "Oh my gosh! I'm so sorry! Did I—did I kick you? What did I hit?"

Jake chuckled, leaning against Zeke for support. "My face, Sammy. You hit my face."

"Oh, no!" Sammy's voice climbed an octave as she reached out, unsure of what to do. "Jake, I'm so sorry. I was just trying to—"

"Dismount with style?" Jake teased, his grin turning lopsided as he winced.

Sammy groaned. "With grace," she corrected, covering her face with her hands. "Clearly, I failed!"

Jake reached into Zeke's saddlebag, pulling out an instant ice pack and cracking it with a practiced snap. But before he could lift it to his face, Sammy snatched it from his hands.

"Hold still," Sammy said, stepping closer with determination. "Let me."

Jake didn't argue, though the teasing glint in his brown eyes made it very clear he was enjoying this way too much.

Sammy pressed the cold pack gently against his cheek, her brow furrowed as she tried to look serious. "This is terrible. You're going to have a bruise now all because of me. I'm officially the worst horseback date in history."

Jake's lips curved into a smile, his dimple making a sudden and unfair appearance despite the sting. "So, can I call this our first date then?"

Sammy's jaw dropped slightly, and she blinked at him, thrown completely off guard. "Wait—*this* is a date?"

Jake tilted his head, that playful spark never leaving his eyes. "You showed up before dawn, we rode horses at sunrise, and you kicked me in the face." He grinned wider. "Sounds like a date to me."

Sammy let out a laugh, unable to help herself, even as her cheeks flushed bright pink. "A very *unique* date," she admitted, shaking her head. "Most people stick to dinner and a movie."

Jake shrugged, his voice warm as he said, "Well, where's the fun in ordinary?"

She rolled her eyes, still smiling as she held the ice pack in place. "I'm not sure *fun* is the word for what just happened."

He didn't flinch, his gaze resting gently on her.His tone softened, the humor melting into something more sincere. "Maybe not fun, but it's memorable. And for the record," he added, his voice dipping lower, "you're a pretty great horseback date—killer kick and all."

Sammy bit her lip to hide a smile, but the flutter in her chest betrayed her. She dropped her gaze, focusing on his cheek instead of the way his eyes seemed to hold hers just a little too long. "If you say so," she murmured.

"I do," Jake replied, his smile lingering, his voice quiet but steady as he took the ice pack. "I wouldn't trade this morning for anything."

Sammy crossed her arms, watching him with a mix of guilt and fondness. "Are you sure you don't want to head back? I mean, I don't want to ruin the morning any more than I already have."

Jake shook his head, his gaze warm as it met hers. "Sammy, you couldn't ruin this if you tried." He gestured toward the horizon, where the first rays of sunlight spilled over the hills. "Besides, we've got a sunrise to catch."

Chapter 20

Jake led her to the fallen tree, its smooth bark a reminder of the storm that had split it long ago. They sat side by side, letting the quiet settle around them.

The sky was brushed in soft pinks and golds, the sun stretching across the horizon in a slow, gentle rise. A breeze carried the scent of wildflowers and fresh earth, rustling through the tall grass like a whisper.

Sammy drew in a deep breath, letting it all sink in. The peacefulness of the morning, the steady presence of Jake beside her—it was the kind of moment she wanted to hold on to.

Something to tuck away in her heart forever.

Jake pointed out different parts of the ranch like the creek that wound through the valley, the pasture where the cattle grazed, and the distant ridge where he and Zeke often raced the wind.

"So, is this what you want to be when you grow up, Jacob Martinez?" Sammy teased, her smile soft as she leaned back against the smooth, weathered log.

A breath of laughter escaped him as he plucked a blade of grass and rolling it between his fingers, the motion easy and familiar. "It's not what I pictured when I was a kid. But life has a way of changing your plans." His gaze drifted to the hills, his voice steady but reflective. "Abuelo raised me after my parents died. And I guess somewhere along the way I fell in love with this ranch too."

Sammy tilted her head, surprised. "I'm so sorry you lost your parents." Her voice was gentle, hesitant. "Do you mind if I ask what happened?"

Jake's fingers stilled on the blade of grass. He stared at it for a moment before meeting her eyes. "It's okay. Really." His tone was even, but she could hear the weight behind his words. "They were high school sweethearts, born and raised right here in Willow Creek. They worked in medical sales and traveled together a lot. One night, they were driving back from a convention in New Mexico. It was late. They never saw the drunk driver coming."

Sammy's hand flew to her mouth. "Oh, Jake."

"The responders said it was instant," Jake said softly, his gaze fixed on the horizon. "For that, I'm thankful. They didn't suffer." He let out a breath, quiet and slow. "The other driver was beat up pretty bad. He landed in the hospital for weeks."

Sammy blinked, unsure what to say, her heart aching for him. "Did—did you see him?"

He gave a subtle nod, his features shadowed with something unspoken. "Abuelo and I went to confront him. I was ready to yell, to let him have it. But when we walked in, there he was—bandaged, broken, and just lost." He paused, the memory shifting in his voice. "Abuelo, though, he stood there for a moment, then walked up to him and said, 'Son, you look so tired and alone. Do you know Jesus Christ?'"

Sammy's breath caught in her throat.

Jake's eyes glistened as he continued. "The guy didn't. He'd grown up following the traditions of his people but said he always felt empty. Abuelo sat beside him, held his hand, and talked about the grace and forgiveness of Christ and left his Bible with him." Jake let out a small breath, shaking his head like he still couldn't quite believe it. "By the end of that visit, we told him we forgave him too, and I really meant it."

Sammy wiped at the tears pooling in her eyes. "That's incredible."

"It was freeing," Jake admitted, his voice cracking just a little. "I didn't realize how much anger I'd been holding until that moment. I was fourteen, but I knew it was the right thing. Watching Abuelo—watching his strength—gave me the courage to say, 'I forgive you.'"

For a long moment, Sammy said nothing. She simply let the quiet settle around them, the sunrise spilling light across the hills as if to remind them both of new mercies.

"Your Abuelo sounds like an amazing man," she said finally, her voice soft.

Pride flickered in his expression, quiet and steady. "He is. That was ten years ago, and he's been my rock ever since." He plucked at the blade of grass again, then glanced at her. "I had plans to leave. To study equine therapy at Texas A&M. But the more I thought about it, the harder it was to imagine leaving him—or this place. I love this life."

Sammy nodded, something warm and tender settling in her heart. "So you stayed."

"I stayed," A hint of satisfaction in his tone. "But not before one last adventure. I spent the summer after graduation backpacking the Rockies with a buddy of mine. It was my chance to spread my wings."

Sammy grinned. "Backpacking in the Rockies sounds amazing. What a way to celebrate."

"It was," Jake agreed with a laugh. "But coming home? That felt right."

They sat there for a while longer, watching the world wake up around them. Sammy breathed in the quiet, her heart strangely full.

The ride back to the barn was peaceful, the horses' hooves drumming a soft rhythm against the earth. Once they brushed down Ellie and Zeke and put away the tack, Jake drove Sammy back to Glory's house.

Sammy let out a contented sigh as Jake pulled into the driveway. The ride home had been peaceful, the kind of quiet that didn't need to be filled with words.

As Jake cut the engine, he lingered for a moment, his fingers drumming lightly against the steering wheel. He glanced toward her, something unreadable in his expression. "I don't usually talk about my parents, but with you, it just feels right."

Sammy turned toward him, her heart softening at the quiet vulnerability in his voice. "Maybe you didn't plan it," she said gently, "but I think it's exactly what the Lord wanted you to share." She hesitated, then smiled. "Thank you for trusting me with that."

Jake held her gaze for a long moment before reaching for her hand. His grip was warm and steady—strong in a way that had nothing to do with the calluses on his palm and everything to do with the kind of man he was.

"Thanks for listening," he said softly.

And then stepped out of the truck and rounding the front to open her door.

Sammy slid down, glancing up at the faint bruise on his cheek. She winced, tilting her head teasingly. "You too, Mr. Martinez. Try to keep that handsome face out of trouble."

He let out a soft laugh, rubbing the spot with exaggerated care. "No promises."

Sammy turned toward the house, but something about the way his voice lingered—just a little softer, a little more familiar—made her glance back over her shoulder.

Jake had one hand on the doorframe, his gaze following her with quiet calm.

A flutter stirred in her chest.

She wasn't sure where this was going, but she knew she could get used to it.

As she reached to open the door, something flickered at the edge of her vision.

Cars. Two, maybe three, parked just off the side of the driveway.

Her brow knit.

They hadn't been there when she left.

Chapter 21

"Yes, last night was fun," Nelda was saying as she sorted through her cards.

"I tell ya, I am so glad Jake is my dance partner every year," Ethel Sue sighed, gazing dreamily out the window. "I love having him twirl me around the floor."

Nelda raised her eyebrows, setting her cards down. "You do know he dances with all of us, right?"

Ethel Sue blinked, brought back to the moment, and waved a hand dismissively. "Well, sure. But that doesn't mean I can't call him *my* dance partner."

The laughter was still echoing through the room when Sammy pushed open the door. She barely had time to take in the scent of lavender and the rustle of cards before she realized every single pair of eyes was on her.

"Well, spill it!" Nelda said, leaning forward with a sparkle in her eye.

"We saw you two dancing last night," Ethel Sue chimed in, her grin mischievous. "And the way he looked at you, Sammy . . ."

"And now," Nelda cut in, gesturing toward the door Sammy had just walked through, "you waltz in with Jake dropping you off this morning. We want details!"

Glory, who sat at the table looking amused, raised her hands. "For the record, I didn't tell them a thing."

"Contrary to us asking," Lora added with mock offense, crossing her arms.

Sammy froze, her cheeks flushing as their eager gazes bore into her. She couldn't escape now. Taking a deep breath, she forced a casual tone. "Ladies, there really isn't much to tell." She shot Ethel Sue a quick appreciative look.

"I never did find your quilt after picking up my water bottle, so I did as Ethel recommended. Thanks for that tip by the way."

Ethel nodded in satisfaction. "You're welcome."

Sammy continued, her voice light and breezy. "I ended up finding a nice tree to sit under and enjoy the fireworks and— " She paused, already seeing the drama play out—"Jake joined me."

The room erupted in a chorus of exaggerated *oohs.*

Sammy rolled her eyes but couldn't fight her smile. "And at the end of the night, he invited me horseback riding this morning."

The ladies leaned forward as one, their cards forgotten, waiting for her to continue.

"We had a great time," Sammy said simply, hoping to end it there.

But the room remained expectantly quiet, and before she could stop herself, she blurted, "And I may have kind of, sort of, kicked him in the cheek as I was getting off the horse." Her cheeks burned as the laughter erupted around her. "I didn't mean to! I was trying to be graceful, and, well, it just didn't go as planned."

"Oh my word!" Nelda gasped, covering her mouth, her eyes wide with delight.

"I know, I know," Sammy said, throwing up her hands. "But he assured me he's fine. He just might have a harder time singing the praise songs on Sunday."

The room dissolved into laughter and Sammy joined them.

"Oooh, what a cute first date memory." Lora beamed, putting her hands to her heart and all the ladies swooned.

"Enough about me," Sammy said with mock exasperation, waving them off as she stepped further into the room. She grabbed a chair and settled in, her curiosity piqued. "What's going on in town these days?"

Lora cleared her throat and set her cards down deliberately, a hint of seriousness replacing the playful mood. "Well, I'm glad you asked."

Everyone stopped to listen.

"I've been thinking about something," Lora began, her tone serious. "It started last week during my quiet time. I realized we've got kids in this town who need more than just summer to keep them busy. I saw Mabel and Ryan at the library just sitting on the reading sofas, like that equaled something to do. And every time I see Roman, he is skinnier than the last time. They need love. Attention. Something to do. Maybe a good meal too. I think that maybe we should do that summer camp idea."

The ladies nodded, murmuring their agreement.

"You're absolutely right, Lora," Glory said, leaning forward. "So what's your plan?"

Lora smiled sheepishly. "Well, that's as far as I've gotten. Step one: Tell y'all. Check."

The group chuckled, and Nelda immediately grabbed a pencil from her purse. "Should we save bridge for another day?" she asked, flipping her score sheet to a blank page and scrawling *Summer Day Camp* at the top.

No one objected. With smiles all around, they packed up their cards and set to brainstorming.

"What if we include a lunch program during camp week?" Sammy suggested. "The food pantry's almost up and running. We could put together sack lunches easy."

Nelda leaned in, her pencil flying over the page. "And we could do craft days, story time, maybe even gardening."

Lora sighed wistfully, setting her cards aside. "You know, I've always thought it'd be wonderful if Willow Creek had a real community garden. A place where folks could learn to grow their own food, maybe even take home some fresh veggies. The kids could dig in the dirt, and we could use what we grow to stock the pantry."

Sammy's heart stirred at the idea. She could almost see it—a stretch of green filled with raised beds, sunflowers nodding over neat rows of tomatoes and carrots. A place where hands young and old could work the soil together.

"That would be amazing," she said softly, tucking the thought away. Maybe one day . . .

Sammy glanced around, watching the excitement ripple through the group, their minds running with ideas. She smiled. "And maybe we could partner with the local library for reading challenges."

The ladies shared knowing smiles, the idea of a week-long camp growing into something truly special.

Laughter and ideas filled the room as the women planned, their excitement spilling over into something bigger than just a summer camp. Sammy listened, her mind already spinning not just for this summer, but for how God might use these small seeds to grow something lasting in Willow Creek.

The house felt different once the bridge club ladies left—quieter, but not empty. Their laughter still lingered in the air, a reminder of how quickly a place could feel like home.

* * *

Sammy stepped onto the porch, her glass of sweet tea cool against her palm. Glory was already there, rocking gently in the porch swing, watching the horizon as the sun began to lower.

"Busy day," Glory said, her voice warm, welcoming.

Sammy let out a breath, sinking into the swing beside her. "That's one way to put it." She took a sip of tea, letting the stillness settle around them before adding, "But a good one."

Glory glanced at her, a knowing smile tugging at the corners of her lips. "So," she began, her tone light, "how was horseback riding with Jake? Really?"

Sammy hesitated, then exhaled slowly. "It was incredible."

Glory chuckled, giving the swing a little push with her foot. "I thought so. Are you two becoming friends or . . . ?" She let the question dangle, her eyebrows lifted in expectation.

Sammy traced the rim of her glass, a small smile playing on her lips. "I don't know." She shook her head slightly. "But I do know he's kind. Thoughtful. He listens—really listens. And most importantly," she added, a wistful laugh escaping, "he asked me to dance. I've never felt so swept away in my whole life."

She hesitated, then exhaled, almost as if admitting it to herself. "Honestly, I just thought we were going for a morning ride as friends." She swirled her tea, watching the ice shift. "But somehow *date* slipped out, and Jake just lit up."

"Well, well," Glory said quietly.

Sammy continued. "I don't even know how it happened. One second, we're talking about the morning, and the next, he's looking at me like I'd just said something he'd been waiting to hear." She bit her lip, a warmth rising in her chest. "And honestly? It didn't feel wrong."

Glory smiled, her eyes twinkling. "Maybe that's because it wasn't."

A comfortable silence stretched between them, the sounds of crickets rising in the night air.

Sammy traced the condensation on her glass, then glanced at Glory with a knowing smile. "And then Edmund asked you to dance . . ."

Glory's cheeks flushed just a little. She waved a hand, but there was no hiding the softness in her eyes. "Oh, Edmund? He's always been such a dear friend."

Sammy grinned. "Mm-hmm. And dear friends often twirl each other around the dance floor under the stars?"

Glory let out a soft chuckle, setting her tea on the side table. "You know, sweet Sammy, even at seventy-two, life still finds ways to surprise me too." She sighed, folding her hands in her lap. "But between you and me? I'd be lying if I said I didn't feel something. I suppose for now, I'll just enjoy the dance and let the Lord—and Edmund—handle the rest."

Sammy smiled, watching her grandmother's face. "I think that's what I'll do too. Wait and see what the Lord—and Jake—are up to."

Glory lifted her glass, and Sammy followed suit. Their tea glasses clinked together, a quiet, knowing giggle shared between them.

"You know," Sammy said thoughtfully, watching the sky darken, "God's timing really is something. Two weeks ago, I couldn't see past the food pantry. And now? It feels like He's opening doors I didn't even know were there."

Glory reached for Sammy's hand, her voice filled with gentle conviction. "Lord," she whispered, "Your timing is impeccable, and we trust You with all of this. In Jesus' name, amen."

As the stars stretched across the night sky, Sammy felt a deep peace settle in her heart.

* * *

If I don't write this down, I might not believe it actually happened. Sammy thought as she reached for her journal, yawning as she settled in for the night.

> Last night I danced under the stars.
>
> This morning I rode horses at sunrise.
>
> And somewhere in between, Jake called it a date—and I didn't correct him.
>
> (Okay, technically, I said *date* first. And technically, I also kicked him in the cheek while dismounting. Not exactly the fairy tale version of a first date, but honestly? I wouldn't change a thing.)
>
> And tonight? I sat on the porch with Glory, sweet tea in hand, talking about how life surprises us when we least expect it.
>
> The bridge ladies are helping plan the summer camp.
>
> Glory might have a little spark with Edmund.
>
> And me? I think I might just be falling for a cowboy.
>
> Lord, I don't know where all of this is leading, but I'm grateful for today.
>
> For new beginnings.
>
> For open doors.
>
> For You.
>
> Help me walk through them with grace (and maybe a little more coordination).

As she closed her journal, a soft smile lingered on her lips. She could hardly believe this was her life.

And yet, somehow it was so much better than she ever could have hoped or imagined.

Chapter 22

Thursday morning, the food pantry committee gathered to finalize procedures for accepting applications and assembling the first distribution boxes happening in just a few days. Toward the end of the meeting, Lora spoke up.

"I'd like to formally announce I want to help make the summer camp idea happen," she began, her voice brimming with determination. "Glory has offered to host an info and brainstorming night at her home tonight, and we need volunteers. Who's in?"

Three hands shot up immediately. Lora nodded, jotting down names in her notebook. Edmund cleared his throat.

"I'd like to help," he said, his tone steady but thoughtful. "Not sure how I can, but I'm willing, and I'm sure Jake and John would be up for it too."

"Alright!" Pastor Mark exclaimed, clapping his hands. "Looks like we're hosting a summer camp. Any resources the church has are yours! Just keep track so we can include it in next year's budget."

Sammy hesitated before speaking up. "We were thinking of spreading the word with flyers during tomorrow's food pantry distribution. Is that okay?"

"That's a great idea, go for it!" Pastor Mark replied enthusiastically. "This camp is long overdue, and I'm confident it'll be a blessing."

Relieved, Sammy smiled. "Thanks! And thank you all for making the food pantry a success. We couldn't do this without you. As for the summer camp, we'll nail down more details tonight. Spread the word, bring a snack, and meet us at Glory's around 7:00 p.m."

Sammy and Glory hustled around the house, tidying up and setting out refreshments. They knew the bridge ladies, two of the volunteers, and

Edmund would be there, but they weren't sure who else might join. As Glory pulled a batch of brownies from the oven, the door creaked open.

"Brownies mean it's official!" Nelda declared as she and Lora walked in, carrying bags of chips and soda.

Ethel Sue arrived shortly after, followed by more members of the church. Edmund entered next with Jake close behind. Sammy and Jake exchanged warm smiles, her heart fluttering slightly when their eyes met.

Then, another figure stepped inside—someone Sammy didn't recognize.

The woman carried herself with an air of quiet confidence, her polished heels clicking softly against the floor. Dressed in a tailored blazer and slacks, she had the kind of presence that turned heads without trying. Sammy couldn't shake the feeling that she'd seen someone move like this before, the sharp posture, the effortless poise.

A few people in the room smiled and waved to her, and she acknowledged each one with a nod and a practiced ease. Whoever she was, she wasn't a stranger to everyone.

Then it clicked. She looked like Michelle. Not in the obvious way, but in the way she carried herself—like she always knew the next step before taking it.

The woman's gaze landed on her. A poised smile curved her lips as she stepped forward, extending a well-manicured hand.

"You must be Samantha."

Sammy accepted the handshake, keeping her own smile polite. "Hello there. Yes, I am, but I go by Sammy."

"Sammy." The woman tested the name, rolling it over like she was deciding whether it suited her.

Before Sammy could think too much about it, Nelda swooped in with a warm grin. "Vivian! So glad you could make it!" She gestured to an open chair. "Come sit by me. You'll have the best seat in the house." As she turned to lead Vivian away, she shot Sammy a quick wink.

Sammy gave Nelda a grin, then exhaled quietly and turned toward the doorway just in time to see someone approaching up the walkway.

It was Sarah.

"Hey!" Sammy greeted, pulling her friend into a hug. "So glad you could make it."

"Wouldn't miss it," Sarah replied as she and Sammy walked inside. "How can I help?"

"Not sure yet—just join everyone in the living room," Sammy said, motioning her inside.

The house quickly filled with warm conversation, the scent of fresh-baked brownies mingling with coffee. Once everyone was settled, Sammy stepped to the front of the packed room.

"Hey, y'all! Thanks so much for coming. I know your time is valuable, so we'll keep this to an hour. I'd like to hand things over to Lora. Her heart for this community and her willingness to say yes is what's making this camp happen."

A ripple of applause and a few encouraging cheers spread through the room as Lora stepped forward, notebook in hand.

"So, we're looking at the last week of July, Monday through Friday, from 9:00 a.m. to noon, finishing each day with lunch together," she began. "Our theme is 'God Is in Everything,' inspired by Psalm 139:7–12. We want to help kids recognize God's presence in both the big and small moments of life through games, art, and simply being together. It's about seeing Him in places we don't always think to look."

A murmur of approval spread through the room.

She continued. "Day one will be a water balloon toss relay. Teams will pass balloons down a line to a bucket while 'Wipe Out' plays. The team with the most balloons wins free pool passes. Vivian, could Sterling Ridge Ranch donate those passes?"

Vivian tapped a polished nail against her notebook, then pulled out her phone. "We are always looking for ways to support the community. Consider it done." She typed something quickly before glancing back up, her smile unwavering. "And Michelle will be available to volunteer. She can take the week off to assist."

Sammy looked down and noticed her fingers tightened slightly around her notebook. *Of course she can.* But she quickly fixed her expression as she looked back up with a nod and smile.

"Wonderful!" Lora replied, making a note on her page. She continued, her energy contagious. "Tuesday's activity will be obstacle courses with bouncy houses. I've got a friend who can loan us a couple, but we'll need help setting them up early in the morning."

Jake raised his hand and said with a crooked smile, "John and I can handle that. Abuelo always says we're full of hot air."

Laughter rippled through the room, and Sammy caught Jake's eye, mouthing, *"Thank you."*

Jake grinned and winked, sending a warmth up her neck that had nothing to do with the crowded room.

"Next up: Wednesday. We'll take the kids to clean up around the community center and library, then reward them with pool passes. Should be pretty straightforward."

"Thursday's still open," Lora added, scanning the group. "Any ideas?"

Sarah raised her hand. "What about a field trip to the skating rink outside of town and McDonald's for lunch afterward?"

Lora's face lit up. "That's a great idea! I love it." She turned to Ethel Sue. "Think your neighbor—the shift manager—could hook us up with a discount or a few free kid's meals?"

Ethel Sue nodded. "I'll ask him first thing tomorrow."

Lora grinned. "Perfect. That just leaves Friday, and then we're all set!"

Then Lora turned to Edmund, her voice hopeful. "And Friday will be the big finale: a campout. What do you think, Edmund?"

Edmund grinned, his eyes lighting up with enthusiasm. "Now that's my kind of project. Count me in, but I'll need plenty of hands to help corral those kids."

Around the room, several hands shot up, volunteers eager to help. Lora jotted down names, flashing a grateful smile. A few more details were ironed out, laughter and conversation spilling over as people gathered their things.

As the last guest left, Sammy leaned against the door, letting the quiet of the house wash over her. "I think this is going to be something special," Sammy said softly, her voice tinged with wonder.

Glory stepped closer, resting a gentle hand on Sammy's shoulder. "When the Lord's in it, Sammy, it's bound to be something special."

Sammy slipped upstairs for the night, and grabbing her journal, she wrote simply:

> Lord, I didn't see any of this coming.
>
> Not the food pantry. Not the summer camp. Not Jake.
>
> But here I am—standing in the middle of all these unexpected blessings.
>
> Thank You. For the hands that are making this pantry a reality. For the fourteen people who showed up tonight, ready to pour into these kids.
>
> You are in the details, Lord, and I see You working.
>
> And I am so, so grateful.

With a contented sigh, she closed her eyes, letting the promise of tomorrow settle over her like a soft blanket.

Chapter 23

I know I counted this multiple times. It has to be somewhere.

Sammy's eyes darted between the inventory sheets and the half-unpacked boxes lining the storage room. The first food pantry distribution was tomorrow, and she had twenty-five pre-confirmed families coming. Likely more would show up.

She exhaled sharply, running a hand through her hair. "Okay . . . canned goods, check. Dry goods, check. But where on earth are the eggs and fresh produce?"

Her pulse ticked up as she shuffled through the paperwork, flipping pages, scanning numbers. She knew she had accounted for them. Hadn't she?

A cold knot of anxiety settled in her stomach. Had she miscalculated? Lost them? What if they didn't have enough?

She pulled out her phone to double-check the email confirmation from the supplier when a voice broke through her spiraling thoughts.

Pastor Mark peeked in, his expression warm. "How's it going, our fearless food pantry leader?" He glanced down at Sammy, now sitting on the floor surrounded by papers, looking every bit the picture of stressed-out determination.

"Not great." Sammy winced. "Distribution is tomorrow, and the eggs and produce aren't here.

She frantically sifted through her notes. Then her eyes landed on something, and her stomach sank. "Oh no . . . oh no, no, no."

"What is it?" Pastor Mark asked, his calm presence grounding her.

Sammy ran a shaky hand over her face. "They had the wrong date. I gave them our original soft launch date by mistake. That's why the delivery never came. Oh man. I really screwed up, Pastor Mark."

She wrapped her arms around her legs and dropped her head onto her knees. "That was part of the plan. The board approved fresh produce and eggs to make sure families had something nutritious—and now they won't have it."

Pastor Mark crouched beside her, his voice steady. "Sammy, listen to me. You've already done more for this town than most do in a year. One mistake doesn't change that."

"But now the participants won't get fresh food tomorrow," she whispered.

He stood up and held out a hand to help her up too. "Sammy, you're allowed to make mistakes."

She hesitated before taking his hand, and as she stood, he pulled out his wallet and handed her a gift card.

She looked at it, confused. "Coffee with Your Cream Café?"

Pastor Mark chuckled. "Look, you've been working nonstop since you got here. I'm technically your boss, and I say you need a break. Go. Right now."

Sammy frowned. "But I don't want to go. I need to fix this."

"You need a break." His voice was gentle but firm. "We need you strong enough to see another day." She started to argue, but he raised a hand. "No buts. For the love of this project and your sanity, please go take a break."

The walk to the coffee shop felt longer than usual. By the time she slid into a booth and stared into her untouched latte, exhaustion finally caught up with her. She should check the pantry schedule, call the supplier again—

No.

She inhaled deeply and pulled out her phone. She scrolled past unread emails, reminders, and texts before tapping open the devotion she had been going through.

"Be still, and know that I am God." — Psalm 46:10 NIV

When searching for your calling, it can be easy to keep looking for clues the Lord is leaving you, but trust His timing and trust the power of this Scripture. When we are still—when we quit striving—it gives God room to move and show up in ways you would never expect, but exactly as He intends.

Today, take time to rest and be open to what God might show you.

Journal prompt: Where in my life am I striving instead of trusting? What would it look like to be still and let God lead?

Sammy exhaled, rubbing her temple. Striving? Oh, she could fill an entire notebook on that subject.

She took a sip of her latte, the warmth spreading through her, cinnamon and vanilla lingering on her tongue. She savored it as she pulled out her journal, flipped to a blank page, and pressed her pen to the paper.

> I know how to plan. I know how to fix. But do I know how to be still? What if I'm holding on so tightly to control that I'm not leaving space for You to step in? What if today was You reminding me I don't have to carry this alone?

She paused, tapping her pen against the edge of the journal, lost in thought.

That's when a voice pulled her from her reflection.

"I hear you've been working yourself into the ground, sweetheart."

Sammy blinked up as Lisa, crossed her arms, eyebrow raised in that way that said she had already won the argument before it even started.

"I—What? No, I'm fine. Just busy," Sammy stammered trying to bring her thoughts back to the now.

Lisa scoffed. "Busy? Or on the verge of passing out?"

Sammy sighed. "Okay, maybe I've been a little overwhelmed."

Lisa nodded, then tipped her head toward the door. "Well, good thing you're not in this alone."

The bell above the door jingled. Sammy turned, and her breath caught.

A steady stream of Willow Creek locals filed in, each carrying a grocery bag or a small box. At first, she just stared, her brain struggling to process what she was seeing. But then she saw what they were holding.

Baskets of fresh vegetables—tomatoes, bell peppers, squash, cucumbers. Someone held up a crate of apples. A little girl clutched a bundle of leafy greens as her mother helped unload bags of potatoes and onions.

And then came Mrs. Harper.

The elderly woman, as feisty as ever, strode in with a determined look on her face. In her arms, a dozen cartons of eggs. Behind her, two more church ladies followed, their arms equally full.

Tears burned at the back of Sammy's eyes.

"Wait, what is this?" she whispered.

Lisa patted her hand, her voice warm. "This, my dear, is the town reminding you that you're one of us now."

Sammy swallowed hard, her vision blurring at the edges. All this time, she'd thought she was holding up this project alone. But she wasn't. She never had been.

When Jake walked in, carrying a heavy box labeled Fresh Produce, his easy grin sent warmth curling in her chest.

"Heard you needed a little backup."

Sammy let out a breathless laugh, emotion thick in her throat. "I don't even know what to say."

Lisa chuckled, nudging her lightly. "A simple 'thank you' and maybe a promise to stop running yourself ragged would be a good start."

Sammy turned, her gaze sweeping over the room. Mrs. Harper adjusted the egg cartons in her arms, her face set with quiet determination. The little girl with the bundle of greens grinned up at her, eyes bright with excitement. Near the counter, Jake shifted the weight of the produce box effortlessly, catching her eye with a knowing smile.

This wasn't just about the food pantry.

This was about them—about neighbors stepping in without hesitation, about hands lifting burdens she hadn't even realized she was carrying. They weren't just church members. They weren't just volunteers.

They were her people.

And today, they had shown up—not just for the pantry. For her.

She exhaled, nodding, her voice barely above a whisper. "Thank you."

The group cheered, and someone shouted, "Now let's get this girl some pie before she faints!"

Laughter rang through the room, and Sammy got up, her legs shaking with emotion. One by one, she went down the line, hugging each person, overwhelmed by their kindness.

By the time she made it back to her booth, Jake was already there, settling in across from her with his own coffee. He slid a plate in front of her—a slice of Lisa's famous lemon meringue pie.

"Oh, you're going to have to help me with this. I'm so overwhelmed by all of this, I'll be lucky to take even a bite or two." Sammy said as she grabbed a fork.

Jake was already reaching for the extra one. "You don't have to ask me twice. Lisa's pies are the best."

As the café slowly emptied and the last of the townspeople drifted out, Jake lingered. He leaned in next to Sammy. "I've got my truck outside. Thought I'd offer you a ride back to the church with all the donations."

"That would be great, thanks," Sammy said, waving goodbye to Lisa as she followed him.

They worked side by side unloading crates of fresh vegetables, stacking egg cartons, and organizing shelves to make sure everything was ready for tomorrow's distribution.

With each box they tucked into place, Sammy felt something inside her shift—a gentle, quiet certainty she hadn't allowed herself to recognize before. Willow Creek wasn't just a stop along the way. It wasn't a placeholder until she figured out her next step. It was more.

The community. The church. Her new friends. Jake.

She was falling in love with Willow Creek, with the rhythms of this small town and the way people showed up for one another—not just when things were easy, but especially when they weren't.

* * *

That night, wrapped in the patchwork quilt Glory had made, Sammy stared at the blank journal page. *Where to begin?*

> Lord, today didn't go as planned. I thought I had everything under control, yet I still fell short.
>
> But You knew.
>
> You provided—through this town, through Jake. I was never alone.
>
> Thank You.
>
> Tomorrow, the pantry opens. Can't wait to see how You show up!
>
> Next time I start striving, remind me to be still and know that YOU are God. You handle things in such beautiful and unexpected ways.

She stretched as she placed her journal on the nightstand and switched off the lamp. Tomorrow would come soon enough. But tonight, she let herself rest.

Chapter 24

"Today's the day!" Sammy exclaimed as she ran downstairs, her excitement bubbling over. She couldn't help the giddy energy coursing through her. It was a big day, the culmination of weeks of planning and prayer. Today was the first food pantry distribution day.

Glory glanced up from her coffee with a smile. "Good morning to you too! You've got quite the pep in your step today."

Sammy laughed. "I'm heading out for a jog. Be back soon!"

"Don't wear yourself out before the main event," Glory teased.

Sammy waved as she dashed out the door. With every step, the steady rhythm of her sneakers on the pavement echoed how far she'd come not just in miles, but also in spirit.

A few months ago, she had felt so lost. Now, every step felt like a quiet victory, proof that she was moving forward.

"Lord, thank You for giving me the strength to jog this block. It is amazing how far I have come. And thank You for today. Help us to serve these families well and to show them Your love."

As she continued down the street, she spotted Mrs. Harper feeding her chickens, just like always. She smiled and waved like she did every day, but today, Mrs. Harper looked up and waved back.

Sammy's smile widened. "And Lord, thank You for yesterday—for every kind heart that gave. Bless each family who donated."

When Sammy arrived back home, she grabbed her coffee and Bible, settling in for her morning quiet time. She opened her devotional and paused at the *Scripture of the Day.*

CHAPTER 24

"For we are God's handiwork, created in Christ Jesus to do good works, which God prepared in advance for us to do."

—Ephesians 2:10 (NIV)

"'God prepared in advance for us to do,'" she whispered aloud, flipping open her Bible. Holding the pen cap between her teeth, she underlined the verse, tracing the words with her finger.

"You knew this would happen, Lord. The pantry, the summer camp, this new life I'm building here. You saw it all coming together, even when I couldn't."

Beside the verse, she jotted: *Food pantry distribution starts today* and added a small heart below it.

"Wow," she said as she took that thought in. *He knew all along.*

She closed her Bible, prayed over the day, and enjoyed her coffee. Excitement mingled with nerves as she imagined the busy hours ahead.

* * *

When Sammy and Glory arrived at Grace Chapel, the parking lot was buzzing with activity. Volunteers were unloading boxes, setting up tables, and organizing the space for the families who would soon arrive.

"Morning, Sammy!" Nelda called, clipboard in hand. "Check-in is ready, and we've got coffee and snacks for the team in the corner. Lora's handling that."

"Thanks, Nelda," Sammy replied, waving as she walked toward the pantry.

Stepping inside, Sammy's breath caught. The shelves were full, neatly lined with canned goods, pasta, jars of peanut butter, and fresh produce. Along one wall, the boxes from yesterday were closed and ready to go to families. Baskets of produce sat on a table near the entrance, and the refrigerator hummed quietly, stocked with milk and eggs.

"Wow," she whispered, running her fingers along the edge of a shelf. "Lord, You really did this."

A familiar voice broke through her thoughts. "Can you believe it? Today's the day."

Sammy turned to see Jake standing in the doorway, wearing a Grace Chapel volunteer shirt and a warm smile. Just seeing him made her nerves settle a little.

"I can," she said, returning his smile. "Thanks again for all your help yesterday. I don't know what I would've done without you."

Jake shrugged, his grin easy. "You would've figured it out. But I was glad to help." He stepped a little closer, his voice dipping to a gentle rumble. "A hug for luck?"

Sammy's breath caught. She hadn't expected that—hadn't expected him to ask, or for the sudden flutter in her chest. "You know what? Yes, please."

As she moved into his arms, time seemed to slow. Jake's embrace was both careful and comforting, his arms strong yet loose enough to let her decide how close to draw. *His* strength and warmth anchored her in the moment, and for just a second, the bustling energy of the pantry—the nerves, the to-do list—melted away.

She lingered a moment longer before pulling back.

She looked up, and the soft look in his eyes sent another flutter through her. "Thanks."

His smile widened, a mix of boyish charm and something deeper. "Anytime."

The sound of her phone alarm going off broke the moment, drawing their attention. Sammy stopped the alarm. Five minutes to opening. She blew out a deep breath, a mix of anticipation and nerves bubbling to the surface.

"It's time," she said, straightening her shoulders.

Jake stepped back, his grin full of quiet encouragement. "Let's do this." He held out his hand for a high-five, and Sammy slapped it with a laugh before they headed to the parking lot together.

Pastor Mark gathered all the volunteers and any families who wanted to join and led them in prayer, asking for God's blessing on the families they would serve. Then everyone got to their stations.

The morning passed in a blur. Families arrived in waves, greeted warmly by volunteers who guided them through the pantry process. The atmosphere was both calm and bustling, filled with the soft hum of conversation and the occasional laugh of a child.

Sammy moved between groups, checking on volunteers and chatting with families. Her heart swelled at the sight of people leaving with full boxes and hopeful smiles.

At one point, a young mother struggled to manage her toddler while holding a box of groceries, so Sammy stepped in without hesitation, offering to carry the box.

"Thank you," the woman said, her voice trembling. "This means so much to us."

Sammy gave her a side hug as they walked. "We're glad to help."

Nelda brought lunch from Chick-fil-A and nudged Sammy to take a break. "I've been thinking about how to keep this running smoothly and wanted to run an idea by you," Nelda began, opening her tablet with the practiced ease of someone who never really retired.

Sammy nodded as she took a bite of her sandwich, grateful for the break.

"I've started collecting email addresses from every family we serve," Nelda continued. "What if we set up an e-vite system? We could get a headcount before each distribution, manage inventory better, and avoid over- or understocking. Plus, it'd let us send reminders so no one misses out."

Sammy's eyes lit up. "That's brilliant!"

Nelda tapped a few notes into her tablet. "And I've been thinking strategically. If we track which items are most popular, we could leverage that data. I've got connections with a few local suppliers through my real estate work, especially with those developing commercial kitchens and markets. I bet I could negotiate some in-kind donations or discounted bulk buys."

Sammy nearly choked on her lemonade. "Nelda, that's amazing. I didn't realize you had such a knack for this."

Nelda chuckled. "It's all about making connections and finding win-wins. And speaking of connections, Sarah Shoreman knows digital marketing. Maybe she could help us with online ads to reach more families in need."

"Nelda! Yes! Thank you! Can I leave that ball in your court for now?"

"Absolutely," Nelda said with a confident nod. "I'll pull everything together and update you next week." She leaned in, her expression warm, and her eyes began to glisten. "Sammy, I just wanted to say thank you for saying yes to this. This food pantry is an answered prayer for so many of us."

Sammy's heart swelled at the words. "Thanks, Nelda. But it wouldn't have happened without everyone's support."

Nelda smiled warmly and gave Sammy a quick hug. "You're the spark that started it all. Don't forget that."

As Nelda walked out, Sammy stood for a moment, so grateful for her new Willow Creek friends and life.

The steady stream of families continued throughout the afternoon.

As Sammy said good-bye to one family, she wiped her hands on her apron and noticed a man lingering near the door, clutching one of the purple flyers. His clothes were worn, his eyes shining with unshed tears.

"Sir, can I help you?" Sammy began.

"I just . . . I wanted to say thank you," he said, his voice thick with emotion. "I didn't think anyone cared, but this place . . . it's a blessing."

Sammy swallowed hard. "You're welcome. We're so glad you're here."

As he walked away, Sammy pressed her hand to her heart, the weight of his words settling deep. This—this was why they'd worked so hard. She blinked back tears, her heart overflowing with gratitude too big for words.

By the end of the day, over forty-two families had been served. The pantry was now half empty but still filled with purpose, a testament to God's provision.

Sammy stood in the quiet pantry, her hands resting on an empty shelf. Beside her, Glory slipped an arm around her waist.

"You did it, Sammy," Glory said, her voice full of pride. "And I couldn't be prouder."

Sammy leaned into her grandmother, her heart full. "We did it, Glory. All of us."

* * *

That night, Sammy curled up in bed, journal in hand, letting the day's events settle in her heart. She took a deep breath and pressed her pen to the page.

> Lord, today, I saw You move.
>
> Forty-two families served. Laughter, gratitude, and full boxes—not just of food, but of hope. And You prepared it all in advance.
>
> I saw You in the hands that packed, the hearts that gave, and the man at the door whispering, *"Thank you."*
>
> I don't have to control everything. You've already gone ahead of me.
>
> For we are Your handiwork, created in Christ Jesus to do good works, which You prepared in advance for us to do. —Ephesians 2:10
>
> You prepared this. You prepared me. Lord it is an honor doing the good works you prepared in advance for me to do.

She read over the words, exhaling slowly. Peace settled over her. *God really was in the details, and it is beautiful.*

Chapter 25

The sound of hammers and the occasional creak of wood filled the warm afternoon air as Jake and John worked side by side, repairing a section of fence on the ranch. Jake paused, leaning on the handle of his hammer, and glanced out toward the horizon, a small smile playing at his lips.

John caught the look and smirked. "Oh my gosh, man. Get it together. You're doing that goofy smile thing again. Are you thinking about Sammy?"

Jake shot him a sidelong glance, but the grin tugging at his mouth gave him away. "Maybe."

John straightened, wiping sweat from his brow. "Well, this is new. I've never seen you act like this before. You're practically floating."

Jake hesitated, his smile softening. "Honestly? I've never felt like this before."

John arched an eyebrow, half teasing but also genuinely curious. "Jake, you barely know her. How can you already be so sure?"

Jake exhaled, considering that for a moment. Then, with a slow nod, he said, "You know what? You're right."

John clapped him on the shoulder, looking satisfied. "Good. Now that I've got my Jakey back—"

Jake let out a breath, rolling his shoulders as if shaking off hesitation. "Actually, I'm going to ask her on a date. Get to know her better."

John blinked, startled. "Wait, what? That's not where I was going with this!"

Jake's grin widened as he adjusted his hat. "Well, it's where I'm going. Because if that hug we had at the food pantry was any indication, it's time I figure out if what I'm feeling is real."

John groaned, dragging a hand down his face. "There's no stopping you, is there?"

"Nope." Jake picked up his hammer, his expression set. "Not this time."

John threw his hands up in surrender. "Fine, fine. Just make sure you bring her back by curfew."

Jake laughed, a warm, easy sound. "You know I will."

John's face turned serious, his voice a little quieter but still warm. "You deserve this, Jake. I mean it."

Jake's smile turned grateful, and he gave John a quick nod. "Thanks. That means a lot."

John's expression softened, but only for a second before he nudged Jake's shoulder. "Now stop daydreaming, lover boy. We've got work to do."

Jake chuckled, shaking his head as he swung his hammer. "Yeah, yeah. Let's get to it."

* * *

After repairing the fence, Jake grabbed some water and sat on the porch swing, staring at his phone. A week had passed since the food pantry—and that hug. He hoped she'd felt the same pull toward him that he did toward her.

The thought of calling Sammy made his pulse quicken, but he shook off his nerves and dialed.

"Hello?" Sammy answered, her voice bright and curious.

"Hey, Sammy, it's Jake," he said, smiling as he imagined her reaction.

"Oh, hey, Jake!" Her tone warmed, easing his nerves.

"I was wondering if you'd let me take you to dinner tomorrow night," he said, keeping his voice casual. "Hank's on Main, around six?"

She hesitated just long enough to make his heart skip.

Then she said, "Sure, that sounds great."

Jake grinned. "Perfect. I'll pick you up at 5:45." He pumped his fist in the air, grateful she couldn't see.

"Alright," she said, and he could hear the smile in her voice. "See you then."

As he hung up, Jake leaned back against the swing, exhaling. He could still hear the warmth in her voice, and for the first time all week, the uncertainty lifted.

Tomorrow couldn't come fast enough.

* * *

The next morning, Sammy slid out of bed and stretched, savoring the rare luxury of a day off. She'd been putting her hundred-dollar weekly paycheck aside for weeks. Now it was time to splurge a little.

First stop: the shops on Main Street.

The morning air was warm, carrying the scent of blooming flowers and fresh bread from the bakery. Sammy parked her bike at the rack on Main Street, smiling as her sandals clicked softly on the sidewalk. The town had a charm that still felt new to her, but the shop owners' familiar nods and waves reminded her she was slowly becoming part of the fabric of Willow Creek.

As she strolled, a shop caught her eye: Merry Days. The painted sign above the door featured a whimsical wreath, and the window display was a cheerful collection of ornaments, snow globes, and twinkling lights that seemed to transport her straight into the heart of Christmas, even in the middle of summer. Intrigued, she stepped inside, the soft jingle of a bell announcing her arrival.

The air smelled faintly of cinnamon, and every corner of the shop seemed to glimmer. Rows of ornaments, garlands, and tiny snow-dusted villages filled the shelves. Sammy was mesmerized, her fingers brushing a strand of tinsel as she wandered deeper into the store.

"Good morning!" a woman's voice called out warmly.

Sammy turned to see a petite woman with short salt-and-pepper hair standing behind the counter. Her blue eyes twinkled as brightly as the ornaments she sold.

"Good morning," Sammy replied, smiling back. "This place is incredible."

The woman laughed, wiping her hands on her apron. "Thank you! I'm Charlotte Walker. And welcome to Merry Days."

"I'm Sammy Thomas," she said. "I'm new to town—or, well, sort of. I'm staying with my grandmother."

"Ah," Charlotte said with a curious tilt of her head. "And who might that be?"

"Glory Thomas."

Charlotte's face lit up. "Glory? Oh, of course! I know Glory well. Nelda's mentioned you too."

Sammy smiled, feeling the threads of her life in Willow Creek weaving together. "You know Nelda?"

"Nelda's the reason I'm here," Charlotte said, motioning for Sammy to join her at the counter. "After my husband passed, I didn't know what to do with myself. Nelda stepped in, offering me this space and saying, 'You've got a gift for making people smile around the holidays. Let them feel it all year round.' And she's been my biggest supporter ever since."

"That's incredible," Sammy began, "And the store . . . It's beautiful. You can feel the love you've put into it."

"Thank you, Sammy," Charlotte said. "That means a lot."

Sammy wandered the store a while longer, enchanted by the displays. Her gaze settled on a small glass ornament painted with a sunrise—the same soft hues of that early-morning ride with Jake.

She traced the glass, smiling at the memory of golden light filtering through the trees . . . and the bruise blooming on Jake's cheek.

She giggled, shaking her head. *Poor guy never even saw it coming.*

She took it to the counter and set it down with a smile. "I think this one's coming home with me."

Charlotte glanced at the ornament and then back at Sammy. "A beautiful choice," she said warmly as she rang up her purchase.

From there, Sammy continued her shopping trip, visiting the boutique next door, Shelby's Boutique, where she found a lavender sundress that looked perfect for dinner with Jake. As she held it up to the mirror, she couldn't help but grin. "Practical and pretty," she reasoned, trying to convince herself the purchase was worth it.

She stepped into Coffee with Your Cream Café, the little bell above the door jingling as she entered.

Lisa glanced up from behind the counter. "Twice in one week? To what do I owe the honor?"

Sammy grinned as she approached. "Just stopping by on my day off."

Lisa smirked. "Day off? Miracles do happen." She wiped her hands on a dish towel before leaning on the counter. "Now tell me the real reason. You're glowing."

Sammy rolled her eyes, but her cheeks warmed. "I'm not glowing."

Lisa gave her an exaggerated once-over. "Mmm-hmm. Right. Just a normal Friday, nothing special? No exciting plans tonight?"

Sammy sighed, knowing there was no use in trying to keep secrets in Willow Creek. "Fine. Jake asked me to dinner, but I am assuming you already know that."

Lisa grinned triumphantly. "And you said yes. Of course you did. You'd be crazy not to." She walked over to the espresso machine and started making Sammy's usual order without even asking.

Sammy grabbed a sandwich from the cooler and set it on the counter. "It's just dinner, Lisa."

Lisa placed the cup in front of her with a knowing smirk. "At Hank's." She raised her eyebrows for emphasis.

Sammy froze mid-sip, then sighed.

Lisa winked. "Have fun tonight, sweetheart."

With a victorious grin, Lisa turned and walked off to help another customer, leaving Sammy shaking her head with a mix of amusement and nerves.

She took her food and settled by the window, letting the warm sunlight spill across her table. Pulling out her notebook, she began jotting down last-minute ideas for the summer camp starting Monday—water balloon relays, obstacle courses, and Friday's campout at Edmund's ranch.

Her pen tapped against the page, but her thoughts drifted. First to the volunteers who had stepped up, and then, inevitably, to Jake.

That "hug for luck" before the food pantry opened had felt almost heavenly. It had steadied her in a way she hadn't expected, and even now, the thought of it sent a flutter through her chest.

And now, with their dinner plans tonight, she couldn't ignore the flutter of anticipation building inside her.

Back at home, Sammy slipped into her new lavender dress, the soft fabric brushing against her skin like a whisper of confidence. She added a touch of mascara and lip gloss, then paused, studying her reflection.

Sammy smoothed her hands over the soft fabric of the lavender dress, stepping back from the mirror. The dress looked . . . nice. Soft, flowing. A little too romantic for her usual taste.

She bit her lip, debating. Maybe she should just go with jeans and a blouse. Something safer. Something more her.

She reached for her dresser, then stopped. With a small laugh, she shook her head.

Who was she kidding? She'd already stepped outside her comfort zone in so many ways since coming to Willow Creek. Why stop now?

And really, when was the last time she let herself feel beautiful just for the sake of it?

She met her own gaze in the mirror, a slow, confident smile forming.

"Not bad, Sammy Thomas," she whispered.

And just like that, 5:45 couldn't come soon enough.

Chapter 26

Jake pulled up to Glory's house in his faded blue 1972 Ford truck right on time at 5:45. He brushed his hands against his jeans as he stepped out, adjusting the collar of his button-up shirt. His palms were clammy despite the cool evening breeze.

Taking a steadying breath, he climbed the porch steps and knocked.

The door swung open, and there stood Sammy—her summer dress swaying softly, catching the light like she belonged to the season. Jake opened his mouth, then promptly forgot how to speak.

"Uh, wow," he finally managed, flashing a crooked smile. "You look lovely."

Sammy's cheeks flushed, and a shy smile tugged at her lips. "Thanks," she said, voice light. She looped her arm through his with a playful nudge as they walked toward the truck. "You clean up pretty well yourself."

The truck rumbled down the quiet streets of Willow Creek. Sammy's laughter filled the cab as Jake recounted the latest misadventures at the ranch—most of which involved John's ongoing battle with a particularly stubborn racoon.

"Let me guess," Sammy said, grinning. "The racoon won again?"

"Every time," Jake admitted, shaking his head. "It's becoming a matter of pride now."

Sammy's laugh was like music to his ears, and Jake couldn't help but smile.

She sobered slightly, glancing out the window. "I can't believe camp starts next week, I just hope everything comes together."

"It will," Jake said, his tone steady. "You've worked hard to make it happen.

The kids are lucky to have you." He opened her door.

Sammy glanced at him, her smile returning, though it was softer now. "Thanks, Jake."

The lively hum of Hank's greeted them as they stepped inside. Exposed brick walls displayed local art, and string lights cast a warm glow over the bustling crowd. Jake held the door open, nodding to the familiar server. "Hey, Jake," she greeted with a grin. "Want your usual table? It's open."

"That would be great, thanks."

Their corner table by the window offered a view of Main Street, where early fall leaves danced in the breeze and the sunset beyond the fields. "This is my favorite spot here," Jake began. "With the view out the window, you can people watch on Main Street or just relax and watch the sunset from here too."

The waitress waited until they got settled and then passed out menus.

"What's your favorite thing here?" Sammy asked, looking the menu over.

"I love the WC Burger with the bacon extra crispy, it's delicious." He looked at the waitress and said, "I would like that tonight with fries."

"That sounds delicious, I will take the same."

"Sweet teas?" The waitress asked.

"Yep."

"Yes, please." Sammy nodded and handed her the menu.

"So," Jake said, lacing his fingers together on the table, "we could talk about how amazing the food pantry distribution went . . ."

Sammy raised her arms in a mock celebratory pose. "It was amazing!" she whispered, her voice dropping into a dramatic crowd cheering tone.

Jake chuckled, shaking his head. "Or," he said, his voice softening, "we could talk about the camp starting Monday. But honestly? What I'd really like is to get to know you, Sammy."

She blinked, surprised by the shift. His hand rested gently over hers. Steady. Warm.

"All right, Jake Martinez," she said, resting her cheek in her palm. "What would you like to know?"

"Well, to start, what brought you to Willow Creek? I mean, why here?"

Sammy paused, uncertain. Did he really want to hear all that? Would he see her differently once he knew?

But the kindness in Jake's expression didn't waver. He waited, open and still.

"That's a bit of a story," she said.

"I've got time."

The waitress returned with their food, placing the plates gently on the table. Sammy used the moment to breathe.

Sammy gazed out the window of Hank's, as the colors of the sunset filtered through the window.

"Why Willow Creek?" she repeated softly, almost to herself. "It wasn't part of the plan," she admitted. "Actually, nothing about my life right now was part of the plan." Sammy paused, taking a sip of water.

Jake leaned forward, waiting without a word, his presence urging her to continue.

"I used to think my life would be small," she said softly. "Not in a bad way. Just quiet. Supportive. Behind-the-scenes. I thought that was enough."

Jake's brows furrowed gently, but he stayed quiet.

She glanced at him, then looked away. "With Richard, he was a guy I dated in college." She laughed to herself and continued, "I thought we were serious, but he never did and honestly we were just a guy and girl that hung out alot, but" she cleared her throat and continued, "With him and his family, it always felt like I was being tolerated. Like they had this polished life already laid out, and I was just trying to find a corner to squeeze into. And the worst part is—" she swallowed, her voice barely above a whisper—"I was okay with that. I told myself being tolerated was close enough to being loved."

Jake's jaw tightened, but he didn't interrupt.

Sammy gave a small, rueful smile. "Now? I don't want to be a footnote in someone else's story. I want to be . . . chosen. Fully. Not just accepted, but *wanted.*"

When she finally stopped, there was a moment of silence between them. Sammy caught her breath as Jake searched for the right words, the weight of her story hanging in the air.

When Jake finally spoke, his voice was steady and sure. "He was a fool. Sammy, you're more than enough for anyone who's smart enough to see it."

Her eyes shimmered. "Thank you," she said, barely above a whisper. "I guess I needed to hear that."

They sat for a long moment in silence. No need to fill it. Jake gave her hand a gentle squeeze.

Jake's voice broke the quiet again. "So, how did you figure out what to do next?"

Sammy drew a slow breath. "Honestly? I didn't." A look of quiet gratitude flickered across her face. "Glory offered me the food pantry position and a place to stay. It felt like a lifeline, and I took it." She looked out the window again, then back at him. "I've reconnected with her more than I expected to. And I'm finally finding a rhythm again. In my days. In my quiet time with God. It's not flashy, but it's solid."

Jake nodded, something like admiration softening his eyes. "And now you're here. Making a difference. One day of camp and one food box at a time."

Sammy laughed softly. "I'm still searching for my purpose. But for the first time, I'm not panicking about it. I think I'm finally learning to trust that God's plan is bigger—and better—than mine ever was."

Jake leaned back slightly. "I've always believed God works in mysterious ways. Maybe everything you've been through was leading you right here. To this town. To this table."

"Maybe," Sammy agreed, biting her lip nervously.

He raised a hand and waved at the waitress.

"Dessert?" the waitress asked as she approached.

Jake glanced at Sammy, a spark of mischief in his eyes. "So, about that famous chocolate cake. One slice or two?"

She laughed. "Two. Definitely two."

Jake grinned. "Smart girl."

And in that moment—beneath the warm lights and shared laughter—it felt like the beginning of something new.

Chapter 27

The chocolate cake disappeared far too quickly, their conversation flowing as effortlessly as the laughter between bites. When the plates were cleared, Jake leaned back in his chair, his smile lingering as he caught Sammy's gaze.

"This has been . . ." Jake exhaled, shaking his head slightly as if trying to find the right words. "Better than I ever could've hoped for."

Sammy's cheeks warmed, and she tucked a loose curl behind her ear. "Me too."

The moment hung between them, soft and unspoken, until Jake broke the silence.

"It's a clear night. How about a walk down Main Street before we head back?"

Sammy's smile widened. "I'd love that."

Outside, the air was crisp, and the string lights hanging above Hank's patio cast a soft glow over the sidewalk, giving the night a magical feel. Jake glanced around, his hands tucked into his pockets.

They fell into a comfortable rhythm, the evening settling gently around them. After a moment, Jake spoke up. "Did I tell you how John and I met? We were roommates at summer camp."

"No," Sammy said, her interest piqued. "But I bet that made for an interesting cabin!" She giggled at the thought.

Jake chuckled. "It definitely did. John . . . he likes a bit of mischief. We pulled the funniest pranks around camp. And the talent show—oh man, we'll have to have John do his skit for you sometime. It was hilarious."

Sammy smiled at the warmth in his voice. "That sounds so fun! Was it a church camp?"

"Well, kind of," Jake said, his tone softening. "It was a Christian camp for kids who had lost a parent."

Sammy's smile faded slightly, replaced by quiet understanding. "Oh," she said, giving his arm a gentle squeeze.

Jake glanced down at her, appreciating the kindness in her expression. "It was the first place I didn't feel out of place," Jake admitted, his voice quieting. "All of us had lost a parent. No awkward explanations, no pity, just kids who understood without needing to say a word. The staff there, they were incredible. They helped us laugh again. Helped us feel like we were allowed to still be kids."

Sammy's heart ached for him, but she could see how much the experience had shaped the man walking beside her. "That sounds like an amazing place," she said, her voice barely above a whisper.

"It really was," Jake said, his gaze distant for a moment. "It taught me that even in the hardest moments, there's light to be found. You just need the right people to help you see it sometimes."

Sammy stayed quiet, letting his words settle in the space between them. She felt honored that he would share something so personal, something so vulnerable.

"It sounds like you and John were lucky to find each other there," she finally said.

Jake looked down at her, his expression soft. "Yeah, we were. But when we first met, if you'd told me he'd be living on my property, working the ranch with me, and like family now—I never would've believed you." He paused, a spark of gratitude in his eyes. "But God had better plans."

A quiet brightness touched Sammy's face. "I hear ya! So, how did John end up at your ranch?"

Jake chuckled. "After he graduated high school, things with his mom started getting tense. They were bumping heads a lot. She wanted him to go to college, and he didn't. John's got more energy than he knows what to do with, and he's happiest working with his hands. Meanwhile, Abuelo and I could use the extra help. So one day, I just texted him, 'Wanna come be a ranch hand up here?'"

Sammy laughed. "And?"

Jake grinned. "John's reply was instant: 'I'll see y'all tomorrow!'"

"No way!" Sammy giggled, her eyes lighting up.

"Yep! Sure enough, he showed up the next day with whatever he could fit in his truck. We offered him a room in the house or the dry cabin behind it. He chose the cabin." Jake shook his head with a fond smile. "That was seven years ago, and I've had a brother living next door ever since."

Sammy smiled warmly. "It sounds like God knew what you both needed."

Jake smiled softly, the warmth in his gaze steady. "John's not just a ranch hand, he's family. He's brought so much laughter and life to the ranch. I don't know what I'd do without him."

Sammy tilted her head, her smile brightening. "It sounds like you've been a blessing to each other. I love that he found a home with you and your Abuelo."

Jake shrugged, rubbing the back of his neck. "We are too. He's the kind of guy who makes life a bit lighter and more fun just by showing up."

A cool breeze swept past, sending a shiver down Sammy's spine. Before she could react, Jake was already shrugging off his jacket, draping it over her shoulders.

"Better?" he asked softly.

She nodded, warmth spreading in more ways than one.

"Come on, let's get you back to the truck."

They walked back in companionable silence, the warm glow of streetlamps casting long shadows as the night breeze rustled the blooms in the flower boxes.

Jake pulled into Glory's driveway, shutting off the engine as the quiet of the night settled around them. Stepping out, he rounded the truck to open Sammy's door. As they walked to the porch, the stillness wrapped around them, warm and expectant.

"Thank you for tonight," Sammy said softly. "I can't remember the last time I felt so relaxed on a date."

Jake's gaze lingered on hers, his expression warm but searching. "I'm glad," he said, his voice low as he slowly took her hands in his. "I feel the same way."

The world seemed to hold its breath as Jake hesitated, his thumb grazing the back of her hand.

"Sammy," he began, leaning in closer, his voice barely above a whisper. "May I . . . ?"

Her heart skipped, and for a fleeting moment, uncertainty flickered. Was this too fast? Was she ready? But as she looked into his steady, patient eyes, her hesitation melted into something softer—something that felt a lot like trust.

"Yes," she whispered, her voice barely carrying above the night's gentle hum.

Jake released her hand, his fingers trailing up to cup her cheek, his touch warm and steady. His thumbs brushed her skin in a quiet, unspoken question. Every movement was deliberate, patient, as if giving her every chance to step away.

But Sammy didn't move. She couldn't.

Her breath hitched as Jake leaned in, his touch gentle, patient. Every nerve in her body seemed to hum, every thought melting away except for one—she trusted him. She wanted this. And as his lips brushed hers, the world around them seemed to quiet, narrowing to just this moment.

His kiss was soft, a whisper of a promise. It wasn't rushed or expectant—just tender, unhurried, and filled with more care than she'd ever thought to find.

A flutter of joy from her heart spread all the way to her fingertips. It was as if everything inside her had shifted into place, and in that moment, standing on Glory's front porch under a sky full of stars, Sammy felt the sweet, unmistakable certainty that this was real.

When they pulled back, Jake's thumb lingered on her cheek, his own expression a mix of awe and quiet joy. Sammy opened her eyes, and the world felt a little brighter, a little softer. She didn't know what tomorrow would bring, but tonight . . . Tonight was more than enough.

When they pulled back, Jake rested his forehead against hers, his grin tugging at the corners of his lips.

"Wow," he whispered, his voice filled with wonder.

Sammy let out a soft breath, her cheeks flushed. "Wow is right."

They lingered, the air between them humming with unspoken possibilities. Finally, Jake stepped back, his hand trailing from hers. "Goodnight, Sammy."

"Goodnight, Jake," she replied, handing him his jacket as she turned to go inside.

Leaning against the closed door, Sammy pressed her fingers to her lips, as if trying to hold on to the feeling just a little longer. The warmth of Jake's touch lingered, but so did something else—uncertainty.

"Lord, thank You. For tonight. For him. I don't know what happens next, and honestly that scares me. What if I let myself believe in something too good to be true again?"

Her breath wavered as the questions swirled, doubt creeping in. But then, another thought surfaced, quiet but steady.

"Be still, and know that I am God."

The verse she'd read so many times lately settled over her, anchoring her heart in truth. She wasn't in control. She didn't have to be.

She exhaled, a slow release of the tension she hadn't even realized she was holding.

Maybe she didn't know what the future held. But she knew the One who did. And that was enough.

Her hands fell to her side, and she stepped away from the door. The questions remained, but they didn't feel so heavy anymore. Hope outweighed the fear.

On the way home, Jake pulled over to the side of the road, his headlights slicing through the darkness. He stepped out, leaning against the hood of his truck as the cool air bit at his skin. Tilting his head back, he let out a breath, his gaze tracing the endless stretch of stars above.

"Wow, Lord, Your sky sure is beautiful tonight."

Jake's cheeks ached from smiling—he couldn't help it. That kiss. That moment. It was all still swirling in his chest. He chuckled softly, shaking his head in awe. "Lord, I think I see what You're doing here."

He paused, gaze lifting toward the stars.

"And wow, Sammy, she is something else." His voice softened as he ran a hand over his jaw. "She's strong in this quiet, steady way. Not flashy, but you feel it. Like you're safe. Like you're home."

He exhaled, the words coming softer now. "She is everything I never knew I always wanted."

Jake let out a slow breath, feeling it calm his heart down. "Thank You for tonight, for her." His voice was barely above a whisper now. "I don't want to rush ahead of You. I don't want to mess this up. But Lord, my heart feels so full."

He let the words settle, as real and unshaken as the stars above.

"Help me honor her. And help me follow You."

The night wrapped around him, still and peaceful. Jake closed his eyes, letting the quiet settle his thoughts. When he opened them, the stars seemed a little brighter, and for the first time in a long time, the future didn't feel so uncertain.

Climbing back into the truck, he started the engine, the familiar hum grounding him. He exhaled once more, a soft smile curving his lips.

Whatever came next, he wanted to give it his best.

Chapter 28

As Sammy slid into her usual pew on Sunday morning, she let the soft hush of the sanctuary settle over her. Glory was off in the choir loft, whispering with Ethel Sue and the others, no doubt debating who brought the best potluck dish last week.

A warm voice cut through the pre-service hum behind her. "Is this seat taken?"

Sammy turned to see Jake, his crisp button-up and easy grin somehow making the bustling pew feel like a private corner just for them.

"Of course not, Mr. Martinez," she teased, scooting over.

"Well, good morning to you too, Miss Thomas," he replied, tipping his hat playfully.

The band launched into the first praise song, an upbeat tune, and the worship leader encouraged all to stand. Sammy noticed Jake's rich baritone rolling through the melody.

The man could sing. His voice was confident and smooth, blending effortlessly with the melody. Sammy, on the other hand, had always leaned more toward the *joyful noise* side of things. Still, as the music swelled, she thought, *Why not?*

She lifted her voice, shaky at first, but then Jake glanced her way with a sideways smile. Just like that, her confidence grew. By the final chorus, she wasn't just singing, she was worshiping, her heart full and unguarded. When the service wound down, Pastor Mark stepped back up to the podium, his warm gaze sweeping over the congregation. "Before we go, I'd like to invite our camp volunteers to come forward. As many of you know, tomorrow kicks off our summer camp, and we want to send them off with our prayers and blessings."

A gentle rustling moved through the sanctuary as Sammy, Jake, and the others made their way to the front. Glory, Lora, and Ethel Sue came down from the choir loft, their smiles beaming as they caught Sammy's eye.

Out of the corner of her eye, Sammy saw Vivian and Michelle slip into the line, along with a few others from the congregation.

To Sammy, each step forward felt like a quiet declaration—I'm with you.

A swell of gratitude rose in her chest, the sense of belonging almost overwhelming. Each person was a thread in the tapestry of her life, weaving together a story of grace, love, and unshakable community.

Pastor Mark stepped forward, his voice kind. "These folks have given their time and hearts to make this week special for our kids. Let's pray over them."

He reached out, and the congregation followed, hands extended toward the front. A hush fell over the room, and Sammy closed her eyes.

"Lord, we thank You for each of these willing hearts," Pastor Mark prayed. "We ask for Your guidance, Your protection, and Your joy to fill them. May this week be a blessing not only to the children but to each of these volunteers as well. Let Your love shine through their actions, and may every moment at camp draw them closer to You. In Jesus' name we pray, amen."

Sammy felt the warmth of the prayers, peace and joy filling her heart and steadying her nerves.

Pastor Mark gave a kind smile as he looked over the volunteers still gathered up front. "And as we go, may we all carry that same spirit of love and service into the week ahead. Have a blessed Sunday. See you all next time!"

The congregation agreed with a warm "Amen," then began gathering their things, the usual Sunday shuffle filling the sanctuary as people made their way toward the doors.

Jake lingered beside Sammy as people came by, wishing her a great week. He waited for a free second before leaning in slightly. "Will we see you Tuesday morning when we are setting up the bounce houses for camp?"

"Absolutely," Sammy said, nudging his shoulder with hers..

"Great. See you then." His grin was easy, a touch of warmth in his eyes. As Sarah stepped up beside Sammy, he gave a quick nod before disappearing into the crowd.

As soon as he was out of earshot, Sarah turned to Sammy with a knowing look. "I'm glad I caught you. Do you have time for lunch? I made a Pinterest-worthy chicken dish and could use some girl time."

Sammy laughed, already looking forward to the familiar comfort of a meal with Sarah. "Absolutely! That all sounds wonderful. I'll grab my things and meet you at your car."

"Perfect." Sarah nodded, then turned to wrangle her kids from an enthusiastic game of tag, while Phillip stood by, shaking his head in amusement.

The parking lot buzzed like a disturbed anthill—kids and parents spilling out of the church, women stopping to chat, men trying to corral the kids, and a line of cars inching forward, drivers practicing their Sunday patience.

As Sammy walked with Glory, her Bible tucked against her chest, the gravel crunched beneath their feet, a quiet rhythm that gave space for her thoughts to wander.

Her mind drifted to Jake. She loved how it felt to have him beside her—the quiet confidence he carried, the way he sang like he meant it, the way his presence steadied her without asking anything in return. He'd simply been there.

No judgment when she hesitated. No impatience when she faltered. Just a steady, gentle presence.

Sammy bit her lip. *I've never felt so seen. But how is that possible? We only just started dating. Heck, we only met a few months ago! Is it too soon to feel this way?*

Richard's memory surfaced, but this time it wasn't with the sharp ache of loss or the sting of frustration. Instead, it came with a gentle acceptance, like holding a balloon by the string and finally letting go.

Isn't it too soon to feel okay with releasing him and all that old drama into the past? Shouldn't it hurt more to move forward?

Or maybe, just maybe, this peace was the answer to prayers she hadn't even known how to speak.

Glory glanced over, her expression soft. "You seem different today. Are you okay, my sweet Sammy?"

Sammy let out a breath she hadn't realized she was holding. "Yeah. I think so." She ran her fingers along the worn edges of her Bible. "It's just . . . I feel this strange kind of peace. Like everything's starting to settle, you know?"

Glory gave a slow nod, her arm brushing Sammy's as they walked. "That's a beautiful thing, honey. Sometimes peace sneaks up on us when we finally stop holding our breath."

A small smile pulled at Sammy's lips. "I was starting to think I'd never find it again."

"Well, the good Lord has a way of surprising us," Glory said, her eyes twinkling. "And I gotta say, it's nice to see you with a little sparkle back."

They both laughed, the sound rising with the breeze, and Sammy couldn't help but think that if the rest of her summer felt anything like this morning—peaceful, playful, and full of possibility—then she was ready for whatever God had in store.

She gave Glory a hug before sliding into Sarah's SUV, ready to enjoy lunch with the Shoreman family.

* * *

The Shoremans' home was the perfect blend of rustic charm and modern elegance. Built from warm Texas limestone, its golden hues glowed under the soft evening light, giving the house a welcoming, timeless feel. A sleek metal roof added a contemporary touch, while the deep front porch, framed by wooden beams, invited guests to sit and stay awhile.

The property was dotted with trees of all sizes, while lush landscaping, neatly trimmed hedges, and colorful flower beds lined the front, adding a burst of life against the natural stone. A long, smooth driveway led up to the entrance, making the whole home feel grand yet undeniably inviting, just like the Shoreman's themselves.

Inside, the house smelled of roasted chicken, vegetables, and fresh bread.

Sammy's stomach growled. "Smells amazing," she said.

"Thank you!" Sarah chirped, pulling the chicken from the oven. She handed Sammy a stack of plates with a mischievous smile. "Now, spill. What's new with you and Jake? You two looked cozy at church today."

Sammy's cheeks flushed. "Was it that obvious?" She set the plates on the counter, the cool ceramic a contrast to her warm hands, and began laying out silverware.

"Girl, the whole congregation noticed," Sarah teased, opening a cabinet and grabbing glasses. She filled each with iced tea, the clink of ice adding a soft rhythm to their conversation. "So . . . details. Start with that dreamy look during the sermon."

Sammy laughed, reaching for the serving spoon Sarah offered. She scooped mashed potatoes onto plates, her movements steady despite the flutter in her chest. "Last night . . . oh, Sarah, we had our first real date."

Sarah gasped, nearly dropping the towel she'd been using. "And?"

Sammy hesitated, wiping her hands on a dish towel before setting it aside. "We kissed."

Sarah's eyes widened. "You what? Sammy Thomas! Why is this just now coming up? Sit." She grabbed Sammy's arm and pulled her onto a barstool. "Tell me everything."

"It wasn't planned. It just happened."

Sarah pressed her hands flat on the counter. "The best kind." Then, narrowing her eyes, she pointed a finger at Sammy. "Okay, slow down. I need details. Where was it? Did he make the first move? Was it fireworks, or sweet and slow?"

Sammy turned red, picking up a spoon to stir the gravy. "We were at my front door, and he asked me."

Sarah practically vibrated. "He asked? Oh, that's it. I love this man."

Sammy smiled. "He wanted to make sure it was okay. And when I said yes, he kissed me like—" She hesitated, spoon pausing mid-stir.

Sarah leaned in. "Like what?"

Sammy set the spoon down. "Like he meant it. Like he wasn't just kissing me—he was choosing me."

Sarah sighed dramatically, hands over her heart. "Oh my gosh, you two are the cutest couple ever! I can't handle it." She wrapped Sammy in a quick hug before grabbing the last of the dishes. "Okay, you know I'd love to hear more, but hungry kiddos wait for no one!"

Sammy laughed, shaking her head as she reached for the serving spoon again. But even as the conversation moved on, a quiet certainty settled deep in her chest—this sweet something between her and Jake was starting to feel very real.

* * *

As lunch wrapped up, Michael tugged impatiently at Sammy's sleeve. "Miss Sammy, can we show you the new swing on the tree house now? Please?"

Laughing, Sammy stood. "A swing? I thought you just had a ladder!"

Michael's grin widened. "Not anymore! Come on, you'll love it!"

As the family spilled onto the lawn, the afternoon sun blazed overhead, casting crisp shadows beneath the oaks. The gentle buzz of cicadas filled the air, mingling with the distant rustle of leaves. A perfect moment in the heart of a summer day.

Phillip gave a proud nod to the swings. "Installed it last weekend. Perfect for summer afternoons."

A gentle breeze stirred the tall oaks, under which sat the famed tree house—a sturdy structure perched among thick branches, complete with two new swings hanging from one of the lower boughs.

Sammy ran after Michael, her sandals crunching over the soft grass. He dashed straight to the swings, grabbing the ropes and grinning back at her.

"Push me, Miss Sammy!" he pleaded, already kicking his legs in anticipation.

Laughing, Sammy stepped behind him and gave him a firm push. The swing lurched forward, and Michael let out a loud whoop as he soared higher.

"Higher!" he called.

Sammy chuckled, watching as Adeline slowly made her way over to the second swing. She carefully climbed on, her little fingers clutching the ropes as Phillip crouched beside her, steadying the seat.

After a few more pushes, Michael leaped off mid-swing, landing in the grass with a triumphant bounce. "Your turn, Miss Sammy!"

"Oh, I don't know—"

"Nope, no excuses!" he said, already dragging her toward the swing.

Sammy gave in, sitting down as Michael and Adeline erupted in cheers. As she started swinging, the breeze lifted her hair, and for a brief moment, she felt as carefree as the kids beside her.

After a few more gentle arcs, she let her feet drag in the dirt to slow herself down and passed the swing to Michael, who hopped in quick and pumped his legs higher while Adeline kicked happily in her smaller swing.

Growing up as the oldest of seven, life had always been loud, messy, and full of responsibility. There was always someone to care for, something to manage, a whirlwind of needs that never quite settled.

But this moment—this easy, sun-drenched simplicity—felt like a glimpse into something different. A hidden world she had only ever dreamed of, one filled with warmth, steadiness, and quiet joy. A life not built on duty, but on something softer.

She let the thought settle. She could get used to this.

Her fingers brushed the cool wood of the bench as she let out a slow breath.

"Lord, can life really be this sweet?"

Just then, a patch of color caught her eye. It was a row of zinnias blooming along the edge of the fence, their bright petals dancing gently in the breeze. Reds, pinks, oranges, and soft yellows, each one different, yet together creating something quietly stunning.

Sammy smiled, her chest tightening in that tender, grateful way.

"Let this season, the one I never saw coming but You knew all along, bloom into something beautiful."

Chapter 29

"Hey kids! Welcome to the first-ever Willow Creek Summer Camp!" Sammy's voice rose with each word, her arms spread wide as if she could scoop up all the energy bouncing off the kids in front of her.

The response was exactly what she'd hoped for—an explosion of cheers. Thirty-four kids stood before her, ranging from seven to twelve. Siblings clumped together, best friends whispered excitedly, and a few wide-eyed newcomers clung to the edges of the crowd. Sammy grinned. For a first day, this already felt like a win.

Behind her, the adult volunteers waited, ready to jump in. Sarah stood beside Blake, Ethel Sue's athletic and good-natured college-age grandson, and his equally enthusiastic friend Trevor.

"All right," Sammy called out, clapping her hands for attention. "Here's how today's teams are going to work. Mr. Blake is leading Team One!"

"YAAAY!" Blake flexed his arms dramatically, earning a wave of laughter from the kids.

"And Mr. Trevor is leading Team Two!"

"Hi," he said sheepishly, which earned quieter but no less amused cheers.

"Miss Sarah will call out a number—one or two—and point to you. That's your team. No swapping, even if your best friend is on the other side. Got it?"

A chorus of grumbles rose from the kids. Sammy cupped her hand around her ear, leaning dramatically toward them. "What? I didn't catch that. Got it?"

"OKAAAAAY!" they yelled, energy renewed as they scrambled to their groups.

The morning flew by in a blur of laughter and water balloons. The kids dashed back and forth in a relay race, trying to carry balloons to their baskets without popping them. Mischievous Ryan took every opportunity to smash a balloon on Blake's arm, mid-pass, each time claiming "It was an accident!" Blake's exaggerated reactions—yelling, flopping to the ground—sent the kids into hysterics.

When the games finally wound down, Sammy and Sarah set up snacks, working side by side as they sliced apples and lined up water bottles.

Sarah arranged napkins into neat rows, a pleased smile spreading across her face. "This is going so well, isn't it?"

"It really is," Sammy agreed, stealing a glance at the kids laughing as they played Duck, Duck, Goose. "I think dividing them into teams was smart. They're really learning to work together. But did you see Ryan's face when he 'accidentally' splashed Blake?"

Sarah burst into laughter. "He didn't even try to hide it! And Blake's such a good sport about it."

After snack time, the kids got to show off their creative sides with sidewalk chalk. Sammy wandered through the groups, admiring their colorful creations. But it was Mabel and Ryan's drawing that stopped her in her tracks.

Mabel had sketched a serene forest scene, complete with towering trees and a bubbling stream, while Ryan added a deer delicately sipping from the water.

"Wow, guys," Sammy said, crouching to their level. "This is incredible. Can I take a picture to remember it?"

The siblings shrugged in unison, Mabel finally muttering, "Sure."

Snapping a photo, Sammy couldn't help but marvel at their raw talent. As Mabel and Ryan dashed off to the jungle gym, she showed the picture to Sarah, Blake, and Trevor.

"Look at this," Sammy said, holding out her phone.

"Wow!" Sarah exclaimed. "How old are they again?"

"Mabel's around eleven, and Ryan's seven," Sammy replied.

Blake shook his head. "Dude, I'm twenty, and I couldn't draw like that if you paid me."

Trevor nodded. "Same. That's seriously impressive."

As lunchtime rolled around, sandwiches and fruit were handed out, and the kids gathered in the shade to eat. The adults finally sat down with their own plates, the hum of children's laughter drifting toward them.

"So, camp ends after lunch today," Sammy said as they watched the kids finishing up their sandwiches. "Y'all have fun plans for the afternoon?"

Blake wiped his brow, leaning back on his hands. "Grandma gave me and Trevor some pool passes, so we are heading to the pool."

Trevor grinned. "Oh yeah. I gotta see which one of these kids can do the best cannonball."

Sammy smiled. "That sounds perfect. Have fun!"

Sarah shot Sammy a mischievous look. "Actually, what do you say, Sammy? Should we join them?"

Sammy hesitated, wiping her brow. "I mean, it does sound pretty good." She laughed, her exhaustion giving way to a second wind. "Yeah, let's do it!"

The afternoon turned into a whirl of splashes and laughter. Sammy found herself at the center of a splash war, kids on every side as they aimed their tiny tidal waves at her.

She joined in the cannonball contest, her less-than-graceful attempt sending a modest splash but earning a perfect score from the kids.

Eventually, the splashes slowed, replaced by kids stretching out on towels and basking in the sun. Sammy and Sarah followed suit, sinking into lounge chairs as the Texas heat slowly dried them. Even as the noise settled, the joy lingered, their laughter still drifting through the air.

* * *

That night, Sammy curled up in bed, touching her warm cheek with her fingers, her skin a little sunkissed. She held her journal in her lap, letting the day's events settle in her heart. Taking a deep breath, she pressed her pen to the page.

> Camp started today and our theme is God is in EVERYTHING! And wow, Lord, did I see You today!
>
> 34 kids, laughter echoing under the sun. Water balloons bursting, chalk dust swirling, little hands creating something beautiful. I saw You in the joy, in the teamwork, in the way walls came down and friendships were built.
>
> I saw You in Ryan's mischievous grin, in Mabel's quiet talent, in Blake's patience, and Sarah's steady presence. I saw You in every scraped knee comforted, every high-five exchanged, every whispered "Miss Sammy, this is the best day ever."
>
> Thank You for letting me be part of what You're doing.

She read over the words, exhaling slowly. *Peace.*

Chapter 30

"Sammy, dear, it's 6:30 a.m." Glory's soft voice floated into the room as she eased open the door. The cool morning air slipped through the crack, carrying the fresh scent of dew and coffee. "I know it's a bit early for you, but I believe today's the day Jake and John are setting up the bounce houses at the park around seven."

Sammy's eyes fluttered open at the mention of Jake's name. With a groggy stretch, she sat up, already more awake than she wanted to admit. "Thanks, Glory," she murmured through a yawn.

By 6:45, Sammy was dressed, her hair pulled into a ponytail. She jogged downstairs, accepting the cup of coffee Glory handed her and brushing a quick kiss to her cheek before darting out the door. The park was only a few blocks away, and she used the brisk walk as a chance for some quiet time with God. She thanked Him for everything He'd done yesterday and for whatever blessings He had planned for today.

The morning air was crisp, laced with the faint scent of freshly cut grass. Dew clung to the blades, shimmering in the early light. As Sammy approached the park, the wide stretch of green came into view, punctuated by the bright, billowing shapes of bounce houses slowly inflating.

Her smile widened when she spotted Jake and John already hard at work. The sight of Jake—hair tousled, an easy grin on his face—sent a warm flutter through her chest. Maybe she was a little too excited about setting up bounce houses, but she wasn't about to overthink it.

"Hey, guys!" she called, her voice light and cheerful. "How's it going? Do y'all need anything?"

Jake glanced up, his smile widening at the sight of her. Something about seeing Sammy this early with coffee in hand and her hair swept back made the morning feel a little brighter. "Hey, Sammy! We're good. Just wrangling these stakes into the ground."

John swiped a hand across his sweaty forehead, shooting her a look of exaggerated misery. "But man, why is it already so hot? It's barely morning!"

Sammy chuckled, the sound light and easy. "I don't know, but I bet in winter you're the first one to ask why it's so cold, right?"

John shot her a perplexed look, but Jake laughed. "He totally does."

"Well, I can't do much about the temperature," Sammy said with a teasing grin, "but how about I just keep y'all company?" She settled onto a nearby bench.

Jake glanced her way, his gratitude evident in his expression. "Thanks," he said simply, warmth in his tone.

As the bounce houses slowly took shape, the three fell into easy conversation.

"So, John," Sammy began, leaning forward slightly, "Jake told me you two met at that camp in Colorado. That's amazing."

John grinned. "Oh, he told you about that, huh? Man, those two weeks were a game-changer. I'd just lost my dad a few months earlier, and I was a wreck—angry, confused, you name it. That camp? It was the first time I didn't feel so alone. I remember sitting under this massive pine tree, listening to someone in our group talk about their parents. It was like, for the first time, I could breathe again."

Sammy nodded, her expression soft with understanding. "Jake mentioned how special that place was to him too. I imagine meeting someone who really understood what you were going through made a huge difference."

"It did," John said, glancing at Jake, who was busy hammering stakes into the ground. "Jake had lost both of his parents a couple of years before I got there, so he got it—really got it. But the guy wasn't just good at listening. He was good at everything."

Jake looked up, smirking. "Here we go."

"Oh, you have no idea," John continued, turning to Sammy. "Hiking, climbing, sports—Jake crushed all of it. So, naturally, I had to hate him a little at first. I was the guy who liked to show off, and then this guy strolls in, all Mr. Humble-and-Talented."

Jake rolled his eyes but smiled. "I wasn't trying to show off. I just needed to keep busy."

"Sure, sure," John said, giving Sammy a playful, wide-eyed look. "Meanwhile, he had every girl at camp swooning by the end of week one."

"Oh, really?" Sammy laughed, eyes sparkling.

Jake cleared his throat, his cheeks coloring slightly. "Y'all, it was camp. I was fourteen."

John leaned back against the bounce house, grinning mischievously. "Yeah, but when you delivered that talent show monologue? Even the counselors were crying. I mean, I had my cowboy skit, and folks were laughing, but Jake here? He went straight for the heart."

Sammy tilted her head, intrigued. "Talent show?"

"It wasn't about the talent show," Jake said, his voice softer now. "I just wanted people to know grief wasn't something to hide. That we didn't have to go through it alone. Honestly? I think I needed to hear it as much as anyone else."

Sammy's smile turned tender. "That's beautiful, Jake."

John held up his hands in mock surrender. "See? This is what I'm talking about. The guy's been out here making the rest of us look bad since middle school."

Jake shook his head, chuckling as he stood to check the stakes. "John moved here after high school, and he's been part of the ranch ever since. He keeps things interesting, to say the least."

"More like I keep you from working yourself into the ground," John shot back. "And you're welcome, by the way."

Sammy grinned. "It sounds like you two balance each other out."

Jake glanced at her, his expression warm. "Yeah, we do."

John's eyes lit up with mock enthusiasm. "Oh! Sammy, have you tasted Abuelo's cooking yet? His brisket tacos? Life-changing."

Jake chuckled.

"Oh, sounds like that's my cue," Sammy said with a grin as the sound of children's laughter filled the air.

She started to leave, then turned back to Jake, her smile quick but genuine. "Thanks for all the help this morning. Hope you have a great day."

"You too," Jake replied, though his gaze held on her for a moment longer.

Before she could pause—before her heart could make too much of the warmth in his eyes—she jogged toward the kids, tossing high-fives as she went.

John clasped his hands over his heart, his voice dripping with exaggerated longing. "'Oh, Sammy, my love! My heart beats only for you! Don't ever leave me!'" He let out a dramatic sigh, fluttering his lashes for effect.

Jake rolled his eyes, though his grin stayed put. "You're ridiculous."

"Yeah, but I'm not the one out here making heart eyes."

Jake laughed, nudging him as they walked toward the truck. "Jealous?"

John scoffed, tossing the last of the tools into the truck bed. "Oh, absolutely. All I've got are my good looks, charm, and an endless supply of tacos from your abuelo." He glanced over, his expression softening. "For real, man. I'm happy for you."

Jake's smile turned grateful, and he gave John a small nod. "Thanks. That means a lot."

"Alright, alright. Enough of this after-school special stuff," John quipped, hopping into the truck. "Come on, lover boy. Let's get back before I say something nice again."

As they pulled away, Jake stole one last glance over his shoulder. Sammy stood in the middle of it all—laughing, light on her feet, completely in her element.

Oh, man. He liked her.

Scratch that. He more than liked her.

Jake exhaled, drumming his fingers against the steering wheel, energy buzzing beneath his skin.

More and more, it was becoming clear that God was in this. In every moment, every unexpected turn, every quiet assurance that this was no accident.

He let out a slow breath, shaking his head with a quiet chuckle as John smirked and cranked up the radio.

Yeah . . . he didn't mind one bit.

Chapter 31

Today was going to be a long day at camp, and Sammy was determined to make it happen. She'd promised the kids the bounce houses would stay up until 2:00 p.m., and she wasn't about to let them down.

After her usual round of morning high-fives, she scanned the park, doing a quick headcount. Sarah's SUV pulled in with Adeline and Michael, followed closely by a familiar blue Jeep.

Sammy's heart dipped as Michelle stepped out, sunglasses in hand.

She waved, hoping to start things off on the right foot.

Michelle's shoulders were drawn tight, like she was bracing against a strong wind. She gave a quick, halfhearted flick of her wrist before turning away.

"Mom, Mom! I have to go 'volunteer.' We can talk about this later," Michelle muttered into her phone. Rolling her eyes, she shoved it into her back pocket, pulled her sunglasses back on, and strode over.

Adeline and Michael, however, didn't hesitate—running straight to Sammy for hugs before darting off to join the other kids on the playground.

Michelle sighed as she stopped beside Sammy, her sleek bun pulled so tight it looked like it might give her a headache. "How do you want me to help?"

Before Sammy could respond, Sarah looped her arm through Michelle's with effortless warmth. "Let me show you what's going on," she said, steering Michelle toward the inflatable obstacle course.

Sammy exhaled, grateful for Sarah's timing. "Thank you, Sarah," she whispered as she climbed on a nearby park bench, adopting her best camp-leader voice.

"Good morning, everyone!"

"Good morning, Sammy!!" the kids chorused back, their voices bright with excitement.

"Are you ready to have some FUN?"

"YAAAAAAAAY!" The kids screamed, pumping their fists in the air.

Sammy laughed, feeling the energy ripple through the group. "Well, we've got an amazing day planned! We're kicking things off with an obstacle course. Does anyone know what that is?"

Mabel raised her hand, her eyes bright. "It's when you go through hoops and jump over stuff and try to get to the finish line first!"

"Exactly right!" Sammy said enthusiastically. "And guess what? This one is bouncy and soft, so it's going to be even more fun!"

A few kids whispered excitedly, pumping their fists.

Trevor and Blake stepped forward as Sammy continued, "Do you remember which team you're on?"

"YEEESS!" the kids shouted, bouncing on their toes.

"Great! Find your team leader, and let's get started!" Sammy hopped off the bench as the kids scrambled toward their groups.

To kick things off, Blake and Trevor demonstrated the course first, stumbling dramatically as they navigated the inflatable terrain. Trevor pretended to struggle climbing the wall, while Blake reached down to pull him up only for Trevor to flop down the slide in exaggerated defeat.

The kids roared with laughter, their excitement building.

Once the demonstration was over, Blake clapped his hands. "All right, now it's your turn! One person from each team goes at a time. When you reach the bottom of the slide, run back and tag the next person. First team to finish wins!"

Trevor chimed in, "But remember, we're also giving bonus points for teamwork! So don't forget to cheer each other on!"

The kids huddled together, whispering strategies.

Sammy spotted an opportunity to involve Michelle. "Hey, Michelle, would you mind doing the 'ready, set, go'?"

Michelle hesitated, then shrugged. "Sure."

To Sammy's surprise, Michelle stepped between the teams and cupped her hands around her mouth. "Are you READY?"

"YEEEEEEEES!" the kids yelled.

"On your mark . . . get set . . . GO!" Michelle shouted, joining the laughter and cheers as the kids took off.

Across the way, Mabel caught Sammy's eye, arms crossed, uncertainty written all over her face.

As her turn approached, Sammy stepped beside her. "Hey, Mabel, you're going to do great," she said gently, bumping her hip against the girl's. "How about a high-five for good luck?"

Mabel grinned shyly and slapped Sammy's hand before running toward the course.

She navigated the obstacles carefully, her face a mix of determination and concentration. But by the time she slid down the final stretch, her expression transformed into pure joy.

She ran back to tag the next person, then glanced at Sammy.

Sammy shot her a thumbs-up.

"Thanks," Mabel whispered, her voice barely audible over the noise.

Sammy's heart swelled. These were the moments that made the exhaustion worth it. Small miracles, unexpected joy—this was what made camp feel life-giving.

The day unfolded in a blur of games, laughter, and teamwork.

By lunchtime, the kids were happily exhausted. As the adults prepared sandwiches, Sarah nudged Sammy. "We've officially mastered the art of sandwich-making."

"Thanks for making us sound like heroes for something so simple," Sammy replied, laughing.

"Hey, when you're a mom of two, even folding laundry deserves a standing ovation," Sarah joked, glancing at Michelle.

Michelle chuckled softly, tension easing from her shoulders.

"Fooooood!" Blake and the kids shouted, sprinting toward the pavilion.

Sammy leaned back for a moment, savoring the chaos and joy around her.

As the kids played on the bounce houses after lunch, Sammy settled onto a picnic table with her journal, flipping to a page filled with scribbled thoughts.

She reread the question she'd been mulling over for days:

What is something that comes natural to you that you enjoy doing?

She tapped her pen against the page. Was this it?

Watching the kids—full of energy, excitement, and just the right amount of wild—Sammy couldn't help but smile.

Blake and his friend had taken charge of a game she'd recommended, keeping the fun chaotic but controlled. Victory.

With a satisfied sigh, she scribbled in her journal:

> I LOVE organizing chaos.

A blood-curdling scream tore through the peaceful afternoon.

Sammy bolted toward the obstacle course, where a small crowd of kids had gathered.

Michelle stood frozen, streaked with mud. A thick glob slid down her pristine white shirt.

Ryan, pale and teary-eyed, rushed up. "Miss Sammy! I'm so sorry! I was playing in the mud, and some of it kinda slipped out of my hands and accidentally hit Miss Michelle. I didn't mean to make her mad!"

Michelle's jaw clenched.

Sammy took a breath—biting back a laugh—and prayed Michelle could hang on for just a few more seconds.

Ryan mumbled a quick "Sorry, Miss Michelle."

Before the tension could linger, Sammy scooped up a handful of mud, letting it smear across her palm. "Were you playing in the mud like this?" she asked, her tone teasing.

Ryan's lips twitched into a smile. "No, Miss Sammy! That's not how you do it!"

Sammy widened her eyes in exaggerated surprise. "Oh really? Then show me how it's done, mud expert."

"You do it like this!" Ryan declared, scooping up a large handful of mud with his clawed hand.

Sammy grinned. "Oh, like this?"

The cool, squishy mud slipped between her fingers. Then, before she could second-guess herself, she let it fly.

The glob sailed past Ryan and landed with a thick splat against Trevor's chest.

For a moment, silence hung in the air. Then the world erupted.

Trevor gasped in mock outrage. "Oh, it's ON now!" He grabbed a scoop of mud and hurled it back, missing Sammy by inches as she ducked.

Laughter rippled through the kids as the first few handfuls of mud launched through the air.

And just like that, the mud war of the century began.

Mud flew high and far, splattering hair, clothes, and shoes. Even Trevor and Blake weren't spared, dodging and ducking while lobbing handfuls back at the kids.

From a safe distance, Michelle shrieked, "Nooooo!" before sprinting away, a few older girls chasing after her in an attempt to escape the mess.

By the time the laughter died down, everyone was coated in mud—shoes, hair, and all.

As Sammy thought the chaos was winding down, a row of cars pulled into the lot.

She wiped a streak of mud from her cheek and muttered, "Of course."

The parents had arrived.

As they stepped out, their faces ranged from shock to amusement. Sammy crossed her arms, bracing for their reaction.

One mom finally broke the silence with a laugh, which quickly spread.

"It was just too tempting," Sammy admitted, shrugging sheepishly.

The parents burst into laughter, pointing at their mud-covered kids. Relief washed over Sammy as she laughed along with them.

As she turned back toward the obstacle course, Michelle approached, furiously wiping at her hair with a paper towel.

In a sharp whisper, she hissed, "Well, Miss Samantha Thomas, sometimes you need to say no to temptation for the greater good!" With one last glare, she stomped toward her car, tossing over her shoulder, "See you Friday."

Sammy watched her retreat, biting back a grin. She shook her head and murmured, "Well, bless her heart."

Shrugging it off, she turned back to the kids, her heart lighter.

Blake, now wielding the hose like a water-spraying warrior, sent a blast of water into the crowd, officially marking the end of an epic mud fight.

* * *

That evening, as the heat of the day faded into a warm glow, Sammy and Glory settled onto the porch swing. The seat creaked gently beneath them as they each cradled a tall glass of sweet tea.

Fireflies blinked lazily across the yard, the last traces of the day melting into dusk.

Glory patted Sammy's knee. "Well, I'd say today was a memorable one. Do you know, we even talked about your epic mud fight at bridge today?"

Sammy chuckled, shaking her head. "Oh, I believe it. Word in this town moves faster than a runaway toddler during a church service."

Glory laughed, her eyes twinkling. "Glad you're having fun, my sweet Sammy."

For a moment, they simply sat there, letting the cicadas fill the quiet.

Then, Sammy exhaled. "I do love seeing the kids have fun. But I don't know. Something still doesn't feel settled."

Glory glanced over, waiting.

Sammy sighed, leaning back against the cushion. "I like helping with the summer camp, but I'm starting to realize working with kids isn't where my heart is forever. Is that awful to say?"

Glory took a slow sip of her tea, then set the glass on her lap. "Not at all, sweetheart. Knowing what God's stirring in your heart is the first step to figuring out what He's calling you to do." She reached over, giving Sammy's hand a reassuring squeeze. "Like Ethel Sue said today, you gotta try on a few hats before you find the right fit."

Sammy nodded, tracing the rim of her glass with her finger. "I keep reminding myself that every experience, good or bad, teaches me something.

But I'm itching for that 'click' in my spirit, you know?"

Glory smiled. "I do know. And you'll get there. In the meantime, it's all part of your story—mud fights included."

They swayed gently, the swing's rhythm matching the slow pulse of the summer night.

Sammy's thoughts drifted back to Michelle—the sharpness in her voice, the way she put up walls the moment things got messy.

And yet, for all of Michelle's bluster, Sammy realized something. She wasn't nearly as bothered by it as she might've been a week ago. Maybe Michelle's sharp edges weren't meant to hurt, but to shield. There was a story there, tucked behind the polished exterior.

Sammy wondered if she'd ever get to hear it.

Glory took another sip of tea before saying, "You'll find your sweet spot. Might take a little time and a few more muddy mishaps, but it'll come together. God's good like that."

Sammy smiled, lifting her glass. "For now, I'll just try to enjoy the beautiful mess He's leading me through."

Glory clinked her glass against Sammy's. "Now that's the spirit."

Chapter 32

Each day had built on the last, and now, finally, it was Friday.

That afternoon, Sammy steered the church van down the hill toward the Martinez Ranch, the sprawling fields stretching endlessly toward the horizon. Jake, John, and a few volunteers were already at work, their laughter drifting across the summer breeze. Sammy turned to the kids piling out of the church van and volunteer SUVs. "All right, campers! Grab your gear, find your group leader, and let's get this party started!"

Excited cheers erupted as the kids raced to their designated areas, sleeping bags slung over their shoulders, backpacks bouncing against their backs. Edmund waved her over, his hands dusty from hauling hay bales for the makeshift seating area. "Hey, Sammy! Everything's coming together. We've got the campfire pit set, tents ready to go, and the horses saddled for later. The kids are going to love this."

"Thank you so much, Edmund," Sammy said, her voice full of gratitude.

Edmund winked. "Just wait until you see them ride for the first time."

Nearby, Jake was stacking firewood. He glanced up as Sammy approached, his smile warm and steady. "Hey, you made it."

"Wouldn't miss it," Sammy replied, her heart doing a little flip at the sight of him. "Everything looks great."

"Well, we've got a good crew," Jake said, nodding toward John, who was attempting to wrangle a tent pole while laughing with a group of boys.

"That's an understatement," Sammy laughed.

With the last of the cars pulling in, Sammy gathered everyone around the fire pit. "All right, campers! Tonight is all about fun, friendship, and celebrating the amazing week we've had together. We've got games, horseback riding, stargazing, and of course s'mores by the fire!" The kids erupted into cheers, their excitement contagious.

Horseback riding was an instant hit. Small groups of kids took turns riding around the fenced pasture under Edmund's watchful eye. The soft crunch of hay underfoot, the creak of leather saddles, and the rhythmic swish of the horses' tails made for something peaceful and exhilarating. Even the more hesitant campers like Mabel found themselves grinning atop gentle horses with names like Daisy and Rusty.

Sammy leaned against the fence, watching the scene unfold. "Look at Mabel go," she said to Jake, who had joined her.

"She's a natural," Jake agreed, crossing his arms. "Ryan's already asking if he can live here so he can ride every day."

Sammy chuckled. "Wouldn't surprise me if he tried to move in."

Dinner was a hit, the smoky scent of barbecue drifting through the camp as laughter rang out around the fire. Sammy had just sat down when Michelle was shaking the Barbecue sauce bottle and it went all over Sammy's shirt. A lot of it.

Michelle's eyes widened in mock surprise. "Oops." She set the bottle down with deliberate care, her smile tight. "Guess I got a little carried away."

Sammy wiped at the stain with her fingers, only making it worse. Of course. She glanced up, meeting Michelle's too-casual expression.

Accident? Maybe. Or maybe not.

Sammy exhaled and gave a small, easy shrug. "Guess I'll smell like dinner tonight."

Michelle let out a short laugh before turning back to her plate. The sauce clung to Sammy's skin, sticky and stubborn, but she refused to let it cling to her thoughts. There were bigger, better things to focus on, like a night under the stars with a bunch of happy kids.

As the sun dipped below the horizon, the campers gathered around the fire pit, their faces illuminated by the flickering flames. Blake and Trevor led a few silly campfire songs, their off-key voices sending the kids into fits of laughter. Even Michelle had joined in. Then came the s'mores.

Sammy passed out graham crackers, chocolate, and marshmallows, showing the younger kids how to hold their sticks over the fire without setting them ablaze.

"Miss Sammy, is mine supposed to look like this?" Ryan asked, holding up a marshmallow that resembled a lump of coal.

Sammy grinned. "Perfect. Extra crispy just means extra flavor."

Ryan beamed and smashed it between two graham crackers before taking a massive bite. Beside him, Mabel rotated her marshmallow with careful precision, whispering to herself, "This is fun."

Sammy smiled. "It really is."

As the evening settled into a peaceful hush, the campers sprawled out on blankets, gazing up at the stars. Blake strummed his guitar, leading the kids in song, while Sarah checked in on everyone. Freshly changed after dinner, Sammy felt like a new woman as she returned to the fire circle, where laughter mixed with the crackle of the flames. Spotting Jake and John on a hay bale at the edge of the group, she made her way over.

"Hey, y'all," she said, hopping up beside Jake.

She took a breath, soaking it all in. The fire's soft glow, the kids' voices mingling with the rustle of the leaves—it all felt so right. For the first time in a long while, she wasn't worried about what came next. She was here, fully present, and it felt like a gift.

"Hey, Sammy," John greeted with a grin before suddenly sitting up straighter, his gaze shifting. "Oh, look, there's Michelle. I need to . . . um, I'll catch y'all later."

Sammy raised an eyebrow as he hurried off. "What was that about?"

Jake shrugged, expression unreadable. "Not sure. But I'm not complaining. I'm glad we've got a moment."

"Why's that?" Sammy asked, tilting her head.

Jake turned slightly toward her, his voice soft. "I've been meaning to talk to you about something important."

Sammy's pulse quickened. "Sure, what's up?"

Her mind raced. *It couldn't be about our date, could it? Or that amazing kiss we had last week? Because I can't stop thinking about it . . .*

Before Jake could answer, a high-pitched shriek cut through the night.

"Eeeeeeeek!"

They both shot to their feet.

Rachel, one of the quieter ten-year-olds, was sobbing, clutching her foot. Sammy dropped to her knees. "What happened?"

Rachel's friend answered breathlessly, "She took her shoes off, and when she went to put them back on, there was a scorpion inside!"

Rachel's sobs grew louder. "It hurts so bad!"

Jake crouched beside her, his brow furrowed. "Be right back," he said, already heading toward Zeke.

Sammy stroked Rachel's hair, humming softly. "You're so brave, sweet girl. It'll feel better soon, I promise."

Moments later, Jake returned with a small bottle of meat tenderizer and his bandana.

"Here," he said, kneeling beside Rachel. "My abuelo swears by this stuff. One summer, I got stung a dozen times helping him clear brush."

Rachel sniffled but followed his instructions. Her face scrunched at first, then her eyes widened. "It's not hurting as much!"

Jake smiled. "Works every time."

As the energy settled, John picked up his guitar, and the campers sang under a sky full of stars. Sammy whispered a prayer. "Lord, what a sweet week this has been. And thank You for always being in the details. I mean, who knew? Meat tenderizer?"

She chuckled, looking up at the stars just as the song faded into the night.

Chapter 33

Sammy woke early to the scent of fresh air and the cool breeze drifting through the big parachute tent where all the girls were sleeping. It felt like the perfect time for a jog. She grabbed her clothes to change and noticed Mabel stirring in her sleeping bag.

"Where are you going?" Mabel asked, her voice groggy as she rubbed her eyes.

"Just for a quick jog before everyone's awake," Sammy whispered. Then, tilting her head with a playful grin, she added, "Wanna join me?"

Mabel blinked in surprise. "Really? You want me to come?" Her voice was unsure but hopeful.

Sammy nodded. "Of course. Let's do this."

By the time Sammy was ready, Mabel was waiting at the trailhead, stretching her legs like she was prepping for a marathon. Sammy chuckled. "Okay, I see I'm jogging with a pro."

Mabel grinned. "Ready?"

"Let's go."

The two ran along the well-worn paths that wound through the ranch. The dirt crunched softly under their sneakers, the morning quiet broken only by the chirping of birds. Sammy had a loose goal of making it to the top of the hill where Jake had taken her before, but halfway up, she was ready to stop.

"You mind if I keep going?" Mabel asked, her face eager.

Sammy waved her on, catching her breath as she found a soft patch of grass and sank down. The breeze cooled her flushed cheeks, and she closed her eyes for a moment, savoring the stillness.

Then, the sound of footsteps drew her attention. Assuming it was Mabel returning, Sammy turned to greet her, but instead she saw Michelle.

"Mind if I join you?" Michelle asked, lingering a few steps away, her voice uncharacteristically soft.

Sammy blinked, her surprise obvious. Of all the people she might've expected to find her here, Michelle was dead last. Still, she nodded and tapped the ground beside her. "Uh, sure."

Michelle exhaled, visibly relaxing as she sank onto the grass. Both women sat quietly, watching the sunrise paint the horizon.

"It's really beautiful out here."

"Yeah," Sammy agreed. "Feels like the world gets a little quieter up on this hill."

Michelle tugged at a blade of grass, twisting it around her finger. "You'd think I'd be good at this whole 'quiet' thing," she said with a small, self-conscious laugh. "I mean, I'm on my horse every morning, watching the sun come up. But this . . ." She glanced around, the weight of the stillness settling over them. "This isn't the kind of quiet I'm used to. When I ride, it's like I'm outrunning the noise of everything coming in the day ahead. But here, it feels like none of that matters."

For a moment, neither spoke.

Michelle's voice broke the silence. "I bet you're wondering why I'm here."

Sammy blinked, startled out of her thoughts. "The thought had crossed my mind," she admitted.

Michelle sighed, her expression softening. "I wanted to apologize about the barbecue sauce. I swear I was just shaking the bottle, but . . . yeah. That went sideways fast."

Ya think?! Sammy thought, but instead raised an eyebrow and said, "Really?"

"Truly," Michelle said earnestly.

Sammy gave her an empathetic smile. "Okay. Apology accepted."

Michelle exhaled in relief. "After John pointed out—"

"You talked to John?" Sammy tilted her head, a small smile tugging at her lips.

Michelle groaned. "Let's just say he didn't mince words." Sitting up straighter, she added, "But he's right. We're supposed to be adults, aren't we?"

Sammy chuckled. "Well, we're the right age, anyway."

Michelle laughed softly, then turned serious. "Look, can we talk? Like really talk?"

Sammy nodded, curiosity flickering through her. "Okay."

Michelle took a deep breath. "First, I'm sorry for being rude last night. Second . . ." Then, meeting Sammy's gaze. "I'm sorry for stealing the last dance with Jake at the Fourth of July Festival."

Sammy blinked in surprise. "Oh."

Michelle raised a hand, stopping her. "I knew it was meant for you. I saw him walking toward you, and I couldn't stand the thought of not being the one in Jake's arms at the end of the night."

Sammy bit her lip. "What's the deal with you two, anyway? You've known each other forever."

Michelle rolled her eyes, laughing at herself. "Yeah, we grew up together. Same classes, same clubs, same everything. The whole town expected us to end up together." She sighed. "And I didn't mind at first. I mean, he's Jake. Practically perfect, right?"

Sammy faintly smiled.

"But here's the thing: I want big and flashy. And Jake? He wants *this*." Michelle gestured to the peaceful ranch spread before them. "I tried to be the perfect simple country girl, but the truth is, I love the galas, the spotlight, and being the center of attention. I want someone who fits into that world, and that's not Jake. It never was."

Michelle let out a soft laugh, lighter than Sammy had ever heard from her. "And that's okay. Honestly, it's better this way." Her gaze drifting over the sunlit hills before meeting Sammy's eyes. "You and Jake . . . the way he looks at you, Sammy. It's like you're the only person in the room. It's obvious to anyone paying attention."

Michelle's smile was small but genuine, a quiet truth resting between them. "It's good. You're good for him. And maybe he's good for you too."

Sammy's pulse quickened. Michelle wasn't one for heart-to-hearts, and hearing her say all this felt . . . unexpected. The tension that had always been between them wasn't gone, but for the first time, it wasn't a fight.

"You really think so?" Sammy asked, her voice quiet.

"I do," Michelle said simply. "And I mean it." She looked away before adding, "But really, what I'm trying to say is, can we start fresh?" Michelle asked, her tone tinged with something like hope. She held out her hand.

For a moment, Sammy sat there a bit stunned, still processing everything. Then, with a soft smile, she reached out and clasped Michelle's hand in hers. "Absolutely."

A few minutes later, Mabel bounded back down the hill, her face alight with excitement. "Guys! Have you seen the view from up top? It is *sooo* beautiful! You've *got* to come see it!"

Mabel's enthusiasm made Sammy laugh as she grabbed her hand, tugging her to her feet. "All right, all right, I'm coming!" she said, realizing how much she genuinely enjoyed seeing Mabel come out of her shell.

Sammy glanced at Michelle, who smiled and stood as well. Together, the three climbed to the crest of the hill. The view was breathtaking—rolling green fields stretched endlessly, kissed by the morning sunlight.

Standing together at the top, Sammy felt the weight of the morning's conversation lift entirely. The breeze swept over them, carrying with it a sense of peace and possibility.

But then, cutting through the quiet, the sound of the morning bell rang out from down at the camp.

It was time.

Chapter 34

As the campers gathered in a circle under the shade of the trees, their overnight bags piled behind them, Sammy took a deep breath, her heart full.

The last week had been a whirlwind of fun and laughter, but this moment felt especially important. It wasn't just the last day of camp; it was a chance to share something that had shaped her life.

"All right, guys, I want to share something with y'all," Sammy began, her voice steady. She looked out at the circle of campers, each one with eager eyes waiting for her words.

She smiled softly. "When I was your age, I had no idea who I was. I tried to fit in, tried to be good enough, but no matter what I did, I always felt like I was missing something. And then, one day, I heard about Jesus—how He loved me just the way I was, how He died for me so I could be forgiven and have eternal life by accepting Him as my Savior and following Him. I remember the exact moment I made that decision. It wasn't a big, flashy thing. No fireworks. But something inside me changed, and it was the best decision I ever made."

She let her words settle, scanning the group. "If any of you have questions about Jesus, about accepting Him as your Savior, or what life is like when you follow Him, you can always ask me, Jake, Sarah, or any of the volunteers here. We love you, and we want to help you get to know Him too."

A few campers nodded, and Sammy felt a smile tug at the corner of her mouth.

"But for right now," she said, shifting the tone, "Where is God?"

“GOD IS IN EVERYTHING!” they shouted in unison.

“Exactly!” Sammy grinned. “Now, I’ve got a follow-up question, and I want you to think about it: Where did you see God this week?”

She repeated the question, letting it hang in the air.

The campers paused, reflecting, and then one by one, they began sharing.

“I saw God this morning in the sunrise. It was beautiful!” Mabel said, squeezing Sammy’s hand.

“I saw God in Joseph when he cleaned up all the dinner dishes last night,” another camper shared.

“I saw God in lunch!” Ryan grinned.

Jake nodded. “I saw God in each of you this week—in how you helped set up, took things down, and looked out for each other.”

“I saw God in SAMMY!” Michael Shoreman suddenly shouted. Letting go of his mom’s hand, he jogged over and threw his arms around her.

The campers kept going: “I saw God in the music we sang this week.” “I saw God in the art we made with chalk.” “I saw God in my horse I got to ride yesterday.”

Sammy smiled, looking around at the campers. “I saw God in the mud fight,” she admitted, chuckling. “It reminded me that God doesn’t need us to be perfect. He loves us, even in our mess.”

She let that sink in for a moment before adding, “The Lord thinks you are amazing, and He has great plans for you. Never forget that!”

The campers squeezed hands, soaking in her words.

“Now,” Sammy said, clapping her hands, “hug the people next to you, grab your bags, and hop in the car you came in!”

Pandemonium broke out. Kids hugged, scrambled for their bags, and laughed as Sammy and Jake pointed everyone in the right direction. Amid the chaos, Sammy noticed a boy stop in front of Mabel, hand her a note, and rush off to grab his bag.

Mabel blinked, staring at the note like it was something precious. Slowly, she unfolded it. *Your drawings are really good.*

Her eyes widened. She turned to Sammy, holding it out like she needed confirmation it was real.

Sammy smiled softly. "You've got this, Mabel," she said, giving her a reassuring side hug.

Mabel's cheeks flushed, and a shy smile spread across her face as she clutched the note and ran to hop in the van.

As the kids settled in, still buzzing with excitement, Sammy lingered for a moment, watching them with a quiet smile.

"Thank You, Lord," she whispered, her heart full. "For every single one of them, and for showing me You in all of it."

The van roared to life. With one last glance at the ranch, she felt a new resolve stir inside her.

God wasn't finished writing her story. Not by a long shot.

* * *

When Sammy finally got back to Glory's, the exhaustion of the week finally caught up with her. The energy of camp still buzzed in her veins, but as she stepped onto the porch and breathed in the scent of wisteria drifting through the yard, she froze. The peace here was a stark contrast to the chaos she'd just left behind.

And Glory wasn't alone.

Nelda sat on the porch swing, her wide-brimmed sun hat perched jauntily on her head, swaying gently beside Glory as they sipped iced tea. The two women looked so at ease, their laughter drifting on the breeze, that Sammy hesitated.

"Well, there's our camp superstar!" Glory called out, her voice warm. "Come on over, sweet Sammy. Nelda's been waiting to chat with you."

Sammy blinked in surprise, glancing at Nelda. "To me?"

Nelda smiled, her sharp blue eyes twinkling with warmth and curiosity. "I know we see each other often, but if you've got a moment, I'd love to talk." She patted the empty chair across from the swing.

Sammy sighed dramatically. "I am practically sleepwalking, but Nelda, I always have time for you." She sank into the chair, stretching her legs out with a sigh.

"I've really enjoyed watching you bring the food pantry to life," Nelda said, her tone genuine. "It's been amazing to see a prayer answered, one we've prayed over for so long."

Sammy felt warmth rise to her cheeks. "Thank you. It's been a pleasure putting it together."

Nelda nodded thoughtfully. "It's been a long time since I've seen someone shake things up around here in such a good way."

Sammy tilted her head, curiosity flickering in her expression.

Glory chuckled, setting down her glass. "Ladies, I need to move the sprinkler in the back. I'll let you two chat."

Sammy gave Glory a questioning look before turning back to Nelda.

Nelda leaned forward, eyes sharp, hope dancing in them. "So, Sammy, tell me. What's lighting you up in this part-time temporary position?"

Sammy watched as Glory watered a row of dahlias in her floppy sunhat. "It's been a whirlwind," she admitted. "A good one, but still—so much has happened so fast. The pantry, the camp . . . I've been so caught up in it all, I haven't really stopped to ask what comes next."

Nelda nodded, as if she'd been expecting that. "It's easy to get swept up in the doing," she said. "But every now and then, you've got to pause and ask yourself, does this fit? I heard you've been working through the Still Becoming devotional about discovering God's calling. Any clarity yet?"

Sammy hesitated. "I'm learning that God's plans are always better than mine. And that the gifts He's given me? They're intentional. Not random. Ephesians 2:10 keeps coming to mind."

Nelda tapped a finger against the arm of the swing. "That's a great verse to chew on, especially as you think about what's next." She studied Sammy a moment longer, then asked, "Do you like building things? Not just helping, but starting something and seeing it grow?"

Sammy's tiredness faded slightly, replaced by something else. She leaned forward. "Yeah, I do. I see what something could be, and it drives me to make it happen." Then she hesitated. "But maybe I just got lucky with these two projects."

Nelda let out a soft chuckle, shaking her head. "No such thing as luck when you're doing what you're called to." She took a deep breath, then stood, smoothing her skirt. "Well, I must be going. But I have a feeling we'll be talking again real soon."

Sammy watched her descend the porch steps, something stirring in her chest.

Glory reappeared just as Nelda's car pulled away.

Sammy turned to her, eyes narrowing. "What just happened?"

Glory chuckled, settling back into her chair. "That, sweet Sammy, was Nelda McGraw doing what she does best—making things happen."

* * *

That night, Sammy curled up in bed, journal in hand, the weight of the week pressing into her bones, but in the best way. She let out a slow breath, her thoughts still swirling from the conversations, the laughter, the moments she didn't want to forget. She pressed her pen to the page.

> Lord, today, I saw You in the quiet.
>
> In Mabel's determined steps up the hill. In Michelle's unexpected honesty. In the way walls—mine and hers—started to come down.
>
> I saw You in the kids' voices, calling out where they saw You this week. In the mud, in the music, in the smallest moments that meant something big.
>
> I don't know exactly where You're leading me. But today, I'm reminded that I don't have to know. I just have to keep following You.
>
> "Trust in the Lord with all your heart and lean not on your own understanding; in all your ways submit to Him, and He will make your paths straight." — Proverbs 3:5–6
>
> You see the whole picture. I just get to say yes. And Lord, I want to keep saying yes.

Sammy read over the words, and a soft smile tugged at her lips.

His plans really were good.

Chapter 35

Tuesdays had always been Sammy's favorite day—distribution day at the food pantry.

She was wrapping up the last check-out when Pastor Mark appeared at her side, his usual cheerful demeanor even brighter today. "Do you have time for a quick chat?"

"Sure," Sammy replied, signing off on the final log. "Give me ten minutes, and I'll meet you in your office."

"Perfect," he said with a nod.

Sammy quickly filed the day's paperwork and grabbed her notebook. She always looked forward to these meetings. Pastor Mark had a way of keeping things structured while leaving room for meaningful discussions.

As she tapped on his office door, he stood to welcome her. "Come in! Thanks for making time. This week's been a bit wild, hasn't it?"

Sammy grinned, sliding into a chair across from him. "It has, but in the best way."

"Well, let's dive in," he said, pulling out his checklist. "First, what's our current family count?"

"We have forty-two families registered, and thirty-nine boxes were picked up today," Sammy reported, flipping to her notes.

Pastor Mark jotted the info down. "What happens to the boxes that aren't picked up?"

"We give the leftover produce to volunteers and put the boxes back in storage and use them the next week," she explained.

"Good system," he said thoughtfully. "But what if we started checking in on those families? Just a quick call to make sure everything's okay. Sometimes a missed box could mean something more serious. I'd be happy to take this task on."

Sammy blinked, surprised. "That's a great idea! I'll add that to the weekly process and have the list ready for you."

"Wonderful," he said with a smile.

They moved down the list, covering volunteer turnout, supply needs, and a few small improvements for efficiency. Finally, Pastor Mark leaned back, setting his pen down with a grin.

"Now, about the summer camp . . ." His smile widened. "Sammy, I can't walk two blocks without someone stopping me to rave about it. Parents are thrilled. Kids are still talking about it. You've made quite an impact."

Sammy's cheeks warmed. "It was such a team effort. Everyone pitched in."

"Well, it's got the whole town buzzing, and it's given us a lot to think about," he said, leaning forward. His tone softened. "Sammy, this position you've taken on is so much more than what we envisioned. What you've done in two months is incredible. You've breathed life into this community in ways we didn't even know we needed."

Sammy blinked, unsure where he was going with this.

Pastor Mark opened a folder on his desk and pulled out an envelope. "After seeing the impact and hours you've been putting in, we've decided to make the role full-time," he said. "It's way more effort and responsibility than we planned for when we offered this part-time, temporary position to you." He handed her the envelope. "All the details are in here, but I'll tell you this: It's not just a paycheck. It's an investment in you and in Willow Creek. Our town is growing, and the work you've done has helped us realize it's time we grow with it."

Sammy stared at the envelope, her heart racing.

"Take the rest of the week off," Pastor Mark said, his tone gentle but firm. "Pray about it. Think about what God's calling you to. No pressure. We'll respect whatever decision you make."

Her throat tightened as she took the envelope, nodding mutely.

Pastor Mark smiled warmly. "You've earned this, Sammy. Enjoy the time off. We'll talk Monday."

Sammy sat in the parking lot, staring at the church's offer inside the envelope. It was generous, more than she ever expected when she first took the part-time role. Yet, as her eyes scanned the details, a small knot formed in her stomach. It wasn't dissatisfaction, exactly. More like hesitation.

She thought back to the past two months: the laughter of kids at summer camp, the relief on a mother's face as she picked up her first pantry box, the late-night talks with Glory on the porch. Sammy loved the connections she'd built here, but something inside her whispered that her journey might not stop with the food pantry.

Shaking her head, she folded the letter and headed home. Maybe some time on Glory's porch would help her sort it out.

* * *

When Sammy got home, bridge was in full swing at the kitchen table. She greeted Glory, Ethel Sue, Lora, and Nelda before heading out to the porch swing, envelope still in hand.

The swing's gentle creak and the warm breeze calmed her nerves, but for some reason, this dream job offer wasn't the easy yes she'd expected it to be.

"Mind if I join you for a moment?"

Sammy looked up, surprised to see Nelda stepping onto the porch. "Of course, sweet Nelda," she said, scooting over and patting the swing beside her.

Nelda settled in, her movements unhurried. Sammy fidgeted with the envelope, unsure where to start.

"That must be the offer from the church," Nelda said, her tone knowing but kind.

Sammy nodded. "It is," she admitted. "And it's a wonderful offer."

Nelda tilted her head, reading between the lines. "But . . . ?"

Sammy hesitated, glancing out at the yard. "I'm not sure it's the right fit. I love what I'm doing at the pantry, but I can't shake the feeling there might be something else I'm supposed to be doing."

Nelda studied her for a long moment before nodding. "Good," she said simply. "That means you're paying attention. Because I've been thinking the same thing."

Sammy blinked. "What do you mean?"

Nelda leaned forward slightly. "As you know, I'm on the outreach committee, so I helped shape the church's offer. But even so, my heart didn't feel peace without at least trying to offer you something else." She folded her hands in her lap. "Sammy, I'd like to offer you a job. Starting as my assistant, but with the potential for much more."

Sammy's thoughts spun. "An assistant?" she echoed.

Nelda nodded. "Yes. But let me take a step back. What you may not know is that I've been a real estate investor for years. I've built a solid portfolio in Willow Creek, trusting the Lord's guidance every step of the way." She met Sammy's gaze. "But I also have a vision for something bigger. And I believe you're exactly the person I need to help bring it to life."

Sammy stared at her, speechless.

"And before you worry about the pantry," Nelda added quickly, "this wouldn't mean giving that up. You'd still have time to volunteer, to be part of the outreach events you care about. But this—this would be your job. And as far as pay goes, it would be double what the church is offering."

Sammy's jaw dropped slightly. "Double?"

Nelda chuckled. "You're worth every penny. But this isn't about money. It's about finding where you shine."

Sammy let out a shaky laugh. "I don't know what to say."

"Don't say anything now," Nelda said, her voice gentle but firm. "Pray about it. Trust that God has the details covered. When you know where He's leading, let me know."

Sammy nodded slowly. "Thank you, Nelda."

Nelda smiled warmly, reaching out to pat Sammy's hand. "You don't have to thank me, dear. Just promise me one thing."

"What is that?" Sammy asked searching Nelda's face.

"Follow your peace, Sammy. You'll know where God's leading when no matter what you see ahead, you feel His peace inside."

With that, Nelda stood and headed back toward the kitchen, where the sound of bridge players laughing and chatting floated through the screen door.

Sammy sat on the swing, staring out at the yard, her thoughts a whirlwind of possibilities. "*Follow your peace.*" The words echoed in her mind, and as she sat there, the evening breeze whispered around her, carrying with it the faintest sense of clarity.

Chapter 36

Sammy woke to the soft creak of the screen door and the scent of damp earth drifting through her open window. She stretched, listening. Outside, she heard the gentle splash of water and the rhythmic rustling of leaves.

She slipped out of bed, tugged on a hoodie over her pajamas, and padded barefoot onto the porch.

Glory stood among the irises, garden hose in hand, misting the blooms with a practiced ease. The early morning light painted the yard in soft golds and blues, the air still carrying the last traces of nighttime coolness.

"Morning, sweetheart," Glory greeted, not turning from her work. "I water now so I don't melt later. You know how Texas heat is."

Sammy chuckled, settling onto the porch swing. "Smart thinking."

Glory finished with the flowers and coiled the hose before joining her. She wiped her damp hands on her apron, then picked up her water bottle from the porch railing.

"You were lost in thought last night," she noted, giving Sammy a knowing glance.

Sammy let out a breath, tracing a knot in the wood with her finger. "I just don't want to disappoint anyone."

Glory hummed thoughtfully. "And who exactly are you afraid of disappointing?"

Sammy hesitated. "The church, Nelda . . . myself, I guess."

Glory sipped her tea, watching her closely. "Sweetheart, there's no wrong choice here. Both paths you're looking at are good ones. It's all about where your peace settles."

Sammy frowned, leaning back against the swing. "But what on earth does 'peace settling' feel like?"

Glory let the question linger, her gaze still fixed on the garden. After a moment, she nodded toward the flowers beside the barn. "You see those daffodils?" she asked, pointing to them. "They don't fight to grow. They don't worry if they're planted in the right spot. They just bloom where they are, soaking in the sun, stretching toward what gives them life." She turned back to Sammy, her expression soft. "That's what peace feels like. Not striving, not second-guessing. Just knowing, deep down, that you're right where you're meant to be."

Sammy swallowed, watching the way the flowers swayed, unhindered by doubt, by expectation—just being.

She exhaled, the tension loosening just a little.

"How do you know so much?" she whispered in awe.

Glory chuckled, shaking her head. "Took me years to learn that, you know. I spent too long pulling up my own roots, afraid I'd planted myself in the wrong place."

They both chuckled, the warmth of the moment settling between them.

Glory patted Sammy's knee. "Come on, let's get some coffee."

* * *

The next day, she got to go on a horse ride with Jake. They were about half way up the trail when the words came tumbling out.

"I mean, isn't it selfish to choose the job that pays double?"

Maybe she should've kept that thought to herself. But something about Jake made her think he might help her sort it out.

Jake turned his head slightly, his brows lifting in surprise. "Selfish?" he echoed. "Or smart?"

She sighed, shifting in her saddle. The horses moved in an easy rhythm beneath them, their steady footfalls blending with the distant hum of cicadas. "Growing up, my family always side-eyed wealthy people. If they had money, we'd watch how they spent it—like it was any of our business."

Jake chuckled, shaking his head. "So, rich folks were automatically the villains?"

"Basically." Sammy smirked, but the old belief still sat uncomfortably in her. "I mean, we weren't poor, but we weren't comfortable either. My parents worked hard, and there was this unspoken rule that 'just enough' was the godly way to live."

Jake adjusted his reins, thoughtful. "I get that. But look at the Shoreman family. They're loaded, and yet they pay for summer camp scholarships, host the church Christmas party, and probably help people in ways we don't even know about."

Sammy let that sit for a moment. "Right! That's what's messing with me. I used to think wealth was bad, but now I'm seeing it's just a tool. A tool that can be used for good."

Jake gave her a knowing grin. "And yet you still feel guilty for wanting it?"

She huffed, tilting her face toward the sky. "Yes! Ugh. Like, if I take Nelda's offer, does that make me a sellout?"

Jake shrugged. "I used to think that too. My uncle turned down a big job once 'cause he thought money would change him. But you know what? He ended up broke and bitter, and still the same guy. Money just makes you more of what you already are."

Sammy turned that over in her mind, staring out over the wide stretch of land ahead of them. The wind tugged at her hair, the late-afternoon sun casting a golden glow over the rolling hills. She'd spent so much time worrying about making the "right" choice, but maybe there wasn't just one right path.

Jake nodded. "You know, money's not the enemy, Sammy. Fear is. And like Abuelo always says—and I bet he learned it from Glory—never make a decision based on fear."

A small smile tugged at her lips. "Yep. I've heard that before too."

They lingered on the ridge, their horses shifting beneath them as Jake pointed out what he and John had been working on lately. Eventually, they turned back toward the barn, Sammy dismounting with a lighter heart.

"So, you've got to make a decision soon?" Jake asked, rubbing Zeke's neck as the horse relaxed under his touch.

Sammy nodded, brushing a strand of hair from her face. "Yep, I have until Monday. But I think I'm ready."

Jake's slow, easy grin made her stomach flip. "It sounds like it."

She managed a small smile in return, but there was still that lingering knot in her chest. Even if she knew what she wanted, there was always that tiny voice whispering, *What if you're wrong?*

They walked the horses back to the barn in silence, the weight of her decision pressing down on her shoulders again. She didn't want to disappoint anyone. She wanted to make the right choice.

Just as the quiet started to feel too heavy, Jake nodded toward the chicken coop. "Hey," he said, a teasing glint in his eye, "want to help me grab some eggs? Might take your mind off things."

Sammy shot him a skeptical look. "Is that your way of distracting me from an existential crisis? Throw me into a coop with angry chickens?"

"They're not angry," Jake said with a chuckle. "They're just . . . territorial. You'll be fine."

Moments later, Sammy found herself standing in the middle of the coop, surrounded by a chorus of clucking hens while Jake leaned casually against the doorway, watching with far too much amusement.

She crouched down, eyeing the nearest chicken with suspicion. "This one looks . . . friendly."

Jake smirked. "That's Mildred. She's the boss."

Sammy raised an eyebrow. "I'm negotiating with the head honcho?"

"Exactly. You have to let her know you're in charge."

"Right . . ." she muttered, half to herself. "I'm pretty sure Mildred already knows exactly who's calling the shots."

With an exaggerated sigh, she reached for the nearest egg—only for Mildred to flap her wings and squawk loudly, sending Sammy stumbling back with a startled yelp. The chicken strutted in a victorious circle, making it clear who was really running the show.

Jake laughed. "Maybe be a little clearer."

Sammy huffed, rubbing her arm where Mildred had nearly pecked her.

"This is ridiculous." She lunged forward again, but the hen darted away. "I'll never get this."

Jake stepped forward, his voice patient but teasing. "Here, let me show you."

As Mildred resettled, Jake moved in calmly. With slow, deliberate movements, he reached down and scooped up an egg, placing it in Sammy's basket with an exaggerated flourish.

"See? Easy," he said with a wink, as if he'd just performed a magic trick.

Sammy watched him for a beat before snorting. "You've been working with chickens longer than I've known how to walk, haven't you?"

Jake stood taller and handed her the basket. "Maybe, but you're getting the hang of it."

Taking a deep breath, Sammy tried again. This time, she moved slower, more confident. She reached down and finally plucked an egg from the nest, a triumphant grin spreading across her face.

"Got it!" she cheered softly, holding it up like a victory prize.

Jake nodded, smiling. "Told you you'd get the hang of it."

Sammy chuckled, dropping the egg gently into the basket. "I wouldn't go that far."

Jake smirked. "Mildred might disagree."

She shot him a playful glare, and they headed back toward the barn, the sound of clucking hens behind them.

Maybe Jake was right. Maybe fear had been running the show for too long.

* * *

As Sammy drove home, she knew there was one more person she wanted to talk through the idea with. She pulled over and got out her phone.

Sammy: *Hey Sarah, have time for a chat?*

Sarah: *Always! Come on over!*

Sammy turned her music up, and then turned her blinker on and took a right to make her way to Sarah's.

"So, you're basically asking if it's wrong to take a job outside the church?"

Sarah's voice carried over the hum of cicadas as they sat on her back porch, sipping iced tea.

Sammy sighed, dragging her finger through the condensation on her glass. "It sounds dumb when you say it like that."

Sarah smirked. "No, it sounds like something a lot of people wrestle with."

Sammy inhaled slowly. "I guess I just always pictured myself doing something *directly* tied to ministry. Teaching, church work, food pantry stuff. Nelda's job is real estate."

Sarah tilted her head. "And why does real estate feel 'less godly' to you?"

Sammy frowned. "I mean, I won't be leading Bible studies or feeding the hungry for work. I'll be managing properties and . . . maybe building stuff."

Sarah gave her a long look before asking, "You think God's limited to church buildings and food pantries?"

Sammy blinked. "Well, no."

Sarah leaned forward, her voice gentle but firm. "Sweet friend, I know for a *fact* that you bring Jesus into every space you enter. If you step into Nelda's world, guess what? *Jesus goes with you.* You don't stop being who you are just because your office is in a boardroom instead of a church basement."

Sammy swallowed hard.

Sarah grinned. "Plus, let's be real. You'd rock at it."

A small, almost hesitant smile crept onto Sammy's lips.

Sarah studied her friend's face. "So, what mountain is still in the way?"

Sammy exhaled, slow and steady. "None." She let the word settle, feeling the weight of it—how light it was, how *right.*

For so long, she had thought this decision required some kind of divine handwriting on the wall, a perfectly mapped-out plan. But maybe God wasn't asking her to *figure it all out.* Maybe He was just asking her to *trust* the steps in front of her.

Maybe peace wasn't about certainty.

Maybe it was about *faith.*

She glanced at Sarah, who was watching her with that same quiet confidence.

Sammy set her tea down, straightening her shoulders. "I don't need permission. And even though there are so many questions, I am certain this is the job I should—and *want*—to take."

Sarah beamed. "Now *that* sounds like peace settling."

Sammy nodded, a deep calm wrapping around her.

She didn't rush to grab her phone or make an announcement.

She let herself be still, letting the weight of the decision lift. No more fear. No more second-guessing. She was ready.

* * *

That night, Sammy curled up in bed, journal in hand, the weight of the decision finally settled. She pressed her pen to the page.

> I have decided. I am taking Nelda's job.
>
> Thanks for being with me on the journey. In Glory's flowers, growing without worry. In Jake's easy confidence. In Sarah's reminder that You go with me, no matter where I step.
>
> For as long as I can remember my life has revolved around some plan I created. How beautiful to see Your plans are better and bigger and more beautiful than I could have ever dreamed up.
>
> And about money . . . I used to think having more meant caring less. But maybe money is just a tool. And if I use it right, it could build something that actually matters.
>
> I finally know what peace being settled in me feels like.
>
> Thank You.

She turned off her light and let the cicadas hum her to sleep.

Chapter 37

Sitting at her desk on Monday, Sammy's eyes drifted to the wall, where photos from the food pantry launch hung next to thank you cards from campers. This church had become home in so many ways—familiar faces, familiar routines. Could she really step away from that? She let out a deep breath. "You've got this," she whispered as she stood up.

A light knock at the door made her jump, and Pastor Mark's friendly face appeared as he peeked in. "Hey, Sammy, you ready for our meeting?"

"Sure am!" she replied with a nervous smile that didn't quite match the pep in her voice. "I was just about to go to your office."

Pastor Mark grinned, sensing her nerves but not pressing. "Perfect. Since this isn't a typical meeting, I thought we could have it in a not-so-typical spot. Coffee sound good?"

Sammy brightened, grateful for the suggestion. "Always!"

"Perfect. Let's go."

Sammy thought back to Jake's words on the ridge just days ago: *"Plans aren't bad, but they're way better when they're God's plans."* She smiled faintly, his steady confidence bolstering her own as she walked into the coffee shop.

Once they got settled Pastor Mark leaned forward, his expression kind but curious. "Okay, Sammy, no pressure, but what have you decided? Would you like to join us full-time as our outreach minister?"

The moment she'd rehearsed for was here. Sammy took a deep breath, steadying herself.

"Pastor Mark," she began, her voice steady but soft, "I can't thank you enough for the offer. It's such an honor, and I've truly loved being part of the church and all the work we've done together." She hesitated, choosing her words carefully. "But something unexpected happened."

Pastor Mark's eyebrow arched slightly, but he stayed silent, giving her the space to continue.

"Nelda offered me a job the same day," Sammy explained, her fingers tracing the rim of her cup. "At first, I was overwhelmed—two incredible opportunities, both life-changing in their own way. But after a lot of prayer, reflection, and seeking God's guidance, I've decided to take Nelda's offer."

When Pastor Mark didn't respond immediately, she rushed to clarify. "I know it's not what anyone—including me—expected. But when I really sat with it, I realized something important. For so long, I've made decisions based on what I thought I should do or what I planned to do." Her voice gained strength. "But Nelda's offer felt different. It's not just a job. It's a challenge. It's a chance to grow, to stretch myself, and for the first time, I feel like God is asking me to step out of my comfort zone and trust Him completely."

Pastor Mark leaned back, his brow furrowed as he considered her words. Sammy's stomach twisted. Was he disappointed? Would he try to talk her out of it?

But then, a slow smile broke across his face—small at first, then growing. "Sammy, that's . . . well, that's not what I expected. But it's clear you've thought this through, and it sounds like you've found something that excites you and challenges you in all the right ways."

Relief flooded through her, and she let out a breath she hadn't realized she'd been holding. "Thank you, Pastor Mark. That means so much to me."

He grinned, leaning forward on the table. "Now, about that food pantry. Any chance you can create a binder with all the details before you go?"

Sammy brightened at the practical suggestion. "Absolutely! I can have it ready by Friday." She hesitated, then added, "And Nelda mentioned I could still volunteer on pick-up days until you hire someone new."

Pastor Mark's smile widened. "That's great to hear. Knowing you'll still be around helps a lot. You've built something really special here, Sammy."

Her heart swelled at his words. "Thank you. It's been such a joy to see the pantry grow. I'll miss being so closely involved, but I know this is the right next step for me."

"Well," Pastor Mark said, lifting his mug, "here's to new beginnings, and to trusting God with the unknown."

Sammy clinked her cup lightly against his, a smile breaking across her face. "To new beginnings."

They lingered a little longer, discussing transition plans and sharing gratitude for all they'd accomplished together. By the time they left, the weight Sammy had carried all week had lifted.

As she walked through Willow Creek's familiar streets, Sammy felt a blend of peace and anticipation. It was time to tell Nelda. She pulled out her phone to text her.

Sammy: *Have time for lunch at Hank's today?*

Nelda: *Absolutely! See you in 30?*

Sammy: *Perfect.*

With lunch plans set, Sammy ducked into the stationery shop for a quick stop before heading to meet Nelda.

This town had changed her in the best way. From her first uncertain steps into the church office to the relationships she'd built, Willow Creek had taught her to trust in God's timing—and to dream bigger.

She hadn't planned to stop, but something in the window caught her eye. Inside, a display of leather-bound journals sat neatly arranged, their covers smooth and waiting. One in particular seemed to call to her—a soft purple journal stamped in silver with Jeremiah 29:11: "'For I know the plans I have for you,' declares the LORD."

It felt like a promise, a tangible reminder that she didn't have to have all the answers right now.

"This is perfect," she whispered, clutching it to her chest.

The words on the cover echoing in her heart. *This is my new beginning—scary, exciting, and full of unknowns. But I'm not walking into it alone.*

"For I know the plans I have for you," she whispered. "And thank goodness someone does."

At the register, a whimsical card caught her eye—one that reminded her of

Amanda, her best friend and former roommate. She smiled, thinking back to their last night together, right after Richard had broken up with her. *Jeremiah 29:11.* Amanda had spoken that verse over her when she felt lost, when the future felt like nothing but fear.

Back then, it had felt impossible to believe.

Now, standing here, seeing how far she'd come, she realized something.

She believed it now.

Pulling out her phone, she set an alarm to call Amanda. They texted here and there, but this deserved an actual conversation.

The bell jingled as she stepped outside, the journal tucked securely under her arm. Sammy paused, looking up at the vast, endless blue sky.

"All right, God," she said, picking up her pace toward Hank's. "Let's do this."

Chapter 38

When Sammy arrived at Hank's, the familiar sounds of the lunch rush buzzed. The scent of sizzling burgers and hand-cut fries filled the air, mingling with the warm, yeasty aroma of fresh rolls, making her stomach rumble. She and Nelda exchanged warm smiles near the hostess station.

While they waited to be seated, Sammy cleared her throat, breaking the companionable silence. She took a deep breath, the weight of her decision settling in her chest. This was it. No more second-guessing. No more wondering if she was making the "right" choice.

She was making *her* choice.

"So, Nelda," she began, her pulse fluttering with both excitement and nerves, "after much prayer and thought, I'd love to accept your job offer."

Nelda's face lit up, her smile broad and genuine. "Oh, Sammy, I'm so pleased to hear this!" She pulled Sammy into a warm hug, laughter bubbling in her throat.

Sammy returned the warm embrace, Nelda's warmth calming her nerves, then took a half step back, still holding Nelda's hands. "But here's the funny part—I'm accepting without really knowing all the details. Can you fill me in over lunch?" She gave a little laugh, half nerves, half anticipation.

Nelda chuckled, gently shaking Sammy's hands reassuringly. "Of course, sweetheart. There are quite a few parts to the job, but I'll give you the overview now. And if you have time after, we can swing by my office to dig into the details."

Sammy blinked. "You . . . have an office?"

Nelda laughed again, her tone rich and warm. "Sweetheart, of course I do.

And soon you will too."

Sammy grinned, tension easing. *One step at a time,* she reminded herself.

The hostess soon led them to a cozy booth in the corner, and Julie, a friendly waitress, appeared moments later with two glasses of sweet tea. Nelda leaned forward conspiratorially. "Oh, and Julie, meet Sammy, my new assistant."

Julie's eyes sparkled as she turned to Sammy. "It's about time you hired someone, Nelda!" Julie said with a warm smile. She turned to Sammy. "Well, you must be pretty special. It's so nice to meet you."

Sammy's cheeks warmed, a mix of gratitude and surprise at the warm reception. "Thank you," she said, her voice soft but sincere. "It's great to meet you too."

Nelda slid her menu toward Julie. "I'll have the usual, and Sammy will have whatever she wants. Put it on my tab."

As Sammy glanced over the menu, Nelda turned to Julie with a knowing smile. "Were you and Lily able to get to that park I was telling you about this past weekend?"

Julie's face lit up. "Oh, we did! And let me tell you, Lily *loved* it. She must have gone down that big slide a dozen times." She shook her head fondly. "I think she would've stayed till dark if I'd let her."

Nelda chuckled. "I had a feeling. And how'd you like it?"

Julie leaned on her notepad. "Honestly? It was nice just sitting in the shade, watching her run around. Sometimes I forget how much I need that too."

Nelda gave her a knowing look. "That's why I mentioned it, sweetheart. You deserve a break just as much as she does."

Julie's smile softened. "I appreciate that, Nelda. Really."

Sammy glanced up from her menu, drawn into the easy warmth between them. Nelda wasn't just a businesswoman. She was someone who truly saw people.

Julie looked to Sammy, and after a brief hesitation, Sammy closed the menu. "I'll have the grilled chicken sandwich with sweet potato fries."

Julie gave a quick nod. "Great choice. I'll get that started." With a warm smile, she turned and headed toward the kitchen.

As she walked away, Nelda leaned forward, her expression soft but earnest. "Sammy, let's start with what I call 'creative stewardship.' I've learned over the years that I've been blessed with resources: properties, investments, connections, and it's my responsibility to use those blessings wisely. Maintaining what I have, finding new opportunities, and sharing them to benefit others . . . that's the heart of it."

She paused, her gaze steady but warm. "And that's why I need you. You have this way of seeing people and projects not just as they are, but as they could be. I saw it at the pantry, at camp, even in the way you connect with people around this town. That gift? It's exactly what creative stewardship is about."

Sammy blinked, caught off guard by Nelda's words. "I've never thought of it like that before," she admitted softly, her voice tinged with awe.

Nelda's smile deepened, full of encouragement. "Well, that's why I'm here, sweetheart. To help you see what God's already planted in you and give you the space to grow it. I'd like to start you as my assistant and, in time, groom you to become my CCO, my Chief Creative Officer. I have no doubt you can handle it, but are you willing to believe it too?"

Sammy nodded, beginning to see just how sharp of a businesswoman Nelda was, while hardly believing this was her life.

"Good," Nelda said, sounding pleased. She leaned in, her voice dropping to a playful whisper. "It's not just about making a ton of money—which we do, by the way." Nelda winked and continued. "It's about seeing potential in every project. Sometimes that means hosting community events or providing a space for someone to start a business. Other times, it's something bigger, like creating or redeveloping properties. But always, it's about making an impact."

Nelda pulled a pen out and began outlining her real estate portfolio on a napkin, explaining how the various pieces fit together. Sammy listened closely, nodding as she started to see the picture taking shape. Her mind buzzed with possibilities, the puzzle of responsibilities coming together in a way that was both exciting and daunting.

"Right now," Nelda continued, picking up her fork, "I've got a special project that needs fresh eyes. It's a plot of land just outside town, prime real estate, but I haven't figured out how to use it yet."

"Okay, I can't wait to hear more about how I can help with this," Sammy replied as she thanked Julie for refilling her glass.

"Good. For now, let's pray and eat!" Nelda took Sammy's hand and prayed and then added, "After lunch, we'll go to my office. I want to introduce you to my team: Cindy, my numbers gal, and Harold, our maintenance guru. Great folks, both of 'em."

Sammy took a sip of sweet tea, the tension in her shoulders easing. "I'd love that."

Nelda beamed. "Perfect. Because once we get you up to speed, you and I are going to make great things happen, Sammy. Just you wait and see."

* * *

After lunch, the early afternoon sun warmed the sidewalk as they strolled a short block down Main Street. Willow Creek's flower boxes were bursting with color, and cheery storefronts drew the eyes of passersby.

Nelda paused outside a stately two-story building nestled on the corner, its large windows reflecting the golden afternoon light. Dark green shutters framed the glass, lending the place a timeless charm.

"Here we are," she said with a knowing smile.

As Sammy followed her inside, the scent of fresh coffee and a hint of lemon welcomed her. The office was compact but inviting, with dark wood floors and a reception desk tucked neatly against one wall.

Behind the desk, a woman with short brown hair tapped away at a laptop, her fingers moving with practiced ease. Without looking up, she said, "Please tell me this is a lunch meeting. I skipped breakfast, and I'm starting to regret it."

Then she glanced up, spotted Sammy, and straightened with an easy smile. "Oh! You must be Sammy."

Her handshake was firm but friendly. "I'm Cindy, numbers whiz, coffee addict, and Nelda's unofficial voice of reason. It's great to meet you."

"It's great to meet you too."

Cindy gave a single nod, sizing her up; not unkindly, just observant, as if already assessing how Sammy might fit into their well-oiled machine.

"Well, Sammy Thomas, welcome to the circus," Cindy said, a playful glint in her eye. "I've heard plenty about you. Pantry miracles, mud fights at camp, sounds like you thrive in chaos. That's good. You'll need it."

Sammy chuckled. "I prefer to think of it as organized chaos."

Cindy grinned. "Even better. That means you might actually survive here." She turned to Nelda. "Did you scare her yet, or should I?"

Nelda let out a rich laugh. "Oh, hush. She's exactly what we need."

As Cindy leaned against her desk, Sammy's gaze landed on a small framed photo beside her laptop, a teenage boy mid-pitch on a baseball field and a close-up of a teenage girl holding a Yorkie. The frame was angled slightly toward Cindy, as if she glanced at it often.

Cindy caught her looking and tapped the frame lightly. "Emma and Lucas," she said with a touch of pride. "Seventeen and fifteen. They keep me busy and are personally responsible for every one of these gray hairs. But I wouldn't trade 'em for anything."

Sammy smiled. "They look like great kids."

"They are," Cindy said, then smirked. "But if you ever hear me muttering about teenage attitudes, just pretend you didn't."

Sammy laughed, feeling the last bit of tension in her shoulders ease.

Nelda patted her shoulder. "Come on, let's go find Harold."

In the back room, Harold Carter stood at a workbench, long arms moving with quiet precision as he repaired a lamp.

He glanced up as Sammy entered, flashing a crooked grin. "You must be Sammy. I'm Harold, resident Mr. Fix-It. Need a lightbulb changed, a chair un-wobbled, or a hole in the wall patched? I'm your guy."

Sammy smiled. "Good to know. I'll try not to break anything too soon."

Harold chuckled, tightening a screw with practiced ease. "Oh, don't worry. Something always needs fixing around here."

They chatted for a moment longer before Nelda gestured toward the staircase. "Now, ready to see where you'll be working?"

Upstairs, the second floor struck a perfect balance between modern and inviting—wood paneling softened the sleek black-framed glass and steel accents, creating an atmosphere that felt both professional and warm.

A glass wall stretched along the hallway, offering an unobstructed view into the conference room. The doors sat in the middle, bold and symmetrical, marking the entrance to a space where decisions were made and ideas took shape.

Nelda gestured toward it with a knowing smile. "This is where the real battles happen."

Inside, a long, dark wood table anchored the room, surrounded by sleek white leather chairs—the kind that looked equal parts stylish and intimidating. A modern pendant light hung overhead, casting a soft, focused glow. Against the far wall, a large TV screen was mounted above a minimalist sideboard, waiting for presentations or impromptu brainstorming sessions.

The floor-to-ceiling glass wall flooded the space with natural light, making it feel open yet private, an ideal mix of transparency and focus.

Sammy could already picture it—scribbled notes on a whiteboard, coffee cups scattered across the table, Nelda pacing as she worked through an idea.

Nelda gave her a sideways glance. "Now, ready to see your office?"

They continued down the hallway, past the conference room. Nelda motioned toward a door with a small plaque.

"That one's mine," she said with a nod. Then, stopping in front of the next office, she turned the handle with a flourish. "And this is yours."

Sunlight streamed through a large window, casting warm patches of light across the dark wood flooring. A sleek but sturdy desk sat in the center, its surface pristine and waiting—ready to be filled with plans, notes, and late-night brainstorming sessions. Against the far wall, a half-empty bookshelf practically begged to be filled.

Sammy stepped inside, trailing her fingers along the desk's smooth surface. Her heart caught in her throat.

"This is mine?" she asked, awed.

"All yours," Nelda confirmed, her eyes twinkling. "Feel free to work wherever inspiration strikes, but this is your base. You've got a lot to offer, Sammy, and I can't wait to see what you'll do here."

Sammy nodded, her hand still resting on the desk, imagining it piled high with notebooks, sketches, and maybe even a framed photo of Glory or the pantry team.

She smiled, excitement and disbelief mixing inside her heart. *You've come a long way, Sammy Thomas. And this is just the start of your new adventure with God!*

As Sammy left the office, she pulled out her phone and texted Jake.

Sammy: *Jake, I did it! I officially accepted Nelda's job and start on MONDAY!!!*

His reply came quickly.

Jake: *That's incredible, Sammy! Can we celebrate on Friday? I'm buried in work on the ranch until then, but I'm all yours after six.*

Sammy grinned, her heart light.

Sammy: *Friday at 6 sounds perfect.*

Jake: *Proud of you. Just promise me this new job won't make you too fancy to collect eggs. :)*

She chuckled, tucking her phone away. As she walked, she let herself take it all in. A week ago, she'd been drowning in uncertainty. Now, her life had a new rhythm, a new direction. And somehow, it felt like she'd been walking toward this all along.

Chapter 39

Jake woke up to the smell of coffee and the sound of his Abuelo's chair creaking softly in the kitchen. He found him staring out the window, coffee cup in hand—his usual peaceful morning place.

"How are you, mijo?" Edmund asked, his voice calm but curious.

Jake grabbed his cup and joined him at the table. "I'm good. I plan to move the cattle today, and then John and I are going to update the flooring in the hayloft while it's empty."

Edmund nodded. "Sounds like a good day." Then, turning to Jake with laughter in his eyes, he raised a questioning eyebrow. "And how are you and Sammy?"

Jake's smile grew. "It's hard to describe how great it is." His grin widened. "I've never felt so . . . right with anyone."

Amusement lit Abuelo's face. "Really? All that after only a few months of dating?"

Jake chuckled, shaking his head. "I know, but yes. I think she may be the one, Abuelo."

A slow, nostalgic smile spread across Edmund's face as he remembered when he knew his sweet Josephina was "the one" for him. He sighed, his gaze growing distant. "Oh, mijo, I'm so happy for you. I remember that feeling well."

"I know it's probably way too early to talk about engagement . . ." Jake hesitated as they both raised their eyebrows. Then, with a chuckle, he continued, "But I kind of want to make sure we're on the same page, that Sammy could see a future for us too."

Edmund looked at Jake, amused, his grin magnifying the sun-leathered wrinkles on his face. “Well, have you told her?”

Jake shook his head and looked out the window. “I don’t want to scare her away.”

“But what if she’s looking for the same thing?” Edmund set his cup down and leaned forward. “If you were her, wouldn’t you want to know you were both heading toward the same . . .” He waved his hand forward, searching for the right word. “Result?”

“Actually, I *would*,” Jake admitted, leaning in.

Edmund nodded. “Then maybe it’s time you let her know.”

Jake stared out the window and nodded, slowly at first, then more firmly. “Yes. I think you’re right, Abuelo.” He shook his head in wonder, excitement growing at the thought of having this talk with his sweet Sammy.

Edmund watched his grandson, fully aware of the privilege of sharing this moment with him. Raising his coffee cup with a twinkle in his eye, he grinned. “Here’s to enjoying the journey, Jake. But buckle up, mijo. This ride changes everything.”

Jake lingered by the kitchen window, his gaze drifting to the barn where he and Sammy had spent many mornings over the past few months saddling up their horses. Just thinking about her brought a smile to his face, a quiet warmth settling deep in his chest. She loved a plan, thrived on knowing what came next, but life had thrown so many changes her way lately. A new job, a new town, and now their budding relationship.

She might not have all the answers yet. *Neither did he.*

But one thing was certain—whatever came next, he wanted to face it *with her.*

The soft *creak* of the chair behind him pulled him from his thoughts. He glanced back at his abuelo, who was watching him with a knowing smile.

Jake gave a small nod, feeling more resolved than ever. “I think you’re right, Abuelo,” he said, his voice quieter, almost to himself.

* * *

Jake leaned forward, resting his elbows on his knees as he sat across from Glory, who rocked gently on her porch swing. The evening air carried the scent of honeysuckle, mingling with the sweetness of the iced tea in their hands.

Glory gave him a knowing look. "Sarah and Sammy just left for the food bank to restock the pantry, so we've got a little time. What's on your mind?"

Jake exhaled, a small smile tugging at the corners of his mouth. "Sammy and I have been seeing each other for a while now, but I want to ask her if she'd like to date with intention."

Glory's eyes twinkled with understanding. "Is that so? Do you mean what my generation used to call courting?"

Jake chuckled, nodding. "Yeah, exactly." He hesitated, gripping his hat a little tighter. "I know she's been through a rough breakup not too long ago, but from what I can tell, it never really seemed like much of a romance. More like two people who were just going through the motions." He glanced down, turning his hat in his hands. "The last thing I want is for her to feel pressured. But I also know how I feel about her, and I'd never lead her on."

Glory studied him for a long moment before nodding. "And how does Sammy feel?"

Jake let out a quiet chuckle. "That's what I'm hoping to find out." His smile dimmed slightly. "I just want her to know this is different."

Glory tilted her head. "And what is it you want from me, Jake?"

His gaze softened. "Your blessing. Your advice." He paused, then added with a sheepish grin, "And maybe a suggestion for where a man can take a girl on a date that's special but not overwhelming."

Glory let out a delighted laugh. "Oh, Jake. You're already halfway there."

Jake raised an eyebrow. "How do you figure?"

Glory reached out, giving his arm a gentle squeeze. "Because you care enough to ask."

She glanced toward the bird feeder as the sun dipped behind the pecan trees. "You want my advice? Make it personal. Make it meaningful. Let her see that you've been paying attention." She smiled knowingly. "And if you really want to make an impression, take her somewhere that already means something to both of you."

Jake's expression shifted—thoughtful, determined. And then, slowly, he smiled.

"I think I know just the place."

Glory patted his arm. "Then go on, Jake. And trust that Sammy's heart knows what it wants, just like yours does."

* * *

The highway stretched ahead of them, long and open, the Texas sun dipping low toward the horizon. Sammy leaned back in the passenger seat, kicking off her shoes and stretching her legs as Sarah eased into the next lane.

They were heading back from the regional food bank with a van full of supplies for the pantry and an embarrassing number of snacks for the ride.

The air in the car was thick with the scent of caramel corn, chips, and whatever the gas station did to make it impossible to leave without at least three things you absolutely didn't need.

"I can't believe you bought that many caramel nuggets," Sammy teased, eyeing the massive bag Sarah had just ripped open.

Sarah shot her a look, popping one into her mouth. "I regret nothing." She chewed thoughtfully, then glanced at Sammy. "Okay, I've been patient this whole ride. We're ninety minutes from home, and once we get there, I go back to being Mom. So while I still have the chance to be your carefree, nosy best friend, I need updates on you and Jake!"

Sammy laughed, running a hand through her hair. "As much as I'd love to dodge this conversation, I do need to talk it out. So, congratulations—you win. Spill zone: activated."

"Of course you do." Sarah said, nudging her shoulder. "Now spill. Where's your head at with all of this?"

Sammy stared out the window, watching the trees blur past. "Honestly? I don't know. It's different with him. I've never had something feel so easy and terrifying at the same time."

Sarah hummed, waiting for more.

Sammy sighed. "I know he cares about me. That's obvious. And I care about him too." She hesitated, biting her lip. "But I also just got out of something that never really felt right. What if I jump into this too fast and don't see something I should?"

Sarah nodded, thoughtful. "Fair. But let me ask you this—are you holding back because of your ex? Or because you're scared of how real this feels?"

Sammy swallowed. "Maybe both." She hesitated before admitting, "But mostly . . . because there was no plan for this."

Sarah glanced at her, waiting.

Sammy stared out at the road ahead. "With Richard, everything was mapped out. We were together for years. It was the 'smart' choice. The logical one." She hesitated, her voice quieter now. "It felt clear, until I realized it was just a facade I created."

Sarah's gaze stayed steady. "And Jake?"

Sammy let out a half laugh, half sigh. "Jake . . . I didn't plan for him. I didn't plan for any of this. But I can't deny how I feel when I'm with him." Sammy grabbed a caramel nugget from Sarah's bag, popping it into her mouth as if chewing could buy her time to find the right words.

"I was never drawn to Richard the way I am to Jake. It's different. It's more. So much more." She swallowed, her voice quieter now, almost like an admission. "Like I have never felt this alive with a guy in my entire life."

Sarah raised an eyebrow, a smirk playing at her lips. "That sounds like a confession."

Sammy let out a breathy laugh, shaking her head. "Maybe it is."

Sarah waited, letting her sit with the thought.

Sammy exhaled, her voice barely above a whisper. "And that's what scares me. Because I think I may actually be falling in love with Jake." She shook her head slightly. "Is that even possible? We're just dating. No big conversations, no defining what this is supposed to be. And yet it feels like so much more."

Sarah's smile was knowing, warm. "And a little unplanned?"

Sammy let out a breathy laugh, finally meeting Sarah's eyes. "Exactly."

Sarah gave her a knowing look. "I know you love plans, Sammy. And quite frankly, the food pantry and summer camp are running so well *because* of your amazing planning skills. But what if the best things in life don't always come with a plan you can control?" She let the words settle, her voice gentle but sure. "What if, sometimes, the things that take us by surprise are the ones God had planned for us all along?"

Sammy let out a slow breath, shifting her legs and lacing her fingers together as if steadying herself.

Jake had a way of seeing her—really seeing her. Not as someone who had to have it all figured out, not as the girl with the perfect plan, but as her. And somehow, that was enough for him.

He listened—not just to her words but to the quiet hesitations, the things she didn't say. He made space for them, for her.

And when she was with him, something inside her settled. Not in a way that made her feel weak, but in a way that made her feel safe. Known. Like maybe God had placed Jake in her life for a reason.

Maybe Sarah was right.

Maybe love didn't have to be mapped out to be real.

Maybe trusting God meant learning to embrace the unknown.

Chapter 40

On Friday, Jake's truck pulled into the driveway, and Sammy's heart skipped a beat. A week had been too long!

As he stepped out and started up the walkway, his familiar smile lit up his face.

"Hey, sweet Sammy," he called, opening his arms as he approached.

Sammy got up from the porch swing and bounded down the porch steps and into his embrace, warmth flooding her chest as she breathed him in.

"Missed you too," he said, delighted, holding her tight.

From her spot on the swing, Glory smiled to herself, watching the sweet exchange. Taking a slow sip of her tea, she sighed contentedly. "Young love," she mused before calling out, "Y'all have fun now!"

"Thanks, Glory!" Jake replied with a grin and a nod, keeping one arm around Sammy as they turned toward his truck.

He opened the passenger door for her, waiting until she was settled before closing it gently. Sliding into the driver's seat, he glanced at her with a playful glint in his eyes.

"This date feels extra special," he said, starting the engine. "Can I take you somewhere different tonight?"

Sammy tilted her head, intrigued. "Ooo, fun! Sure! What did you have in mind?"

Jake's grin widened as he shifted into gear. "You'll see. It's a surprise."

As they drove out of town, the familiar sights of Willow Creek gave way to quieter country roads. The setting sun bathed the fields in a golden glow, and Sammy found herself relaxing into the moment.

"Are you going to give me *any* hints?" she teased, glancing at him sideways.

Jake chuckled, shaking his head. "Nope. You'll just have to trust me."

Sammy rolled her eyes playfully, but she couldn't stop the smile tugging at her lips.

As they crested a hill, Sammy's breath caught. She recognized the view immediately. It was the ridge on Jake's ranch, the one they'd ridden to on horseback many times this summer.

Jake pulled the truck to a stop near the trailhead where they usually left the horses. Hopping out, he walked around to open her door. "What do you think?" he asked, holding out his hand.

Sammy giggled as she slid out, slipping her hand into his. "It's perfect! I didn't even realize where we were going until we were right on top of it. That is *some* backroad, Jake."

Jake laughed, his grin wide. "Oh, there are *a lot* of backroads when you've got 120 acres to roam."

Just beyond the familiar knocked-over tree, a picnic setup took Sammy's breath away. An old quilt was spread out, a basket sat waiting, and lanterns hung from the branches above, casting a soft golden glow. The scene felt magical, like something out of a storybook.

"You did all this?" she asked, wonder in her voice.

Jake rubbed the back of his neck sheepishly, his cheeks slightly flushed. "Well, I had a little help from John with the lanterns. But yeah."

Sammy turned to him, her eyes dancing with joy. "Jake, it's perfect."

Before heading to the picnic, Jake gestured for her to sit on the log with him, face to face.

"When you said somewhere different, I thought you meant the Italian place on the way out of town," Sammy teased with a laugh. She squeezed his hand and added, "But this? This is even better."

Jake's expression softened, his fingers lacing with hers.

"Sammy," he began, his voice low and steady, "I've been thinking about us, and I wanted to talk about it. But I thought a place like this—somewhere quiet, just the two of us—would be best."

She took a steadying breath, meeting his gaze. "Okay," she said softly, open but cautious.

Jake hesitated, his thumb brushing lightly over her knuckles. "Sammy, I've dated before—"

Sammy's brows lifted, reflexive humor slipping in. "Well, that's one way to start."

Jake chuckled, shaking his head, the warmth in his eyes softening the weight of his words. "Fair enough. But what I mean is, I've never felt this way about anyone. You make me laugh, you make me think, and you make me want to be the kind of man God intended me to be—the man you deserve."

A slow, unsteady breath escaped her as his words settled over her heart. Was this real? Could it be? No one had ever said something like this to her—not like this. Not without expectation or pressure. Just . . . love. Real, steady, certain love.

She searched his face, willing herself to find hesitation, a trace of uncertainty, something to protect her from the free fall of hope. But there was nothing. Only quiet confidence, steady as the earth beneath them.

Jake took a breath, his fingers tightening around hers, his voice sure. "Sammy, I love you, and I'd like to date you with the intention of someday marrying you."

The world seemed to still, the only movement the gentle rustling of leaves overhead.

She had heard words like these before. But never like this.

Never with this kind of tenderness. Never with this kind of certainty. Only with false hope and quiet control.

No, she reminded herself. This isn't Richard. This is Jake.

Jake, who had never made her feel like she had to measure up to some invisible standard. Jake, who saw her not for what she could give, not for how well she fit into a future already mapped out, but simply for who she was.

Her breath hitched as she looked up at him, his eyes steady, filled with a love she hadn't dared to believe was possible.

Jake must have noticed the hesitation because he squeezed her hand, his thumb brushing gently over her knuckles. His voice was steady, patient.

"I've thought about what you said—about the life you thought you'd have before your breakup with Richard." He took a breath, his gaze holding hers like a vow. "And Sammy, I don't want you to ever feel like you're just being tolerated or living in someone's shadow. I want you to be celebrated, for exactly who you are."

Tears filled her eyes as his words wrapped around her heart like a hug, soothing wounds she hadn't even realized still ached.

Jake's grip on her hand tightened slightly, grounding her. "I know that sounds serious, but I want you to understand what I mean. Dating intentionally doesn't mean rushing into anything. It means we're not just going through the motions. It's about building something real, something with purpose. Getting to know each other deeply. Your dreams, your fears, your quirks, all of it. Because if I'm ever lucky enough to call you my wife, I want the whole package."

He hesitated, searching her face, then added softly, "And I hope you want all of me too."

Tears blurred her vision. A shaky laugh slipped out before she could stop it. "Jake, I love you." She bit her lip, emotions colliding all at once. "And yeah, I want all of you too."

His breath hitched, his fingers tightening just slightly around hers.

Jake gave her hand a small squeeze, a knowing smile tugging at his lips. "I know you love a good plan, so maybe you can help us figure out how this might look?"

That earned another laugh, softer this time. That was Jake. Meeting her where she was. Not rushing her, not demanding an answer she wasn't ready for—just inviting her into something real.

She swallowed hard, her voice quieter now. "I don't have it all figured out yet, but I know I don't want to do this with anyone else."

Jake exhaled, something like relief flickering across his face. And then, in one smooth motion, he stood, gently tugging her to her feet.

He kissed her knuckles before pulling her into an embrace that felt like home.

His voice was warm, full of something steady and unshakable. "So glad you feel the same, Sammy. I've been praying for this. For us."

She smiled against his chest, the words settling deep in her heart. "Me too."

Jake reached into his pocket and pulled out a delicate silver necklace, its pendant a single pearl nestled inside an intricate wire nest.

"This was my mom's," he said quietly. "I don't have many memories of her, but I remember she wore this often. I'd like you to have it."

Sammy's fingers brushed over the charm. "Would you put it on me?" she asked softly, pulling her hair to one side.

Jake stepped behind her, clasping the necklace gently. He breathed in the sweet scent of her hair, committing this moment to memory.

Turning back to him, Sammy pressed her hand to her heart. "I love it. Thank you."

"You're so welcome, sweet Sammy, there is no one else I could ever imagine giving it to." Jake's lips curved into a smile as he gently took her hand, leading her toward the picnic setup. "Now, for your dining pleasure, we have the finest gourmet meal—fancy chips, sandwiches, and for dessert, chocolate cake from Hank's."

Sammy grinned as she settled onto the blanket, tucking her legs beneath her. "Ah, a true culinary experience. You've outdone yourself, Mr. Martinez."

Jake chuckled, pouring her a glass of tea before leaning back on his hands, his expression full of mischief. "So, tell me something about you I don't know."

Sammy tilted her head, narrowing her eyes playfully. "Only if you go first."

Jake laughed. "Fair enough. Did I ever tell you about the time I tried to train a goat to pull a cart?"

Sammy nearly choked on her tea. "A goat?"

"Yep." Jake shook his head, grinning. "I was here one summer, about nine years old, and I was convinced I could start my own little delivery service. I built a cart out of scraps and figured all I needed was a reliable steed." He paused dramatically. "Enter Pancho the goat."

Sammy covered her mouth, already giggling. "Oh no."

"Oh yes. Let me tell you, goats are not exactly team players. Pancho had his own ideas about where to go, and none of them involved pulling a cart."

Sammy laughed. "What happened?"

Jake's grin widened. "After several failed attempts where he either ran in the opposite direction or just sat down and refused to move, Abuelo finally came outside, watched for a minute, then walked up with a carrot and said, 'Mijo, try giving the goat a reason to move.'"

Sammy hugged her knees, delight lighting up her face as she pictured the scene. "Did it work?"

"Oh, it worked all right. That goat would follow a carrot anywhere. I thought I was a genius." Jake sighed, shaking his head. "Of course, the moment I ran out of carrots, Pancho went right back to doing things his way."

Sammy laughed so hard she had to wipe a tear from her eye. "I can just picture it. Little Jake, proudly leading his carrot-crazed goat through the yard. Adorable and slightly chaotic."

Jake shrugged with a mock-serious expression. "What can I say? I was an industrious kid. I believed in innovation." He turned the question on her, leaning forward. "Your turn. Tell me something I don't know."

Sammy smiled, settling back onto her elbows. "Okay, I'll tell you the first time I remember meeting Nelda. It was one Christmas while I was staying with Glory. My brother Chris and I—eight and six at the time—thought we were so grown-up because we finally had permission to walk to the bubblegum store all by ourselves."

Jake raised a brow. "Bubblegum store?"

She grinned. "That's what we called the Wilson Pharmacy. Anyway, on the way back, we got completely turned around. I mean, hopelessly lost. We wandered for what felt like forever, and eventually, we just sat down on a curb and cried."

Jake, mid-bite of his sandwich, nearly choked. "You? Crying on a curb?"

Sammy laughed, nodding. "Oh yeah. Full-on waterworks. Then, out of nowhere, this sweet old lady came out of her house, took one look at us, and asked what was wrong. Turns out, it was Nelda! She called Glory and walked us home herself. Then she stayed for our *White Christmas* sing-along."

Jake chuckled, shaking his head. "Of all the curbs in Willow Creek, you had to land on Nelda's."

"Right?" Sammy smiled, looking out over the ridge. "Small towns have a way of putting you exactly where you need to be."

For a while, they sat quietly, watching the sky deepen into a breathtaking blanket of shimmering stars. The only sound was the soft rustling of the trees and the distant chirp of crickets.

Sammy sighed, tilting her head back. "Wow. The sky sure is clear up here."

Jake leaned back on his elbows beside her. "Yeah. We're far enough away from it all that you can really see everything."

A tiny flicker of light caught Sammy's eye, then another. "Wait, is that a firefly?"

Jake smiled. "Sure is. They'll be around for a few more weeks."

Sammy's face lit up. "When I was a kid, we used to catch them in glass peanut butter jars at Glory's. Then we'd release them, like we were setting tiny stars free."

Jake chuckled, amusement dancing in his eyes. "Oh, so fun! I did too." He fell quiet for a moment, watching the fireflies flicker around them like tiny stars. Then, his fingers brushed lightly against hers. "How about tonight, instead of catching them, we dance under them?"

Before Sammy could respond, he pulled out his phone, scrolled for a moment, then pressed play. A soft, familiar melody filled the air.

He stood, holding out his hand. "May I have this dance?"

Sammy felt her cheeks flush as she smiled up at him, her heart fluttering. "You may."

She placed her hand in his, and he pulled her gently to her feet. As they began to sway, the warm glow of the lanterns, the flickering fireflies, and the quiet night wrapped around them, making the world feel smaller. Just the two of them and the stars.

Jake spun her slowly, his laughter warm and low. "You're a natural."

Sammy giggled, closing her eyes for a moment to soak it all in—the music, the night air, and the steady, grounding presence of Jake's arms around her.

But beneath the sweetness, a quiet voice stirred. *Can this last? Is it too soon?*

Jake must have felt the unease because he slowed their movements and leaned back, studying her face. "You okay?"

Sammy looked up at him, her eyes shimmering with emotion. She hesitated for just a moment before nodding. "I am so much better than okay," she said softly, a small grin tugging at her lips. "It's just . . . this feels too good to be true."

Jake's smile deepened, his voice reassuring. "Oh, my sweet Sammy." He pressed a gentle kiss to her forehead, then met her gaze, steady as ever. "I can hardly believe I've been so blessed to find you too. But we'll take it one step at a time."

As the music faded, Sammy rested her head against his shoulder, letting his words settle in her heart.

She wasn't sure if it was too soon or exactly on time. But here, wrapped in Jake's arms beneath the fireflies, she decided—just for tonight—she'd let herself believe in something this good.

Chapter 41

Saturday night, Glory passed the basket of warm bread across the table, her eyes twinkling. "Alright, sweetheart, catch me up. Your life has been moving so fast lately, even the Willow Creek gossip mill can't keep up."

Sammy grinned, taking a roll and setting the basket back down. The golden crust was warm against her fingertips, and the scent of butter and yeast wrapped around her like a hug. She tore off a piece, letting the comfort of it settle her nerves. "Well, for starters, I finally finished my food pantry binder. And Monday's my first official day working for Nelda."

Glory's face lit up. "Oh, honey, that's wonderful." She reached across the table, giving Sammy's hand a squeeze. "I'm so proud of you."

Sammy laughed softly, turning her hand to squeeze back. "It still doesn't feel real. One minute, I was volunteering at the pantry, scraping by on a hundred bucks a week, and now I'm working alongside Nelda in 'creative stewardship'—whatever that means." She chuckled. "I'm making more than I ever dreamed, and I haven't even started!"

Glory studied her for a moment, tilting her head. "And how do you feel about that?"

Sammy let out a breath, running a hand through her hair. "Excited. Nervous. A little overwhelmed, if I'm honest." She picked up her spoon, absently stirring her soup. "Nelda has all these big ideas, and somehow, she's convinced I'm the one who can bring them to life."

Glory nodded, reaching for her own spoon. "She's a sharp woman, that Nelda. If she sees something in you, it's because it's already there. You just have to believe it too."

Sammy bit her lip, her heart swelling at the encouragement. "I want to. I really do."

Glory smiled knowingly. "Then you're already halfway there."

Sammy hesitated, tearing her bread into smaller and smaller bits. "Speaking of big things . . ." She took a breath, brushing the crumbs from her fingertips. "Jake asked if I'd be interested in dating with intention. To maybe, someday, marry him." She glanced up, her voice barely above a whisper. "And I said yes."

For a moment, Glory was still. Then her eyes softened, something flickering behind them—something knowing. Slowly, a smile bloomed across her face, one so full of warmth and understanding that it made Sammy's breath catch.

"Oh, bless." Glory pressed a hand to her heart, her voice thick with emotion. "Honey, that's wonderful."

Sammy frowned slightly. "You don't seem surprised."

Glory chuckled, reaching for her glass of tea. "That might be because a certain young man sat on my porch a few nights ago, hat in hand, asking for my blessing." She gave Sammy a pointed look. "And my advice."

Sammy's breath hitched. "He talked to you?"

"Mm-hmm." Glory set down her glass, leaning forward as she took Sammy's hand. "Wanted to be sure he was doing right by you. He told me he didn't want you to feel pressured, that he just wanted you to know this was different."

Sammy swallowed hard. "He said that?"

"Oh, sweetheart." Glory gave her hand a gentle squeeze. "That man is smitten, through and through. And he wanted to make sure you knew that, without a single doubt."

Sammy let out a shaky breath, pressing her free hand to her necklace.

Glory smiled knowingly. "And I told him what I'll tell you now: Trust that your heart knows what it wants. Just like his does."

A moment of quiet passed between them. Then, with a twinkle in her eye, Glory reached for the butter and nudged the dish toward Sammy. "So, this whole 'dating with intention' thing, how do you feel about that?"

Sammy's smile softened. "Excited. Nervous. A little overwhelmed."

Glory chuckled. "I think I'm sensing a theme."

Sammy groaned, shaking her head. "You and me both."

Glory blew lightly on her soup before taking a careful sip. "Let me ask you this. Do you feel an inner peace, even if it feels like a lot right now?"

Sammy picked up her glass, rubbing her thumb over the cool surface as she thought. "Yeah. I really do, more than I ever have in my whole life."

Glory gave a satisfied nod. "Then trust that. It's okay to take things one step at a time, sweetheart. New job, new relationship—just let yourself enjoy the process."

Sammy let out a slow breath, some of the tension in her shoulders easing. "You always make things sound so simple."

Glory grinned. "That's because I've already done all the overthinking for you."

Sammy laughed, warmth filling her chest. "I appreciate that."

They finished their meal in easy conversation, the soft clinking of spoons against bowls filling the kitchen. As Sammy reached for her plate, Glory nudged her gently.

"I'll handle the dishes. You go on and get some fresh air. I'm thinking we need a peach cobbler for the church potluck tomorrow. Gonna break out those peaches we froze this summer."

"Thanks, Glory."

* * *

Later, as the dishes clinked in the sink and Glory hummed a hymn in the kitchen, Sammy stepped onto the porch with a throw blanket in hand. The night air was crisp, carrying the scent of damp earth and distant hay fields.

She sank into the swing, her fingers tracing the rim of her tea glass, letting the quiet settle over her before pulling out her phone.

It was time to catch up with Amanda.

"So, how's my favorite Michigan girl?" Sammy asked, twirling a loose thread on her blanket. "And can I just start by saying text is so not enough for us to keep tabs on each other!"

Amanda laughed. "I couldn't agree more. Let's make this a monthly thing, minimum. But oh, Sammy, it's good. It's really good being back home. Although . . ." She hesitated. "I say *home* loosely."

"What do you mean?" Sammy frowned.

Amanda let out a slow breath. "Well, last week, I got home from work, and my parents sat me down and told me they're selling the house and moving to FLORIDA."

"Florida?!" Sammy nearly dropped her phone. "Oh no. But what about you?!"

"Right? That's exactly what I said!" Amanda groaned. "And you know what they told me? 'You can move with us if you want.'"

"So what are you going to do?"

"I think I am going to stay here in town. I love my job!"

Sammy smiled, shifting onto her side. "I love hearing that. Tell me everything."

Amanda groaned playfully, and Sammy could practically picture her stretching out on her couch, probably with a cup of tea in hand. "Well, let's see. Steady income, a solid 9-to-5, and the best part? No angry pet parents today, which is always a win."

Sammy grinned. "You must not have dealt with any dog parents today, because I figure all the angry ones are dog parents. Cat people just accept their fate."

"Ha! Truth," Amanda said with a laugh. "But honestly, my job at the vet clinic is kind of amazing. The other day, I got to watch a horse give birth."

Sammy shot upright, her blanket pooling around her waist. "No way! That's incredible!"

"I know! It was unreal." Amanda's voice brimmed with excitement. "I mean, I've seen videos, but being there in person? The moment that foal stood up on those wobbly little legs?" She let out a breath. "I was done. Completely melted."

Sammy swooned, pressing a hand to her heart. "Awww."

Amanda chuckled. "Right?! Anyway, you texted me over the summer asking for prayer about some camp you were doing. I thought you were running a food pantry?"

Sammy laughed, tucking her legs beneath her on the porch swing. "Oh wow, it *has* been a while! Camp was amazing. Want the highlights?"

"Absolutely."

Sammy smiled, her voice warm with the memory. "We had about forty kids show up each day, there was an epic mud fight, and—bonus treat for me—Michelle called a truce."

"FINALLY!" Amanda exclaimed.

Sammy sighed, shaking her head with a small laugh. "I know, right? But honestly, she surprised me. She was kind, humble, and I could tell she really meant it. Since then, when we see each other—usually at church—we smile and wave. Nothing big, but . . ."

Amanda softened. "Baby steps."

"Exactly." Sammy pulled the blanket a little tighter around her shoulders. "But I have news to catch you up on!"

"No way!" Amanda gasped. "Wait, did you take the job with Nelda?"

"Sure did," Sammy said proudly. "I start Monday. And get this—she wants to groom me into her Chief Creative Officer."

Amanda let out a high-pitched squeal. "Stop it! Sammy, that's amazing!"

"I know! I mean, it's kind of overwhelming, but it feels right, you know? Like God just keeps opening these doors, and I'm just walking through them, trying not to trip."

Amanda laughed. "You? Tripping? Never."

"Oh, hush." Sammy grinned. "But really, life here has been so good." She hesitated, heart thudding just a little. "And Jake and me . . ."

Amanda's voice sharpened with interest. "Oh? Do tell."

Sammy let out a breath, a soft smile tugging at her lips. "Amanda, I wish you could've seen us this morning. We went horseback riding again, just after sunrise." She closed her eyes for a second, the memory still fresh—the golden light filtering through the trees, the crisp air, the steady rhythm of hooves against soft earth. "You know how much I love it, and he just . . . lets me be me. No pressure, no expectations. Just the two of us, riding through the fields like something out of a dream."

Amanda practically melted. "Sammy, that sounds amazing."

"It was." She hesitated, her fingers playing with the edge of her blanket. "And, Amanda, when he hugs me, the world slows, and I can finally breathe. His warmth, the steady rise and fall of his chest—it's just so safe."

Amanda made a soft, knowing sound. "That's how you know, Sammy."

Sammy smiled, warmth blooming in her heart. "And when he kisses me . . . Amanda, the few times we have, it just—" She let out a small, breathless laugh. "It completely takes my breath away."

Amanda huffed out a laugh, pure amusement in her voice. "I *knew* it. You're a goner."

Sammy grinned. "I really might be."

Amanda laughed, but then her tone turned teasing. "Okay, but you're totally holding out on me. There's more, isn't there?"

Sammy bit her lip, heat creeping into her cheeks. "Maybe."

"Sammy!"

"All right, all right!" She laughed, shaking her head. "Last night, he took me on this picture-perfect date. I mean, Amanda, it was *unreal*—twinkle lights, music, the whole thing." She paused, her heart skipping at the memory. "And then he asked if I'd like to date him. With the intention that maybe, one day, we'd get married."

Silence.

Then Amanda nearly shrieked. "NO. WAY." Amanda let out a dreamy sigh. "That's all I ever wanted for you, Sammy."

Sammy swallowed past the unexpected lump in her throat, her fingers brushing the wire nest on her necklace. The weight of Amanda's words settled deep.

"I didn't think I'd ever get this close to something that feels so right."

A comfortable silence stretched between them, the kind only years of friendship could hold.

Then Amanda spoke, her voice quieter, almost hesitant. "So, can I tell *you* something now?"

Sammy sat up straighter. "Always."

Amanda exhaled, hesitating for just a second too long. Then—softly—she said, "Sammy, I think I might be falling for someone too."

Sammy gasped. "AMANDA. WHO?"

Amanda laughed softly. "Relax. I reconnected with an old friend. We go dancing every Friday to celebrate the week and, well . . . you *know* how much I love to dance."

Sammy practically bounced in place. "Oh. My. Gosh. Is this a *thing*? Are we talking about a *thing*?"

Amanda hesitated, as if she wasn't sure whether to say it out loud. "Not yet, but maybe."

Sammy's grin widened. "Amanda. This is *so* exciting! What's he like?"

Amanda was quiet for a beat. "He's great. Easy to be around. No pressure, just fun. And . . ." She hesitated, as if saying it out loud would make it real. "He makes me laugh in a way I haven't in a long time."

Sammy's heart softened. "Oh, Amanda."

Amanda let out a breath, almost as if she'd needed to tell someone. "I don't know what it is yet, but it feels different."

Sammy pulled her blanket a little tighter. "That's how it started with Jake too."

Amanda was quiet for a moment before murmuring, "Well, whatever this is, I'm enjoying it."

Sammy's smile deepened, her heart swelling with joy. "Oh, Amanda, I'm so happy for you."

They talked for another hour, laughter and stories filling the spaces between them, before finally deciding to be responsible adults and call it a night.

Chapter 42

When Sammy walked into her new office on Monday morning, a nervous thrill buzzed in her chest. She'd chosen dark-wash jeans, a simple teal top, and a long caramel cardigan—a mix of comfort and confidence that felt just right for the day ahead. Around her neck, Jake's necklace rested softly, its weight a steadying reminder of the support she now had in her life.

The faint scent of freshly brewed coffee greeted her as Cindy looked up from her desk with a welcoming smile.

"Good morning, Sammy! First day. How's it feel?"

"A little surreal," Sammy admitted with a laugh. "But good. Excited, mostly."

Cindy nodded approvingly, sliding a stack of papers toward her. "We just need to get you on the books. I-9, W-4, all the boring stuff. And this"—she tapped a stapled packet on top—"is your contract. Take your time, look it over, and get it back to me whenever you're ready."

Sammy picked up the stack, feeling the official weight of her new role. "Thanks, Cindy. I'll get this done soon."

"No rush. Oh, and Nelda's waiting for you in the conference room. She said she has your first big assignment ready."

Sammy's heart skipped. "Thanks for the heads-up!"

"Morning, Sammy!" Nelda said, her tone as bright as her smile. "Ready to dive in?"

"As ready as I'll ever be," Sammy replied, sliding into a chair with a grin.

"Good answer," Nelda said, passing her a folder. "This is your first assignment. It's big, but I think you're ready for it."

Sammy opened the folder, scanning the pages inside. Her brows furrowed slightly. "The land outside of town?"

"Exactly." Nelda leaned against the table, her expression growing thoughtful. "It's been sitting unused for years. The city council's interested, but I want us to present a plan before they get too many ideas."

Sammy nodded slowly. "Do you have something specific in mind?"

Nelda smiled. "Not yet. That's where you come in. I want your fresh perspective. Take the week. Talk to people, research, dream a little. Let's regroup next Monday, and you can share what you've come up with."

Sammy blinked, the weight of the task settling on her shoulders. "You trust me with this?"

Nelda's smile softened. "Absolutely. You've got the heart and vision this project needs. Now, it's time to put them to work."

A mix of excitement and nerves swirled, but she nodded firmly. "Okay. Let's do this."

Nelda gestured to a stack of photos and documents on the table. "These might help you get started—photos of the site and examples of what the space could become. Let's go over a few ideas."

As Sammy flipped through the images and listened to Nelda's explanations, her excitement grew. This wasn't just brainstorming. It was dreaming big, turning possibilities into realities. And somehow, she was getting paid a generous salary to do it. *Who knew adulting could be so fun?*

By the end of their time together, Sammy felt a surge of confidence. "All right," she said, closing the folder and meeting Nelda's gaze. "I'll have some ideas ready for you next Monday. Should I work from my office here, or . . . ?"

Nelda waved her hand with a warm smile. "Honey, go wherever your creative juices flow best! Take your time, think big, and don't hold back." As she stood, she placed a reassuring hand on Sammy's shoulder. "Sometimes the best ideas don't start with answers, but with the right questions."

Sammy left the conference room with the folder tucked under her arm and a spark of determination lit in her heart. By the time she reached her desk, she was already jotting down notes: *Sometimes you don't start with answers.*

You start with questions.

At the top of her notebook, she carefully wrote:

What does this land need to become?

Beneath it, she added a prayerful thought:

What does Willow Creek need from it? What does God want to see grow here?

Her mind flickered to her first days in Willow Creek—the uncertainty of starting over, the whispered prayers, the quiet hope that things would one day make sense. Step by step, God had led her here.

Now, hope had taken root. She didn't have all the answers, but she trusted that in God's perfect timing, the right path would bloom.

Sammy leaned back, gazing out the window. Below, shoppers strolled Main Street, pausing to chat or browse in the cheery storefronts. The quiet rhythm of Willow Creek life was simple and steady.

She tapped her pen on her notebook, the weight of the task settling in. If this idea was going to take root, it had to start where it mattered most—with the heart of Willow Creek. Its people.

Chapter 43

Sammy woke the next morning with a renewed sense of purpose. Lacing up her sneakers, she pushed herself to jog farther than usual, exploring quiet streets and hidden corners of Willow Creek. By the time she returned home, breathless but triumphant, she could feel it in her bones. This day was going to be different.

During her quiet time, she read a passage from Isaiah that stopped her in her tracks: "See, I am doing a new thing . . ." The words stirred something deep in her heart. A new job. Maybe even a deeper connection with someone. And something bigger—a change for Willow Creek itself.

Sipping her coffee, Sammy flipped through the notes she'd scribbled the night before. Her mission was clear: to listen to Willow Creek. What did the people hope for? Dream about?

Armed with her notebook and a few open-ended questions, she set out to discover the heartbeat of the town.

The scent of fresh coffee wrapped around Sammy as she stepped into Coffee with Your Cream Café,, the town's unofficial gathering place. Spotting Mrs. Jacobs by the window, surrounded by a stack of books, Sammy slid into the chair across from her.

"Good morning, Mrs. Jacobs," Sammy said with a warm smile. "Mind if I pick your brain?"

Mrs. Jacobs's eyes twinkled over the rim of her coffee cup. "Depends. Is this about getting mud out of clothes again? Because you already got my best tips last time."

Sammy chuckled, flipping open her notebook. "Not this time. And for the record, they worked!"

"I never doubted it." Mrs. Jacobs beamed.

Sammy grinned. "I'm asking around. If you could add something new to Willow Creek, what would it be?"

Mrs. Jacobs set her cup down, considering. "Well, I've always thought we need a proper event space. Weddings, concerts, even barn dances—it'd be nice to have somewhere modern but still charming. The community hall is fine, but it's outdated."

As Mrs. Jacobs returned to her book, Sammy glanced toward the counter. The morning rush had died down, and Lisa was wiping down the espresso machine, her movements easy and familiar.

Sammy leaned against the counter, her best *curious journalist* face in place. "Lisa, what about you?"

Lisa snorted. "What about what, Miss Sammy?"

Sammy grinned, knowing Lisa prided herself on being the town's unofficial news hub. "For once, I might have a piece of town news you *haven't* heard yet, and I definitely want your thoughts."

Lisa let out a half laugh, propping her elbows on the counter. "Well now, that's a bold claim." She smirked. "Good thing I'm an expert on my own opinion. Lay it on me. What's the question?"

Matching her stance, Sammy leaned in. "If you could add *one* thing to Willow Creek—something for locals, maybe something for tourists—what would it be?"

Lisa glanced past Sammy, out the café's large front windows, her expression thoughtful. "Main Street's pretty full, and Nelda and the others have curated it beautifully, but honestly?" She turned back with a knowing grin. "This town could use *another* coffee shop."

Lisa's voice carried, sharp and sure, as she straightened up and gestured around her café. "Now, don't get me wrong. I *love* my little shop. But let's be real, Sammy. I can't be the only source of caffeine in this town." She smirked, waving a hand as if that idea was *absurd*.

Sammy chuckled. "You think we need another coffee shop?"

Lisa scoffed. "Honey, have you *seen* this place at 8:00 a.m.? I got people lining up out the door, bless their caffeine-deprived souls. And don't even get me started on Saturdays during the farmers' market. Nelda nearly staged a riot last month when we ran out of scones by ten."

Sammy laughed, picturing Nelda leading a brigade of outraged early risers. "Okay, fair point. But do you really think a second shop would work? I mean, wouldn't it be competition for you?"

Lisa waved her off. "Please. This town's growing, and folks love options. A second place—maybe one with a little more seating, a cozy fireplace, something that makes you wanna sit and stay awhile? That'd be good for everyone. Besides, I wouldn't mind a day off where I could sit and sip my own coffee instead of making it."

Sammy tapped her pen against her notepad, intrigued. "So, you're saying we need a rival coffee empire?"

Lisa grinned. "Nah, let's call it a *friendly* caffeine alliance." Then, with a pointed look, she added, "And before you ask, no, I *do not* want to run it. I got my hands full right here, thank you very much."

Sammy smirked. "Noted."

Lisa folded her arms, studying her. "Alright, now my turn."

Sammy blinked. "Your turn for what?"

Lisa tilted her head, eyes twinkling. "How was Hank's the other night?" she asked, raising her eyebrows with a playful bounce.

Sammy felt the warmth rise in her cheeks, but she knew better than to let Lisa's teasing fluster her. Lisa had a way of mothering all of Willow Creek's young adults in her own playful way, and dodging the question would only make her more relentless. So, with a small, knowing smile, Sammy replied, "It was lovely."

Lisa studied her face and nodded. "The look on your face says everything I need to know." She tossed the towel over her shoulder and turned back to the espresso machine. "Mmm-hmm. Love's brewing in Willow Creek, and it ain't just the coffee."

Sammy groaned again, but despite herself, she was smiling.

Lisa glanced over her shoulder, her voice turning just a touch softer. "For real, though, Jake's a good one. Steady. Genuine. You could do a whole lot worse."

Sammy let out a breath, her smile settling into something smaller. She touched her necklace. "I couldn't agree more."

Lisa nodded, satisfied. "Good. Now, go finish your little town survey, and try not to daydream too hard while you're at it."

Sammy rolled her eyes, but her heart was light as she turned back to her notes.

Lisa, as usual, was right.

Next, Sammy visited Wilson Pharmacy, where Mr. Wilson was arranging a new card display.

"You know what Willow Creek needs?" he said, leaning over the counter. "A permanent farmers' market. Right now, it's hit-or-miss, depending on who's organizing. A dedicated space could bring in fresh produce, crafts, even visitors from nearby towns."

"That's fantastic," Sammy said, adding it to her growing list.

At the park, a group of mothers on a bench shared their wishes. "A place that would be fun for the kids to play!" one said, her voice brimming with excitement.

Another added, "It gets so hot in the summer, make sure it has lots of shade!"

"Speaking of hot, what about a small local movie theatre?" another mom added. "So we could take the kids somewhere air-conditioned too?" The moms all nodded in hopeful agreement.

Sammy thanked them, carefully noting every detail. Their enthusiasm was contagious.

Her next stop was Hank's Diner, where she was greeted by the scent of fresh coffee and sizzling bacon. The morning rush had slowed, leaving only a few scattered customers lingering over their meals.

Julie was behind the counter, wiping down a tray. When she saw Sammy, she grinned. "Hey, stranger. What's got you out and about this early?"

Sammy slid onto a stool, putting her bag on the counter in front of her. "Just gathering ideas, and you are just the person I hoped to run into here." She smiled and pulled out her notepad, tapping the cover with her pen.

"Hypothetically, let's say the town *might* be considering a new center on the outskirts. And *maybe* it'll have restaurants."

Julie arched a brow, leaning on the counter. "Might? Maybe?"

Sammy shrugged. "Nothing's set in stone yet, but I'm getting input. Seeing what people might want, what could work."

Julie nodded slowly. "Alright, I'm listening."

Sammy leaned in slightly, her voice laced with curiosity and hope. "So, have you ever considered taking your pies to the next level?"

Julie paused mid-wipe, blinking. "My *pies*?"

Sammy smiled nodding.

"Yes, ma'am. You're already selling them at Coffee with Your Cream Café, and people can't get enough." She leaned in, resting her chin on her hand and raising her eyebrows with a playful grin. "We're going to have restaurants there. Any chance you'd be interested in getting your pies on a few of their menus?"

Julie blinked again, the dish towel in her hands momentarily forgotten. "Wait, you think my pies could be in restaurants?"

Sammy grinned. "I know they could be."

Julie huffed out a breath, shaking her head. "Well, sure, folks like them, but selling to actual restaurants? That's a whole different ball game."

Sammy tilted her head, her voice steady. "Why not, though? You're already halfway there."

The bell over the diner's door jingled, cutting Sammy off.

Julie glanced toward the entrance, then back at her, brows furrowed in thought. "Hold that thought, Sammy."

Sammy smirked, closing her notebook. "Oh, I'm not going anywhere. Think on it."

As Julie stepped away to greet a customer, Sammy tapped her pen against the counter, a knowing smile playing on her lips.

Chapter 44

Julie bit her lip, clearly turning the idea over in her mind. "It would be nice to make a little more doing something I love," she admitted. Then she laughed, shaking her head. "I swear, Sammy, you've got this way of making people believe they can do anything."

Sammy grinned. "Because you can."

Julie exhaled, tapping her fingers against the counter. "Alright," she said finally. "I'll think about it. But if I end up buried under a mountain of pie crust, I'm blaming you."

Sammy laughed. "Fair enough."

Julie smirked, wiping her hands on a dish towel. "Now, since you're here, do you want a slice of peach pie? Fresh out of the oven. I'm testing a new recipe while it's slow today."

Sammy placed a hand over her heart, mock-serious. "Julie, I thought you'd never ask."

As Julie moved to grab a plate, Sammy jotted a note in her notebook: *Julie's Pies—restaurant supply potential?*

She smiled to herself. Willow Creek wasn't just growing. It was thriving. And, for the first time in a long time, she felt like she was thriving too.

At the post office, Mrs. Tanner suggested a community garden. "It'd be wonderful for folks to grow veggies or flowers, and teach kids about sustainability."

At the barber shop, Mr. Lyle didn't hesitate. "You know what we really need? More parking. No one likes hunting for a spot when the diner's full."

With each conversation, a pattern began to emerge—Willow Creek needed spaces for connection, fun, and practicality.

At Cooper's Hardware, Sammy approached Mr. Reynolds, a retired farmer known for his bluntness.

"What does this town need?" he repeated with a huff. "Nothing. Willow Creek's fine as is."

Sammy hesitated, pencil hovering over the page. "You don't think there's room for improvement?"

Mr. Reynolds crossed his arms. "Last time someone tried to 'improve' this place, we got those parking meters no one could figure out. If that's progress, I'll pass."

Sammy hesitated, tapping her pencil against her notebook. "But what if it was something that brought people together? Something that fits the character of Willow Creek?"

Mr. Reynolds grumbled, but his tone softened. "Depends on what it is. Just don't go making this place look like Austin or Dallas."

Sammy smiled. "Got it. Thanks for your thoughts."

"Hmph," he muttered, but there was a glimmer of approval in his eye as he shuffled off.

By late afternoon, Sammy found herself at Shelby's Boutique, sitting in a plush chair as Shelby twirled a scarf between her fingers.

"A mixed-use space," Shelby mused. "Shops, restaurants, maybe an art gallery. Somewhere people want to linger." She grinned. "And a good selfie spot. Teens love that."

Sammy's pencil flew across the page. "I love that idea. It could be a draw for both locals and visitors."

* * *

That evening, Sammy stepped onto the porch, tucking a freshly curled strand behind her ear. The scent of honeysuckle lingered in the air, carried by a soft breeze. And then, there was Jake.

Basket in one hand, a grin on his face, he climbed the porch steps effortlessly.

She blinked. "What's this?"

Jake lifted the basket slightly. "Sweet corn. We had a great harvest this year, and Abuelo wanted to make sure y'all got some of the best of it."

A slow smile spread across Sammy's face. Some things, like golden summer corn and Jake Martinez, only got better with time.

"Glory's going to be thrilled. She swears there's nothing better than fresh corn straight off the stalk."

Jake chuckled, setting the basket down. "She's not wrong." Then, reaching for Sammy's hand, he added, "Are you ready? I've got a table reserved for us."

The Italian bistro on the edge of town was everything she'd imagined—soft candlelight, the aroma of baking bread, the comforting hum of conversation.

"I've always wanted to try this place," she admitted, running a finger along the edge of her menu.

Jake smiled, eyes crinkling. "Then you're in for a treat."

As they ordered—pasta for her, steak for him—Jake leaned back, studying her with quiet curiosity. "How's the project with Nelda coming along?"

Sammy took a sip of water, choosing her words carefully. "It's exciting but busy. I've been gathering ideas from folks around town, things like a few chain stores, farmers' market, event space, a playground. But not everyone's on board."

Jake nodded, thoughtful. "Small towns can be slow to warm to change."

"That's exactly it." Sammy let out a slow breath, absentmindedly running her fingers over the charm on her necklace—the one Jake had given her. "This change—addition, really—is good, but how do I do it and not lose the heart of Willow Creek?"

Jake reached across the table, his hand warm and steady over hers. "You won't. You care too much for that."

Something in his voice, steady and certain, settled deep inside her.

Over dessert, Jake twirled his fork absently in his hand, watching her with that unreadable expression that always sent something warm through her.

Finally, he leaned forward. "Abuelo always says the best way to harvest is to do it together. Maybe that's the key for the land too—make sure folks feel like they're part of it."

Sammy's pencil hovered over her journal, heart catching on his words. "That's actually a really good point."

Jake shrugged with a grin. "I have my moments."

Sammy laughed, but her heart was doing that ridiculous thing again—beating too fast over the way he looked at her like she was the only thing in the room.

"What are you doing tomorrow?"

Sammy glanced up from her notebook. "Tomorrow?"

"Yeah. I'm teaching that monthly line dancing class at 10:00 a.m. in the senior center." He smiled, a little sheepish. "I think you'd really enjoy it. Plus, it'd give you a chance to hear from more folks in the community."

Sammy grinned, pulling out her phone. "I'm totally available. Adding it to my calendar now." She paused and looked up at him. "What should I wear?"

Jake chuckled, clearly pleased by her enthusiasm. "Great! As for what to wear . . ." He leaned back, giving her a once-over with an exaggeratedly thoughtful look. "Something comfortable. Boots if you've got 'em. But most of the ladies show up in their sneakers, so you'll fit in just fine either way."

Sammy tapped the details into her phone, then glanced up at him with a teasing smile. "So, should I be preparing myself for a lot of two-stepping and do-si-do-ing?"

Jake laughed. "It's not that fancy. Just some basic steps, lots of laughter, and if you're lucky, a few of the seniors might share some of their best life advice in between dances."

Sammy's expression softened. "That actually sounds perfect."

His gaze lingered on her for a beat longer than necessary, something unreadable flickering across his face before he shook his head with a grin.

As they stepped out into the cool night air, the conversation lingered between them, easy and unhurried. The drive home was filled with quiet moments, the occasional hum of an old country tune playing through the speakers.

Jake walked her to the porch, picking up the now-empty basket. A lone envelope rested inside, the name scrawled in familiar handwriting.

"Edmund," he murmured, slipping it into his back pocket. "I'll take this home, then."

She exhaled, steadying herself. "Hey, Jake?"

He turned, eyes steady, expectant.

Before she could second-guess herself, she made her choice and closed the space between them not because she had to, but because she wanted to. Her hand found his shoulder, and from her step above him, she was almost at eye level.

She leaned in and kissed him.

Jake froze for half a beat before responding, his free hand finding her waist—warm, steady.

When they pulled apart, she was smiling, and so was he.

Jake exhaled, a slow, contented sound. "Well, you just made my whole night."

Sammy's voice was soft. "I didn't want you to leave without knowing how I feel."

Jake cupped her cheek, his voice steady. "I already know. But anytime you want to remind me, I won't mind."

* * *

Sammy flipped open her journal that night, her fingers running over the worn pages before she clicked her pen.

> "Faith is being sure of what you hope for, certain of what you cannot see." —Hebrews 11:1
>
> She paused, letting the words settle.
>
> Lord, I don't always see the full picture. But I know You do. And I trust You're leading me in this project exactly where you want it to go.

She closed the journal, turned off the light, and pulled the blankets around her.

As she drifted to sleep, the words of Hebrews 11:1 wove through her thoughts like a quiet promise.

Chapter 45

The Willow Creek Senior Center buzzed with energy, its high ceilings echoing with laughter and the faint twang of a country song playing through the speakers. The polished hardwood floors gleamed under the fluorescent lights, the scent of lemon cleaner and lavender mingling in the air—a perfect blend of order and nostalgia.

Glory and Ethel Sue were already at the front, deep in conversation with Lora, who was fanning herself despite the air conditioning. A few younger faces peppered the room—twenty- and thirty-somethings who had likely been roped in by an enthusiastic grandparent or enticed by the promise of free snacks afterward.

By the sound of it, no one regretted showing up.

Near the portable speaker, Jake, in a well-worn flannel and boots that had seen their fair share of dirt and dance floors, fiddled with his phone, scrolling for the next track. At the sight of Sammy and Nelda, his grin spread slow and easy.

"Glad you made it."

Sammy set her purse down on a folding chair. "Wouldn't miss it."

Glory clapped her hands together. "Alright, let's get to it before my knees decide they've had enough."

Ethel Sue patted her shoulder. "That's what knee braces are for, darling."

Lora adjusted her glasses. "Are we doing the same routine as last time? Because I still haven't quite recovered from that spin move."

Jake chuckled. "Don't worry, we'll start easy."

Nelda leaned toward Sammy, whispering conspiratorially, "Last month,

Ethel Sue tried to add her own flair to the routine and nearly took out a whole row of chairs."

Ethel Sue huffed. "It was an *enthusiastic* side step. Those chairs were too close together anyway."

Jake, clearly accustomed to their antics, clapped his hands. "Alright, everyone. First-timers, don't worry. Just follow along. If you get it wrong, make it look like you meant to."

The music kicked up, the twangy chords filling the air as the group moved into step.

Step, step, heel tap, turn.

"Now add a clap!" Jake called.

Some clapped on time. Others were a full beat late, setting off a domino effect of off-rhythm claps that had the entire room dissolving into laughter.

Jake shook his head, grinning. "Alright, let's try that again."

Glory whooped in delight when she nailed the next turn. Ethel Sue threw her arms up victoriously, and poor George Cummings, who had been dragged here by his wife, stared down at his feet like they'd betrayed him in a time of great need.

When the song came to an end, the group cheered and clapped, breathless but grinning.

Jake turned to Sammy, his eyes twinkling with mischief. "Fun, right?"

Sammy gasped for air, laughing. "So fun."

George wiped his brow, looking exasperated but amused. "I don't know about fun, but I do know I'll be needing a nap."

Lora patted his arm, all reassurance. "That's just the adrenaline talking, dear."

Jake clapped his hands again. "Who's up for one more round?"

Ethel Sue groaned dramatically. "Oh, bless it."

Glory grinned. "You know you love it."

The music started again, and Sammy let herself sink into the moment—the laughter, the movement, the simple joy of being part of something bigger than herself.

As the final song ended and the last stomp of boots echoed through the hall, the group broke into scattered applause.

Lora fanned herself with both hands. "Whew! That was better than any exercise class I've ever taken."

Ethel Sue nodded. "And a whole lot more fun."

Jake tucked his hands in his pockets, his expression turning thoughtful. "Before we wrap up, Sammy's got a question for y'all."

Sammy stepped forward, flipping open her notebook, the pages already filled with notes and ideas. "I have something I'd love your thoughts on." She took a steadying breath. "When you hear the phrase, 'The best way to harvest is to do it together,' what does that mean to you?"

A thoughtful silence settled over the room.

Lora adjusted her glasses again. "Farming, of course. Harvesting takes a team."

Ethel Sue nodded firmly. "But it's more than just crops. It's legacy. You pass down what you know, what you've built, what you've worked hard for. Whether it's farming, a family business, or just showing up for your neighbor—you don't do it alone. Not if you want it to last."

George, still catching his breath, rubbed his chin. "My father used to say you never plant just for yourself. You plant so your neighbor has enough too. Back in the day, we didn't call it charity. We just called it being a good neighbor."

A wave of agreement murmured through the room.

Lora tapped her chin. "It's like raising kids. We always say it takes a village. A town works the same way. It thrives when people pitch in."

Sammy scribbled furiously, capturing their words.

You never plant just for yourself.

A town works best when everyone plays a part.

Stronger together.

A legacy lasts when people invest in it.

She finished writing and glanced out the window, where the sun spilled over the sidewalk leading up to the center. A hint at the missing piece she hadn't known she was looking for.

Ethel Sue eyed her knowingly. "Sammy, this isn't just about farming, is it?"

Sammy smiled softly. "No, ma'am. It's not."

Jake watched her, his expression warm and steady. "Looks like you found your answer."

Sammy met his gaze, something settling deep in her heart.

Not quite yet. But she was close.

As Sammy stepped out of the senior center, their words lingered—legacy, community, planting for others. The vision was forming, but how did it all come together? She needed clarity. And caffeine. Definitely caffeine.

* * *

Coffee with Your Cream Café, was as inviting as ever, with its striped awning and the soft clink of ceramic mugs behind the counter. The chalkboard sign today read:

Today's Special: Hazelnut Latte & A Slice of Kindness.

Sammy stepped inside, breathing in the rich aroma of fresh coffee and vanilla. A few locals sat at the tables, chatting quietly, and a couple of tourists browsed the display of homemade jams and hand-poured candles near the window.

Lisa set the steaming cup in front of Sammy, a delicate swirl of foam floating on top. "So, what's next on this big project of yours?"

Sammy wrapped her hands around the warm mug, letting the heat soak into her palms. "I've got a few more interviews this week. I'm trying to get a real sense of what the community needs and how we can actually make it happen."

Lisa leaned on the counter, her expression thoughtful. "That's ambitious. But if anyone can pull it off, it's you."

Sammy's cheeks warmed. "I hope so. Right now, it feels like this giant puzzle, and I'm not even sure I have all the pieces."

Lisa smirked. "That's how the best things start." She tapped a finger on the counter, her voice turning thoughtful. "When I opened this place, I didn't have a grand business plan—just a dream and a coffee pot. It took trial and error, and plenty of long nights wondering if I'd made the right choice. But you know what? One day, it just clicked. Because when something's meant to be, you figure it out as you go."

Sammy nodded, her fingers tracing the rim of her mug. "That's exactly how I feel about this project. I want it to be a place where people feel connected. Where they belong." She grinned. "And, okay, maybe a little retail therapy wouldn't hurt either."

Lisa laughed. "That's the spirit." She pointed at Sammy's mug. "You're doing the work, and you've got your heart in the right place. The rest? It'll come together. Just give it time."

Sammy took a final sip of her latte, then pushed back from the counter. "I better get back to the office."

Lisa held up a finger. "One sec." She grabbed a small pastry bag, tucking a warm scone inside. Then, with a quick flick of her pen, she scrawled something on the bag before handing it to Sammy.

"This is for Cindy," she said, her voice softer now.

Sammy took the bag, glancing at the note Lisa had scribbled on it: *For when the day needs a little extra sweetness.*

A lump formed in her throat. Lisa always noticed.

Not just the big things, but the little ones too—the unseen heartaches, the weary sighs people thought no one heard.

Cindy had been struggling, and Lisa? She didn't ask. She just acted.

Sammy smiled, tucking the bag into her purse. "You're the best, you know that?"

Lisa shrugged, wiping down the counter like it was no big deal. "Just keeping my caffeine alliance running strong."

Sammy chuckled, giving her a grateful nod. "See you later, Lisa."

As she stepped outside, the morning air crisp around her, Sammy clutched the bag a little tighter. It wasn't just about the project. It was about people—and making sure no one felt alone.

As she made her way back to the office, she pulled out her phone.

A plan was forming, but she needed a fresh perspective to help shape it.

Sammy: *Any chance I could buy you lunch at Hank's today?*

Glory: *Oh goodness, what for?!*

Sammy: *I need an insider's point of view, and I think you're just the gal I'm looking for.*

Glory: *Well, with that being the case, I would be honored. See ya in an hour?*

Sammy: *Perfect.*

With renewed energy, she picked up her pace, she had things to do to prep for her important lunch date.

* * *

At Hank's, the familiar clatter of dishes and warm hum of chatter filled the air. Sammy leaned in, her notebook open between her and Glory as Julie delivered their drinks.

Sammy drummed her fingers lightly against the notebook. "I've been bouncing a lot of ideas around lately, but I realized I need someone who really knows the heart of this town."

Glory's brows lifted with interest. "Let's hear it, sweetheart."

Sammy nodded, flipping open her notebook but hesitating for half a second before sliding it toward Glory. "Here's what I've got so far."

Sammy flipped to a simple sketch of the project and turned it toward her grandmother. "It's looking like a commercial community space. A place for everyone to gather and feel connected. A pavilion for events, a permanent farmers' market, a playground with a splash pad, and plenty of shaded seating."

Glory studied the sketch, her brow furrowing thoughtfully. "It's a good start, Sammy. I can see the heart in it already. But what's the why behind it? Why do you think Willow Creek needs this?"

Sammy glanced down at her notes, then back at Glory. "Because Willow Creek is special, but it's growing. This project isn't just about expansion. It's about preserving what makes us who we are while creating something that keeps our light shining for generations to come."

Glory tapped a finger against her glass, nodding slowly. "That's a strong vision, sweetheart. But how are you going to keep it from turning into just another commercial shopping spot?"

Sammy's eyes lit up. "Great question!" She flipped to a new page, turning her notebook so Glory could see. Several collage-style sections filled the page, images clipped or sketched in different spaces.

"These," Sammy pointed to the first set of images, "are specifically designed for gathering, not retail. No storefronts, no pressure to buy anything. Just spaces where people can come together."

Glory leaned in, studying the layout. "Like what?"

"Think outdoor seating under big shady oaks, a central pavilion for events—concerts, weddings, even church picnics," Sammy explained. "And here?" She tapped another section. "A permanent community garden."

Glory smiled, something proud and knowing in her gaze. "Now that's the kind of place folks will keep coming back to."

Julie returned with their plates, flashing a friendly smile. "Y'all talking about Sammy's big project? Can't wait to see what you come up with!"

As Julie walked away, Glory leaned forward, her voice warm. "You're on the right track, Sammy. I can already see it. A place where folks find more than they expected—connection, memories, even a little hope."

A lump rose in Sammy's throat, but she smiled through it. "Thanks, Glory. That means everything." She hesitated, her fingers toying with the edge of her notebook. "I am a bit nervous about presenting this to Nelda."

Glory gave a knowing smile. "Well, just like a garden, you start with seeds. You tend to them, give them room to grow, and trust that in time, the strongest ones will bloom."

Sammy let out a breath, nodding as she closed her notebook. "Guess it's time to start planting."

Glory squeezed her hand gently. "And trust that in time, the right things will bloom."

As Sammy gathered her things, she felt a peace wash over her. The seeds were planted. Now came the next step—sharing it with Nelda and seeing which seeds were ready to bloom.

Chapter 46

"Happy Monday, Sammy!"

Cindy's voice carried across the front office, bright and chipper as ever. "Nelda's been talking about your meeting all morning. She's ready for you. Just go right in."

Sammy gripped the leather strap of her bag a little tighter. *Here we go.*

"Thanks, Cindy," she said, mustering up a smile as she walked toward Nelda's office.

The door stood slightly ajar, and with a quick knock, she pushed it open. Nelda sat at her desk, flipping through a ledger, but as soon as she looked up, her expression softened into a welcoming smile. "Sammy! Come on in."

The warmth in her tone did what deep breaths couldn't—it steadied her.

"I've been looking forward to this," Nelda continued, setting aside her paperwork and moving toward the conference table by the window. "You ready?"

Ready? No. But God had opened doors she hadn't expected, and she wasn't about to step back now.

Sammy nodded, sliding into the chair across from Nelda. "I hope so."

Her fingers traced the smooth edges of the folder in front of her. Inside were her notes, collages, sketches. Conversations. Ideas. This wasn't just a proposal; it was her heart on paper.

Nelda laced her fingers together, studying her. "How's your first week been?"

Sammy blew out a breath, leaning back. "Good. Fast-paced. I've met so many people and heard so many perspectives. It's been a lot to take in. Some ideas excite me. Others . . ." She hesitated. "Feel overwhelming."

Nelda's mouth curled into an approving smile. "That's exactly how a big vision should feel at the start. Overwhelming and impossible until you put it at the Lord's feet and take the first step forward."

Sammy's nerves relaxed. She opened the folder and slid two packets forward. "Willow Creek is growing. And with that growth comes a need—a space that brings people together. A hub. A heartbeat for the town."

She flipped open the first page of the design layout. "I'm calling it *The Grove.* It's a commercial space, yes. But at its core, it's a community space. A place where people can gather and connect, and where Willow Creek's charm is preserved, not lost."

She turned the next page. A detailed illustration of the center took shape between them. "At the heart is the Community Green Space—large, open, shaded by our existing oak trees. It's designed for concerts, outdoor movies, weddings, even church picnics. A place where families can come, sit, enjoy, and share life."

Nelda's sharp blue eyes flicked over the sketches. "Keep going."

Encouraged, Sammy pointed to the surrounding areas. "Lining the green, we'd have a mix of retail shops and restaurants, including a farm-to-table restaurant that sources local produce. Over here"—she turned the page—"a permanent community garden, where folks can grow veggies, swap gardening tips, and contribute to the town's sustainability efforts."

Sammy's pulse kicked up as she reached the final page. *The best part.* "And here, a dedicated play area. A splash pad for the summer. A shaded playground for year-round use. Every generation would have a place in The Grove."

Nelda sat back in her chair, fingers steepled. "It's impressive, Sammy."

Sammy held her breath.

"But," Nelda added, "what's the heart of it?"

Sammy met her gaze, exhaling slowly as she gathered her thoughts. "It's about belonging."

She thought of the laughter at the senior center, the way Lisa always knew when someone needed a little extra kindness, the way Mr. Reynolds grumbled about change but never failed to show up for his neighbors.

"It's about giving people a place where they feel rooted—where they can share their lives, their milestones, and even the everyday moments that make a town feel like home. The Grove wouldn't just be another development. It would be a reflection of what makes Willow Creek special. A place where people find connection, community, and a sense of belonging. Whether they've been here for generations or are just passing through, they'll know this is a place they can call home, even if just for a little while."

Nelda studied her a moment longer before nodding. "I like it."

Relief washed over Sammy in a whoosh.

"But," Nelda continued, "the city council will want more than a pretty pitch. They'll ask about budget. Logistics. They'll wonder if the community will support this."

Sammy nodded. "That's why I'm planning to hold a community Q&A before anything's finalized. Let people voice their thoughts. Make sure this feels like theirs, not just mine."

Nelda nodded. "Smart." She shuffled through the pages, and then added, "I can hardly believe this is your first pitch. It is really thought through well, but I feel like there is just something missing."

Sammy hesitated, then pulled out a separate folder. "There's one more thing."

Intrigued, Nelda leaned in. Sammy slid a page across the table, filled with images of pathways—brick-lined, engraved walkways, dedication plaques. "I kept thinking about something Edmund Martinez said: 'The best way to harvest is to do it together.'"

She tapped the page. "What if we created a *Legacy Pathway*?"

Nelda lifted a brow.

"A walkway through The Grove, made up of bricks people can buy—engraved with family names, businesses, dedications. A way for Willow Creek to invest in its future."

Nelda's fingers grazed the image of an engraved brick. "A pathway of names . . ."

Sammy nodded, heart pounding with excitement. "And every brick purchase would support the food pantry. The Grove would match a portion of donations every year as a long-term commitment to this town." She swallowed. "It's not just a fundraiser. It's an investment. A way to say, 'I was part of this. I believe in this town.'"

Silence stretched between them. Then, a slow smile broke across Nelda's face. "Sammy, I think you just found the missing piece."

For the next hour, they strategized—mapping out how to present the idea to the city council, discussing partnerships with local businesses, and brainstorming ways to bring the vision to life.

Sammy left the office with a to-do list a mile long, but the excitement in her chest made it feel doable.

* * *

As Sammy sank into the porch swing beside Glory, she let out a slow, contented breath, filling her lungs with the crisp, mid-September air. The warmth of the day had faded into a perfect coolness, the scent of earth and faintly lingering honeysuckle weaving through the breeze.

Glory studied her, a knowing smile tugging at the corners of her lips. "You look like someone with a heart full of hope."

Sammy twisted Jake's charm on her necklace between her fingers. "That's exactly how I feel."

Glory's eyes twinkled. "Nelda liked it?"

"She did. But now comes the hard part—making it happen." Sammy hesitated. "What if I mess it up?"

Glory's expression softened. "Sweetheart. Anything built with love and care will always feel like home."

She reached beside her and handed Sammy a rectangle wrapped in brown kraft paper.

Sammy peeled it open, and the moment her eyes landed on the lettering, her breath caught.

Cream-colored wood, slightly worn at the edges, as if it had already carried years of truth.

Her fingers traced the painted words:

"For I know the plans I have for you," declares the LORD, "plans to prosper you and not to harm you, plans to give you hope and a future." —Jeremiah 29:11

Something inside her settled.

She blinked quickly, willing away the tears. "Oh, Glory . . ." Her voice wobbled. "This is perfect."

Glory squeezed her hand. "Just a little something for your office. A reminder that the plans may be in your hands, but the future's in God's."

Sammy hugged the sign and then hugged Glory.

Because somehow, deep in her heart, she knew—

This was only the beginning.

Chapter 47

Sammy woke early the next morning, the memory of her presentation to Nelda still fresh and a sense of purpose humming in her chest. Stretching, she smiled, feeling as though the weight of her dreams had shifted into focus. Today called for something different, she decided

After pulling on her running clothes, she grabbed her Bible, journal, and Glory's car keys. "Going somewhere special?" Glory called from her spot at the kitchen table, her mug of coffee steaming beside her.

"Just a little road trip," Sammy replied with a grin. "I need to clear my head."

Glory nodded knowingly. "Well, drive safe and don't forget to listen while you're out there."

Sammy chuckled. "Always."

The drive out to the site where The Grove would one day stand felt peaceful.The morning sun bathed the fields in gold as a breeze stirred the roadside grasses. As Sammy pulled into the open space, her heart swelled with possibility. This land, quiet and unassuming now, would soon hum with life and connection—a place where people would gather, laugh, and make memories.

* * *

Sammy stepped out of the car, slipped in her earbuds, and started her jog. Her feet pounded a steady rhythm along the property's perimeter, her breaths syncing with the beat of her favorite worship playlist. With each step, she prayed.

"Lord, guide this place. Let it be a blessing. Let it be a space where people feel loved, seen, and known."

As the music faded, her steps slowed to a walk. She wandered through the center of the lot, letting her imagination bring the space to life. *Over here,* she thought, *families will lay out blankets for summer movie nights. And there—right there—is the perfect spot for the farm-to-table restaurant.* She could almost see couples strolling arm in arm under twinkling lights, their laughter floating on the breeze.

In the distance, she pictured the play area, bright with colors and filled with the joyful squeals of children. Sammy smiled, imagining little Adeline darting through the splash pad, her giggles blending with the chatter of nearby parents.

At the back of the property, she stopped and closed her eyes. In her mind, the space transformed—rows of vibrant vegetables and blooming flowers, neighbors working side by side. She could hear their laughter and the quiet hum of camaraderie.

Returning to her car, Sammy grabbed her Bible and journal. She made her way to the spot she'd mentally marked as the future community green space and settled onto the grass. The warmth of the sun kissed her skin as she opened her Bible to where she'd left off: Hebrews 11.

Her eyes were drawn to a repeated phrase: by faith, by faith, by faith. She began circling the words, her heart quickening with each one. It felt as though the Holy Spirit was weaving a message just for her.

Sammy paused, looking around at the open, desolate space. It was so quiet, so still, and yet her heart overflowed with visions of what this place could become. By faith.

Opening her journal, she began to write.

> By faith . . . so many have gone before me, chasing their purpose.
> And now, I feel like I'm finally stepping into mine.

Her pen hovered as memories flooded in, and she began listing her gratitude, one moment at a time.

Her throat tightened as she let her heart lead.

> **Sarah**—her unwavering support. The way she always knew what to say.
>
> **The food pantry**—the elderly man who whispered thank you and clutched her hand that first week.
>
> **Summer camp**—the day of the mud fight, where she laughed until she couldn't breathe.
>
> **Michelle**—forgiveness and healing she never saw coming.
>
> **The porch talks with Glory**—prayers whispered under the stars, cups of tea, life slowed down enough to be savored.
>
> **Glory's bridge gals**—women who wrapped her in family when she didn't even know she needed one.
>
> **Nelda**—a woman who believed in her, pushed her, challenged her to dream bigger.

She hesitated, then wrote the last name, her heart skipped a beat.

> **Jake**—his steady presence. His quiet way of seeing her. His deep, genuine goodness and faith. Getting to have a real relationship with an amazing guy.

Sammy exhaled, tracing her finger over the ink.

Somehow, some way, God had written Jake into her story, and she hadn't even seen it coming.

She turned her gaze to the sky.

"Ephesians 3:20 is right. More than I could hope or imagine." She whispered the words, a small smile tugging at her lips.

She hugged her knees to her chest, letting the moment settle deep.

The quiet, the hope, the faith in what she couldn't yet see.

A breeze stirred the pages of her Bible, and she smiled.

God was here. In all of it.

* * *

When Sammy returned home, Glory was waiting on the porch swing with two cups of coffee.

"Well?" Glory asked, patting the seat beside her.

Sammy grinned, settling onto the swing. "It's going to be amazing, Glory. I can feel it. In my study time, I kept seeing 'by faith.' I am just certain this is going to be so great!"

Glory sipped her coffee, a quiet smile playing on her lips. "By faith, sweetheart. That's how all the best things start."

Sammy breathed deeply, letting the moment settle around her like a quiet promise.

By faith.

That's how all the best things start.

And this?

This was just the beginning.

Epilogue

The May sun dipped behind the newly constructed buildings, casting a golden glow over The Grove. Sammy stood near the community green space, checklist in hand, her gaze drifting across the progress. The commercial and retail spaces were on schedule and already fifty percent leased. The play area was nearly finished, the splash pad's tiles gleamed in the late light, and the garden beds had just been tilled—fresh and ready for planting.

Everything was coming together, just as she'd dreamed.

The sound of gravel crunching beneath boots pulled her attention. She turned to see Jake walking toward her, a basket in one hand and that familiar smile lighting up his face.

"Hey, sweet Sammy," he called, voice warm and familiar.

"I was so glad when I got your text that you were bringing dinner," Sammy replied as her stomach rumbled. "I'm starving!"

Jake grinned and held up the basket. "I aim to please," he said, greeting her with a kiss. "Thought we could enjoy a little picnic right here to celebrate everything you've accomplished."

Her heart swelled as he nodded toward the picnic table beneath the old oak tree. Together, they spread out a tablecloth, and Sammy settled in as Jake unpacked Edmund's tacos, tortilla chips, and jars of homemade salsa.

"This is perfect," Sammy said, biting into one. "You're spoiling me, Jake Martinez."

"Not spoiling," he replied with a teasing grin. "Just blessing you—and cheering you on."

As they ate, they chatted about The Grove, the latest town news, and the new outreach minister starting next month. But Sammy couldn't shake the feeling that something about Jake was different tonight. He seemed both calm and nervous, like a quiet excitement was simmering just under the surface.

When their meal was finished, Jake stood and extended a hand to her. "I want to show you something," he said, his eyes warm and inviting.

Curious, Sammy stood and brushed the crumbs from her jeans. Jake kept her hand in his, leading her to the center of the green space.

"Can you believe it's only been a year since we met?" Jake asked softly.

Sammy smiled, her heart tugging at the memory. "Barely a year, and yet so much has changed."

He stopped and turned to face her, his gaze locking on hers. "A year ago, I couldn't have imagined this—this past year or you. But now I can't imagine life without either."

Her heart skipped a beat as Jake reached into his pocket and pulled out a small velvet box. His grip on her hand tightened gently.

"Sammy," he said, voice steady but thick with emotion. "You've brought so much light into my life. You've taught me how to dream again. How to trust. How to love. I don't want to spend another year—or another day—without you by my side."

Then, he dropped to one knee.

He opened the box to reveal a simple, elegant diamond ring that shimmered in the soft light. The world seemed to pause, the evening hush settling around them like a held breath.

"Will you marry me?"

Sammy's breath caught as emotion surged—disbelief, joy, gratitude.

The moment wrapped around her like a promise, tender and breathtaking. She thought of the countless small steps the Lord had guided her through to bring her here, and how this past year with Jake—from rooster wrangling to morning rides and evening dances beneath the stars—had been the sweetest season she'd ever known.

Her hand flew to her mouth, eyes brimming with tears. Her chest tightened with the sweet ache of it all. "Jake," she whispered, voice trembling. "Yes. Yes, of course!"

The words had barely left her lips when cheers erupted from behind the trees. Sammy turned, startled, only to see Glory and Edmund, Nelda, Sarah and her family, Ethel Sue, Lora, Pastor Mark, and others stepping out from their hiding spots, clapping and grinning.

Sammy laughed through her tears as Jake slipped the ring onto her finger, then stood and wrapped her in a strong embrace while the crowd cheered around them.

"You planned this?" she asked, her voice thick with emotion.

He smiled against her hair. "I couldn't imagine asking without everyone who loves you here to celebrate."

Glory approached first and pulled Sammy into a tight hug. "Oh, sweetheart, I've been waiting for this moment since the day you arrived." She stepped back, then turned her phone screen to Sammy. "And say hi to the family!"

Her mom, dad, and siblings filled the screen, all of them waving and beaming.

"We're so happy for you, Sammy!" her dad said proudly.

"Yeah, we are," Chris added with a half smirk. "But I still need to meet this guy," he said, shooting Jake a raised brow.

"Oh, you will!" Sammy replied, laughing. "And hopefully soon!"

Then Nelda stepped forward, taking Sammy's hands in hers. "You deserve every bit of happiness coming your way, Sammy."

As the rest of the group crowded around, Jake kept an arm around Sammy, holding her close. The sun dipped below the horizon, and lanterns hanging from the oak trees began to glow, casting a magical light over the scene.

Later, after the last hug had been given and the crowd had drifted home, Sammy walked the new walkway with name after name on the bricks, Jake at her side. She took his hand lightly in hers.

"You okay?" Jake asked softly, his fingers brushing hers.

She glanced around, breathing in the scent of fresh soil and cut wood from the buildings going up, the cool hush of twilight wrapped around her like a prayer answered.

"I'm more than okay," she said with a smile.

Jake slipped his hand into hers again. "Good."

For a long moment, they stood in comfortable silence, watching the stars peek out one by one.

Jake gave her hand a soft squeeze. "Penny for your thoughts?"

Sammy turned to face him, her heart full to the brim. She'd been thinking about the long journey of the past year and how the woman I used to be might not even recognize the one standing here now.

Her eyes dropped to the ring on her finger, then lifted back to the man in front of her—the one who had become her safe place, her best friend, her greatest blessing.

She stepped closer, placing a hand against his chest, feeling the steady beat of his heart beneath her palm. "I think I finally found what I was looking for," she whispered.

Jake's brow lifted gently. "Oh yeah?"

She smiled, soft and sure, and gave a small nod. "It wasn't about having the perfect plan," she said. "It was about following God's plan. And in doing that . . ." Her voice caught as tears welled in her eyes. "He gave me the most beautiful gift."

Jake cupped her face in his hands, his thumb brushing gently along her cheek. "What gift is that?"

Her smile wobbled as tears slipped down her cheeks—tears of gratitude, of peace, of finally knowing she was home. "A place to belong," she whispered.

Jake pulled her into his arms, holding her close. And in that quiet embrace, beneath the starlit sky and the echo of all they'd walked through, Sammy finally exhaled.

She had spent so long searching.

But in the end, she hadn't needed to chase down answers or map out every detail.

God had written a better story than she ever could have planned, and it had led her here.

Right where she was always meant to be.

Note from Melissa

Do you wish you could have looked over Sammy's shoulder and read that Still Becoming devotional she was going thru?

Yeah, me too. :)

So, I created it.

You can find it at **melissaalyse.com**/stillbecoming

May you always have the courage to follow the call on your heart, even when the path is winding. Because if you do, you'll be blessed to discover that it truly is *far more than you could ever hope or imagine* (Ephesians 3:20).

Sending you grace + big hugs,

-melissa.

PS. Ready to hear Michelle's story? Because that's book two.

Turn the page to get a sneak peek because, she saw the proposal too.

Get the 7 day Still Becoming devotional here, my free gift to you. ⟶

Fifteen Minutes After Sammy and Jake's Engagement

Michelle Harper didn't cry in public.

Not at events.

Not at church.

And certainly not in the middle of a construction project with half of Willow Creek watching.

So when she reached her car, she didn't slam the door.

She didn't fall apart.

She simply sat.

Hands still folded in her lap. Back straight. Breathing measured.

Like she had done a thousand times before.

Through the windshield, the last of the crowd lingered, laughter carrying through the warm evening air. Someone shouted Sammy's name. Another voice called for pictures. The celebration stretched on, effortless and bright.

Michelle stared straight ahead.

She could still see it.

Sammy's face—open, overwhelmed, completely unguarded.

The way Jake had looked at her.

Like there had never been a question.

Michelle swallowed, her throat tight.

"Of course he did," she murmured under her breath.

Of course Jake would choose someone like Sammy.

Someone who didn't have to think about every word before she said it.

Someone who didn't carry the weight of an entire legacy on her shoulders.

Someone who didn't feel like she had to be perfect just to be enough.

Her fingers tightened slightly against her skirt.

It wasn't jealousy.

Not exactly.

She was happy for them. She really was.

But there was something else, too.

Something quieter.

Something harder to name.

Her phone buzzed in the cupholder, the sharp sound cutting through the stillness.

Mom.

Michelle closed her eyes for half a second before answering.

"Yes, ma'am."

"I saw the photos already," her mother's voice came through, crisp and composed. "The Benson girl posted them within minutes. Honestly, no sense of timing."

Michelle glanced toward the crowd again. Sammy was laughing now, her hand still wrapped around Jake's.

"They look very happy," Michelle said carefully.

"They do," her mother replied. A pause. "Which means we need to be mindful of appearances this weekend. Your birthday celebration is at full capacity, and people will be watching."

Of course they would.

"They always are," Michelle said softly.

"I've already confirmed your dress," her mother continued. "The blue one. It photographs well, and it sends the right message."

Michelle's grip tightened around the phone.

"Right," she echoed.

"Exactly. And Michelle?" Her mother's tone softened just enough to sound intentional. "You represent the Harper family. There is no need to be perturbed over this."

The line went quiet.

Michelle lowered the phone slowly, setting it back in the cupholder.

For a long moment, she didn't move.

Then, almost without thinking, her gaze drifted back to the celebration one last time.

Sammy leaned into Jake, laughing at something Glory said, her whole face lit up with something Michelle had never quite been able to hold onto.

Ease.

Belonging.

Love that didn't require performance.

Michelle's chest tightened.

"What would that even feel like?" she whispered.

The question lingered in the quiet car, unanswered.

Outside, the celebration carried on.

Inside, something small—but undeniable—shifted.

And for the first time in a long time, Michelle wasn't thinking about what was expected of her.

She was wondering what it might feel like to want something for herself.

Scan the QR code to get Michelle's story, Letting Go of Perfect. It's a heartfelt journey about expectations, identity, and the courage it takes to create the legacy you long to live.

Ready to return to Willow Creek? Michelle's story continues in Book 2.
Download it here.

Acknowledgments

This story would not exist without the grace of God, whose timing, plans, and love are far greater than anything I could ever imagine. So grateful He helped me find the words to tell this first story on my heart.

To my husband, Luke: Thank you for believing in me when I doubted myself, for encouraging me all along to finish Sammy and Jake's story, and for being my steady place in every season. You're my favorite chapter.

To my precious kiddos, who aren't really kiddos anymore: Thank you for encouraging and inspiring me more than you could ever know.

To my sweet mama, Cindie Vaughan: You are my biggest fan and strongest cheerleader. Thank you for praying for me, for being my very first beta reader, and for proofreading this book not once, but twice. Your love and support mean more than words can say.

To the incredible gals of the Front Porch Preview Team—your early reads, sweet encouragement, and overflowing support meant the world to me. You made this journey feel like a cozy gathering of friends with open hearts. Thank you for loving this story so well.

To Laura Ann, thank you for being a light on this path. Your encouragement, guidance, and genuine kindness has meant more than you know.

Thank you to my editor, Bethany Lenderink. You are a gem to work with!

With love and gratitude,

-melissa :)

Book Club & Reflection Questions

1. *Themes & Story Discussion*

Porch swings & pivotal moments: Sammy has some of her deepest realizations on Glory's porch swing. If you had to pick a "porch swing moment" from your own life—a time or place where things clicked into perspective—what would it be?

When plans fall apart: Sammy's carefully laid plans fall apart, but something better emerges. Have you ever experienced a "failed" plan that led to an unexpected blessing? Share your story!

Glory's wisdom: Glory mentors Sammy with gentle faith and practicality. Who's been your "Glory"—someone who guided you without pushing? What's the best advice they gave you?

Sarah's friendship: Sarah becomes Sammy's cheerleader. What's one trait of a *true* friend (like Sarah) that you value most? Bonus: Share a time a friend helped you see your worth.

Willow Creek's charm: The small-town setting almost feels like a character itself. What's a book or movie with a similar cozy vibe that you love? Would you want to live in Willow Creek? Why or why not?

2. Personal Reflection & Connection

The Lies We Learn About Money: Sammy hesitated to take the better-paying job because of what she believed about wealth and what it says about a person. Was there something you were taught about money growing up that you've since started to question or see differently?

Scripture spotlight: Jeremiah 29:11 and Ephesians 3:20 anchor Sammy's journey. Do either of these verses resonate with your life right now? Is there another verse that's been meaningful to you lately?

His Plans vs ours: This story shows how our plans often pale in comparison to the ones God has for us. Can you think of a time when something didn't go according to *your* plan—but in hindsight, led to something better that only God could have orchestrated?

The prayer box idea: Sammy wanted to add a prayer box to the food pantry. If you could leave *one* prayer or hope in a box like that today, what would it be?

3. Creative & Fun Extras

Casting call: If *A Place to Belong* became a movie, who would you cast as Sammy? Glory? Sarah? (Extra points for dramatic readings of your favorite scenes!)

Soundtrack pick: What song would you add to the book's playlist to capture its themes of belonging, faith, or fresh starts?

Title talk: The title plays on physical *and* emotional belonging. Where's your "place to belong"—a location, community, or even a state of mind?

Sequel pitch: If the story continued, what do you imagine for Sammy's next chapter? (A new career? A romance? A mentorship role?)

Book twin: Does this story remind you of another book (or TV show)? What similarities do you see?

Bonus Icebreaker

If you could join Sammy for coffee at the Willow Creek café, what would you order—and what one question would you ask her?

www.ingramcontent.com/pod-product-compliance
Lightning Source LLC
LaVergne TN
LVHW010645110826
845149LV00014B/2953

* 9 7 9 8 9 9 8 6 7 8 7 1 4 *